THE Other Ladies of Georgetown

Corazon N. De La Santa

Cover design by:
Jel Montoya Reid
Jose Luis Garcia Chavarria
Erika dela Santa

Published through Opus Self-Publishing
Politics and Prose Bookstore
5015 Connecticut Ave. NW
Washington, D.C. 20008 www.politics-prose.com / / (202) 364-1919

To my Parents
Miguel dela Santa
&
Mercidita Nepomuceno

Special Thanks to:

Ms. Marilyn Henry, my editor and long time friend.
Ms Katherine Sherwick. Her input and suggestions on how
to keep the story going inspired me to finish my book.

Contents

Introduction

THIS STORY CHRONICLES THE ADVENTURES OF a group of Filipino women who are domestic workers in and out the exclusive community of Georgetown in the nation's capital.

Home to a community in Washington DC, Georgetown is a bastion of old money and people on the threshold of power before, during and after the Second World War. It is bounded on the South by the Potomac River, Rock Creek Park to the East, Burleith and Glover Park to the north, with Georgetown University on the West (Wikipedia, April 14, 2014). David Heyman, in his book "The Georgetown Social Ladies Club, described the area as a patchwork of gardens, meandering tree – lined lanes and red brick Federal and Victorian townhouses, Georgetown is not so much a place as a state of mind."

The late Washington Post publisher Philip Graham described it as a "home to the great, near great and once great in government and journalism (Heyman, p.10)." It was home to the late Katherine Graham, John and Jacqueline Kennedy, Pamela Harriman.

Former Secretaries of State Henry Kissinger, Madeline Albright and John Kerry have made Georgetown their home. Politicians, celebrities have also, and continuous to call Georgetown home.

Another group comprising most of Georgetown are the members of the diplomatic corps, officials and ranking staff of the World Bank, the International Monetary Fund, the International Finance Corporation and CEOs, expats and businessmen from all over the world. Finally, there are think tanks, media personalities, lobbyists flowing in and out of the area.

Georgetown, however, would not be complete without the hundreds of domestic workers from all over the world who serve its residents and maintain their homes. They are vital to the beautiful existence of the area and its people. Their employers may provide them with a visa but in return these workers walk their dogs, babysit their minor children and care for aging parents. They double as chauffeurs to take their children to every imaginable after school activity and sports practices. They also tend to the gardens, cook and serve meals, and deal with the brunt of family issues like divorce and infidelities. Like the rich employers they serve, their individual lives are interesting and complex too.

Their story depicts how they choose to overcome the monotony and drudgery of working for others – to finding pleasures through fun-filled weekends of birthday and holiday celebrations, luncheons, sightseeing and shopping trips together as a group. They learned to celebrate each other, exchange loads of gossip and to simply enjoy their lives.

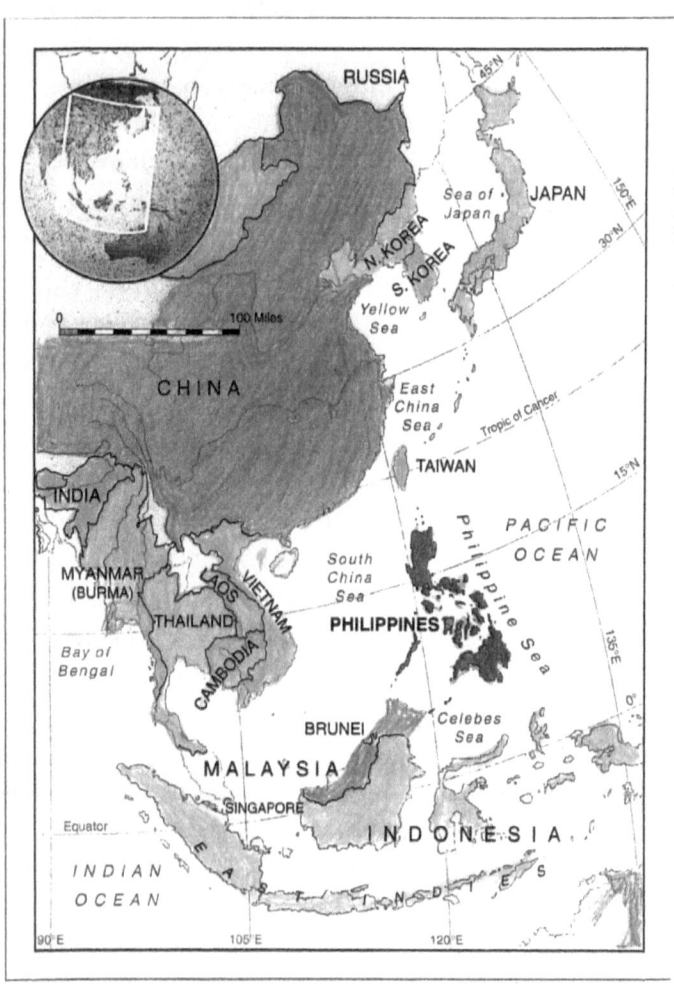

The Philippines is a collection of islands in Southeast Asia, spanning 780,000 square miles (2 million square kilometers) of the Pacific Ocean and the South China Sea.

Thomas Lang, Steadwell Books World Tour Philippines

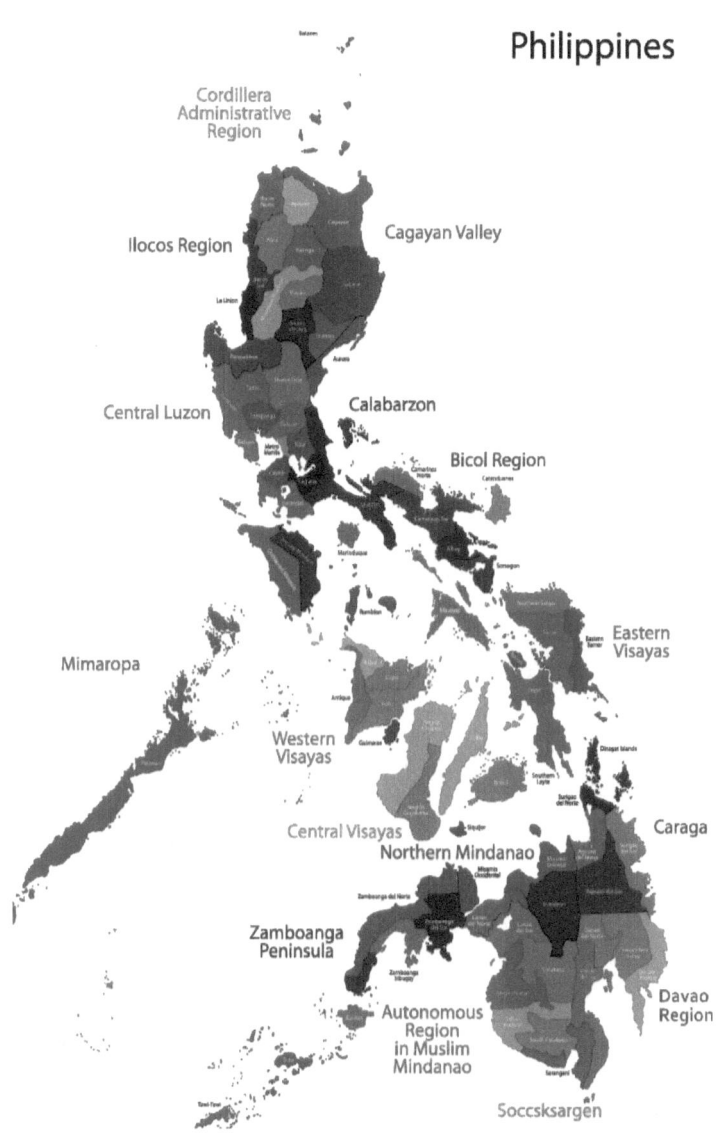

Philippines

Cordillera
Administrative
Region

Ilocos Region

Cagayan Valley

Central Luzon

Calabarzon

Bicol Region

Mimaropa

Eastern
Visayas

Western
Visayas

Central Visayas

Caraga

Northern Mindanao

Zamboanga
Peninsula

Davao
Region

Autonomous
Region
in Muslim
Mindanao

Soccsksargen

Art.com

Characters

The Golden Group

TINA (CRISTINA) AND CHEDENG (ROSARIO) GALVAN—sisters who worked as freelance maids meaning no permanent employer, and live in Glover Park

BLANCA SAMONTE—a former reporter of Philippines' Daily and neighbor of sisters Tina and Chedeng

CITA (PACITA) REYES—a live-in maid in Georgetown and a widow, first hired by a World Bank Staff

CHLOE REYES—teenage daughter of Cita Reyes

PACO (PACUNDO) BONIFACIO—defense contractor employee and Cita's friend

LANIE (LOLITA BALBAO)—a live-in maid in Georgetown and a widow

LULU (MARILOU PACION)—a live-in maid in Georgetown who also claimed to be a widow

RISSA (LARISSA CRUZ)—a live-out maid and a trained dancer married to an economist from India.

CLARA (CLARISSA DIAMANTE)—married and a live-in maid in Georgetown

JELENE (YELENA DAYOT)—single and a live-in maid of a World Bank Staff

TANYA SERENO—a live in maid in Georgetown, godmother of Jelene and friend of sisters Tina and Chedeng

MARIE LEVA—Filipino Clinique Counter lady at Lord and Taylor, also worked as a maid

CELY (CECILIA PEREZ)—a live-in maid of a US ambassador and childhood friend of sisters Tina and Chedeng

Employers

MRS. DANA ROBINSON—Cita's employer and resident of Georgetown

MS. SANDRA WAXMAN—Lanie's employer and resident of Georgetown

AMBASSADOR ANTHONY RICHMOND—Clara's employer and resident of Georgetown

MRS. SALLY LELAND—Chedeng's employer, real estate company owner and resident of Chevy Chase, Maryland

The Other Ladies of Georgetown

Corazon N. De La Santa

1

The Sisters at 22ⁿᵈ Street

After finishing a graduate program at nearby American University (AU) in 2005, Blanca Samonte would walk from AU to her home in Glover Park whenever she could. Her resolve to take life slow came from years of running around town as a single mother and caring for her daughter Miren. "Now that the kid is out of the house and will perhaps one day get married and live somewhere else, it is time for me to enjoy life and appreciate even the simple task of leisurely walking home. I walk down New Mexico Avenue, turn right on Tunlaw Street walk up the hill and I'm home in 45 minutes. Not bad exercise for a 55 year old lady," smiled Blanca.

As she was climbing hilly Benson Street one fall day in 2007, she heard a voice. "Hello, do you live here now?" said the voice. "Yes", Blanca replied. *Filipino ka Day?* (Are you Filipino in Visayan dialect), asked by a lady Blanca assumed as the voice. *Dili uy* (no in Visaya), said Blanca.

"I'm just kidding *Day* (lady in Visaya not known to you). I'm Filipino and *Tagalog* speaking from *Luzon*. I understand why you ask if I am a Filipino American. I am always mistaken for a Chinese or even a Hispanic. Please do not be fooled by me speaking *Visaya*. I went on vacation in *Cebu* when I was in college so I picked up some of the basic expressions like, *Day*.

3

But this is as far as I can go with your *Visayan* dialect," smiled Blanca apologetically.

The lady spoke and said *"Walang bale yan Day* (it does not matter in Visaya). By the way, I am Tina, Tina Galvan, and I am Filipino."

"I am Blanca Samonte. Nice to meet you," sighed Blanca reaching out to shake Tina's hand.

"I used to see you on MacArthur Boulevard either by Citibank or Penny Saver. I work for someone in the area in the morning and I go to Georgetown in the afternoon. I suppose you ride the D bus," said Tina.

"Yes, I do. Bus D2 goes in the neighborhood of Glover Park," replied Blanca.

"How long have been living here?" Tina asked

"I've been here since 2000. We had an efficiency (studio) apartment in MacArthur then we moved to a one bedroom. The building was rent-controlled. That was really a great help to someone new to the US. Luckily, I discovered a housing program in DC for low income folks like me. With help from the district, I was able to buy a one bedroom here on Benson in 2000. So we are now neighbors. By the way, do you live in that building across mine?" Blanca asked.

"No, my sister and I live on 22nd Street which is three blocks from where we are standing right now Benson Street," Tina replied.

"Oh! I get it. I'm sorry but I haven't gone around in the neighborhood. It is never too late to do it especially now that my daughter has left for college. See you around Tina," said Blanca

"*Sa muling pagkikita* (till we meet again)," said Tina.

As she lay down her work bag on the table Blanca realized she missed Tina's name. "I will make it up to her when I see her next time. I don't want her to think I'm a snob because I'm not a maid. No more with that Filipino social status attitude," Blanca murmured.

Several weeks later, Blanca ran into Tina again.

"*O, ikaw ulit* (it is you again), "said Blanca. "So you walk from AU and gets home between 5:30 and 5:45 in the afternoon every day?" asked Tina.

"It looks like we have the same schedule in going home," said Blanca

"The fall season is upon us and it will soon get dark as early as four in the afternoon. Why don't you come this Saturday for dinner? My sister cooks a big meal every Saturday night. Housekeeping is a tedious work so Saturday night starts our downtime. If you are free, you're welcome to join us. It is easy to look for our place because it's only three blocks from Benson Street.

First, you go down Benson then up walk three blocks from bus stop at the corner of Benson and Calvert, the first building on your left is where we live. Press for 301 and will let you in. See you this Saturday," said Tina with a smile as she walks away.

Tina's invitation took Blanca by surprise. She called Tina that Friday to confirm she would come to dinner, even if the invitation was *nakakahiya* (a Filipino trait of modesty and propriety). "Tina did not seem to care what I do for a living. I am tired of my own cooking and would love to eat some authentic Filipino *ulam* (dishes)," thought Blanca.

With no idea of what to bring to the dinner because Filipino get-togethers are always complete, including dessert, Blanca went empty handed. *Bahala na* (cast your luck to the wind), the host will understand.

"*Maayong gabii sa imong tanan* (Good evening to everyone in Visaya)", said Blanca.

"*Maayong gabii din* (Good Evening too in Visaya)," replied the sisters. Joking, Tina asked, "Did you have a hard time finding our place? Did you run into traffic on your way to 22nd?"

"Guess what? I followed the aroma of your cooking and I knew I was in the right building. *Daghan salamat* (thanks a lot in Visaya) for inviting me. Who is the lady in the kitchen?" Blanca asked.

"Oh! That's Chedeng my older sister, "replied Tina.

"No! I am the younger one and Tina is older than me,"

"Oh! Oh! I hope there is no fight tonight," said Blanca.

Blanca looked around for a place to sit down but was ushered into the living room. She immediately saw two big *balikbayan boxes* (return to your country care packages) situated in one corner of the apartment. The boxes were bigger than the ones she sends to her family every now and then.

"Are they ready for pick-up by your forwarder?" shouted Blanca.

"Yes. One box is for Tina's family and the other is for mine," Chedeng replied

Blanca commented on the layout of the sisters' apartment. "I notice that the first thing one can see upon entering your apartment is a space to receive your visitors then a dining area adjacent to the kitchen. The living room is somewhat hidden. It is a lovely set up with the kitchen and dining room as the center of activity especially tonight, right Chedeng?" asked Blanca.

"You are correct. Dinner is ready, so dig in," replied Chedeng.

As Blanca expected when she saw the big pot in the kitchen early on, Chedeng served *beef bone sinigang* (sour beef bone stew). She knew it would be a fantastic meal.

"We hope you like it. I get these beef bones with plenty of meat from Penny Saver on Wisconsin Avenue. They have the best *bulalo* (beef bone marrow) like we have back in the Philippines. Of course, it is not the same but what they sell is the closest to the real thing for *sinigang na baka* (beef sour stew). Be careful, the stew is still very hot," said Chedeng.

"How do you get rid of the foam and the blood from the bones? I want to try cooking your way. I know how to do the fish with veggies. My daughter Miren loves it," said Blanca.

"So your daughter eats Filipino dishes like most Filipino kids?" Tina asked.

"Let's put it this way. I introduced her to our food early on so she could acquire the taste. Besides, it was hard switching back and forth because of the different cultures she was exposed to. We had to adjust when were in Hong Kong in the late 80's. That was Cantonese Chinese. She had to attend British schools for kindergarten because we are not Chinese. Then my work transferred me to Vancouver, Canada.

But there was no need to change what we ate daily in those places because Miren's *yaya* (nanny) is Filipino. She cooked Filipino meals for us and I learned new ones during her stay in Hong Kong. My daughter is now grown and likes most of our cooking except *dinuguan* (blood soup of the pig)" explained Blanca.

"You don't need to explain. Now going back to the *sinigang*, to clean the beef bone from blood etc., you need to boil them first and get rid of the foamy broth. Then boil the beef again in medium heat. This would be your clean broth. Once those bones are all done meaning the meat is loosened from the bone, it's time to add the flavoring. I use lemon instead of the Knorr *sinigang* package we get from the Asian or Filipino stores. It is natural and really sour. I substitute spinach for the veggies and do not forget the *gabi* (tarrow root like yam). The *gabi* adds sweetness and thickness to the soup. Bon Appetit", urged Chedeng

The three ladies finally sat down for dinner. Tina took the *kabisera* (head table seat) while Blanca and Chedeng sat across from each other. Chedeng gently ladled the stew into each bowl while Blanca looked scared passing the bowls. Tina slurped the broth then burst into laughter because it was so hot.

"Why did you make it so sour? Your *sinigang* is so intense to the nose and throat that I don't have to worry about the coming flu season. It's like an agent that clears your nose and you throat. *Sus Ginoo* (Jesus Christ in Visaya) Chedeng! Please tone down the *asim* (sourness) next time," Tina said to her sister.

All three ladies burst into laughter. "I can't promise but don't you think it is good to have hot lemon with some meat coming down your throat Blanca?" asked Chedeng.

"Well, I have no right to complain about your *sinigang*. I go by the rule of my late father every time we complained about food served on the table. "If you did not cook, you have no right to complain about it. I've always go by that rule. But your *sinigang* is great. I haven't had anything like it in a long time. Thank you for preparing it," Blanca responded.

During dinner, the sisters asked Blanca questions like what part of the Philippines she was from and why she came to the United States. The sisters wanted to know if she has a husband and what was she doing before she moved to the United States.

"Oh! We moved to the United States in August 1992. It was a petition that my mother filed in 1985. I did not take it seriously because I was working as a reporter for Philippines' Daily since 1978. My goal was to become a foreign correspondent and I became one. I was sent to cover the situation of the Overseas Filipino Workers (OFWs) in Hong Kong from 1987-1990. Then the Daily had me transferred to Vancouver, Canada where most OFWs moved from Hong Kong and Middle East.

Do you want me to talk more about the OFWs and the Philippine Overseas Administration (POEA) tonight too?" said Blanca as she tried to cut short her story for the night.

"Not tonight please. Maybe some other time but go on with your story on how you ended up in America," begged the sisters.

So I was in Vancouver on an assignment for the Daily when I got a letter from the US Consulate saying I need to come for an interview. I also had to prepare documents like birth certificates etc. to establish my relationship with my mother and my daughter to me. The interview and physical examination went well. The AIDS test was added to the usual lung test to check if we have TB.

An immigrant visa with an expiration date was issued to us after three weeks. We had to get ready fast so my daughter could enroll for the September opening of schools in the States. Did I think twice in my decision to move? Not really because I wanted my daughter to have stability in terms of schools, friends and neighborhood.

I hope I did the right thing because she is graduating next year. She enjoyed our life at Macarthur Boulevard and got that exposure to the cultural scenes of Washington DC. It was a sacrifice to move and start over again. But I am a parent and that's what parents do – care for your child the best way you know how. After getting settled, I stopped looking back at my previous working life with the Philippines' Daily. Otherwise, I would just be wondering what I would have become had I stayed. I just had to keep going and going like that pink rabbit battery commercial," said Blanca with a smile.

Tina stood up, walked around parodying the rabbit commercial on TV. All three ladies laughed with the comparison.

"Your choices for dessert are ice cream, or boiled *kamote* (sweet yam)," Chedeng announced.

Blanca and Tina asked for the *kamote.*

Then, Blanca asked the sisters if they were current with events in the Philippines.

"No. We don't have *TFC* (The Filipino Channel). That's an added expense on top of the rent. Besides, those *Teleseryes* (Filipino soap operas) will also take up much of our time instead of taking care of our place. We want to keep it clean too just like the houses we clean everyday," Chedeng replies.

"So who is a *Noranian* here?" asked Blanca.

"Not me. I am a *Vilmanian*," Tina smiling.

"What about you Blanca?" asked Chedeng.

"I will not reveal who I've been rooting for at the height of their popularity in the 70s but instead let me explain why the rivalry was even. Looking back, *Vilma Santos* was a child actress and bloomed to be a good one through the years. *Nora Aunor*, on the other hand was *promdi* (from the province), uneducated, dirt poor but was a gifted singer. She also could act. All things considered, she was the real superstar because she could sing and act," Blanca replied.

Chedeng and Tina were surprised how well Blanca remembered those days of the 70s and 80s when fans were screaming and fighting over the Nora and Vilma rivalry.

"Can we talk about the love-teams during those days?" asked Tina.

"Maybe next time because it's getting late," replied Blanca.

"Come back next Saturday at 7 because Chedeng will be working in Dupont Circle not in Georgetown," Tina said.

"Okay. Do I follow the same route to go back to Benson?" asked Blanca.

"We're glad you figured out right away the route back to your place," smiled Tina.

"I will call you by Wednesday to confirm. Is that alright with you? Blanca asked.

"No problem. Chedeng will be cooking like she always does every Saturday night. I just do not know yet what she plans to cook," Tina replied.

"Good night and thank you very much. I had a good time, "Blanca said as she hugged the sisters.

Sunday is church day for most Filipinos in the Glover Park and Georgetown areas of DC. The Bread of Life Church and St. Theresa are the closest to those living along the Wisconsin Avenue and Glover Park northwest. Once again, Blanca ended up with the sisters and their other friends at the after mass coffee hour at Bread of Life Church.

"Are you going home after coffee hour? You know, we have a ride," asked Tina.

"I am going home and thank you. Is the driver somebody I know?" Blanca wondered.

Tina hurriedly introduced the driver. "By the way, this is our neighbor Sandra who is also from *Leyte* (a province in the Visayan region of the Philippines)."

Tina took the front seat while Chedeng and Blanca went for the passenger seats. It was a short drive to Glover Park.

Sandra drove with a stern face, hardly a smile and did not join the conversation of the other three ladies. Blanca took her attitude with a grain of salt. She has had bad experiences with Filipinos who get very uppity once they start driving in North America. "Sandra could be one of them. *Sabit lang* ako (Blanca is a tag along because of friendship with Tina and Chedeng). I should be grateful for the ride," Blanca whispered to Chedeng.

The three ladies got off at 22nd Street while Sandra drove in rush leaving Blanca wondering why she drove with such furious speed. "Wow! *Umuusok ang tambutso ni Sandra* (exhaust from tail pipe got smoky because the pressure put on gas),"Blanca asked Tina.

Tina quickly explained and said Sandra needed to get back to work at nearby New Mexico Avenue to walk the dog. And that Sandra gets paid extra for doing it on a Sunday.

"Sandra is gone but let me ask you a question. Do you really take the short bus ride to Bread of Life?" asked Tina.

"Yes, but sometimes I would rather go to St. Theresa Church in Tenberry because the bus ride to Bread of Life is often shorter than the wait. So I might as well go on further to Tenberry on the same bus. It has shopping and eating places I can to go to after church. But I would rather go to Bread of Life most of the time. I like the after mass social with donut and coffee. I get to know new folks from the neighborhood including other Filipinos. It's nice to meet and talk with other people. Don't you agree?" asked Blanca.

"Since you like to go to Bread of Life Church, I will teach you a short cut from our place. As soon as you reach the end of Tunlaw Road, make a right until you reach the end of the hill. Walk a little further and you will see Massachusetts Avenue and the church. Can you repeat the route for me," smiled Tina.

The three ladies burst into laughter again. Blanca rolled her eyes as she blurted out Tina's instructions resulting in more laughter. "Thank you for giving me another short cut tip"

"Don't forget this Saturday," said Chedeng.

"I won't," Blanca replied.

That Saturday, Blanca purposely left to see the sisters a little bit late. She was afraid there would be no one in the apartment if she went too early.

Chedeng was in the kitchen and told everyone to wait until the spaghetti was al dente. A young couple joined the ladies for dinner. Tina introduced Blanca to the other guest while they were waiting for the spaghetti with pesto sauce.

"Hi, I am Minnie and this is my friend Bong Yat. You are *Tita* (a polite way of addressing an aunt recently met and who is not related) _____?

"Oh, call me *Tita* Blanca. I also live in the neighborhood," said a relaxed Blanca.

"Minnie is also from Leyte and the daughter of our friend Cely. Her mother comes once in a while to visit because she is a live in maid. However, she gets a long vacation whenever her employer goes back to Italy. The lady of the house is an Italian while the husband is an Amerian from Oklahoma. I am sure you will meet Cely one of these days.

"Bong Yat and Minnie have been friends for some time. He is from Cambodia," Tina further explained.

"Ladies and one gentleman, dinner is ready," Chedeng announced.

"Your pasta is great *Manang* (Filipino sign of respect for an elderly lady one is familiar with). You are good in whipping up something anytime. This is really delicious.

No offense meant Manang Tina," said Minnie.

"You are right Minnie and no offense to you Tina," Blanca smiled.

"I understand. Wait till you taste my Shepherd's pie!" Tina boasted.

"It must be to die for," said Blanca.

Everyone laughed as they passed around their plates for the pesto. After dinner, Minnie and Tina went to the living room from what's look like a private talk. Chedeng served ice cream for dessert and told everyone that the two will join them later. The couple left after Minnie had a bit of the dessert.

"I will be going soon too. There isn't much light in the street on my way back. I might have a fall and no one is around to help me. Thank you for the pasta dinner. It was delicious," said Blanca as she embraced the sisters to say good bye.

"By the way, we've been invited to a party this coming Saturday so *wala munang* dinner (no dinner this Saturday)," said Tina.

"No problem. Maybe I will see you in church on Sunday," replied Blanca.

"No dinner this Saturday would be a good break for them. *Nakakahiya na* (it's getting to be embarrassing)," Blanca mused, talking to herself on her way home.

Feeling guilty and stuck without any contribution for the Saturday night dinner invitation from the sisters, Blanca kept thinking of ways to reciprocate the hospitality of the sisters. She recalled all the Filipino dishes she could do but had doubts if she could pull it off given how well the sisters cook.

"My *lumpia* (spring rolls) were okay with my *Gringo* boyfriend (White American) when we were dating. He loved my *pansit* (noodles) and shrimp with coconut sauce. My Gringo friend and his cousin were also delighted with my Filipino dessert *halo-halo* (a mixture of sweetened bananas, beans, and jackfruit with shaved ice and milk). Will these be okay with the ladies?" Blanca asked herself.

Still full of doubts and possible embarrassment, Blanca decided to have a pizza night with the sisters. She called them in the middle of the week and invited the sisters. "Filipinos love pizza so I won't go wrong.

"I'm inviting you and your sister Chedeng for pizza this Saturday. What kind of toppings do you want? What is your preferred drink? I know a lot Filipinos like Coca Cola but I do not want to assume you like it too," asked Blanca.

"Pizza would be a good idea on Saturday night. I like pepperoni and cheese. Chedeng likes Hawaiian with pineapple and ham. Coke goes well with pizza and Chedeng prefers Sprite,"

"Is there a brand that you like, Papa John, or Dominoes? Blanca asked Tina.

Is Pizza Hut okay with you? There is one close by on Wisconsin Avenue near the dry cleaner?"

"Oh yes, there is no need to go far because it might just be a long wait," said Tina.

"So I guess we are all set for Saturday. Call me in case you cannot make it." Blanca replied.

Pizza night came and it turned out to be a different kind of fun for the ladies. No one was cooking hurriedly but instead they waited for the pizza delivery guy. Blanca was also happy to see Chedeng relaxed and smiling more. Chedeng struck her as the more serious one of the two sisters. Tina on the other hand, was more fun loving and quirky.

After the pizza dinner, Blanca asked the sisters if they cared to watch a movie. The sisters were surprised about how she got the movie. Tina wanted to know if she rented it or bought it. Blanca explained that she had a Netflix sub-scription and that her plan allowed her to get one movie every week.

"How does Netflix work? Do you have to return the movie the following day or pay a daily fine like we did for Blockbuster?" Tina asked.

"No. Netlfix is convenient because you get the movies in the mail and return the movie the same way. You set up an account in your computer with an email address, credit card and you're set," replied Blanca.

"That sounds easy but we do not have a computer. So everything has to be done online," said Tina.

"I think a computer is a must to set up an account. I am not sure if your phone would work. I will check the Netflix website but in the meantime let us enjoy the movie. Our movie for tonight is Bridget Jones. I hope you like it," said Blanca.

As the movie was playing, Blanca kept looking at the sis-ters to be sure they were comfortable with the movie of her choice." I forgot to tell you Bridget Jones is a British movie," said Blanca.

"But Bridget Jones is American. Is that not Renee Zellwe-ger?" asked Chedeng.

"Well, how do you know the actress?" Tina asked her sis-ter.

"Access Hollywood my dear Sister," replied Chedeng.

Everybody laughed.

"Well that's how versatile Renee is. I read somewhere she had to put on weight to play this role and to practice speaking with a British accent. Can you tell the difference when she talks with the British actor Colin Firth? " added Blanca.

"You two are really up to date when it comes to celebrities past and present," said Tina.

Chedeng and Blanca laughed and high fived each other. They found common interests and topics to rally around. Chedeng said Tina was never into celebrity gossips. She felt those people do not care about us. Tina is also not one of those Filipinos who would line up to see a Filipino show when they come to the US. "Their tickets for most of the time are very expensive so why bother?" said Tina.

"But Tina listens to the gossip too which I find hilarious," said Chedeng.

"We will have more showbiz gossip next time. It's getting late," said Tina.

On their way out, the sisters asked Blanca's if they could have the remaining slices of pizza as *baon* (for take home).They said Bridget Jones was a fun movie to watch especially the part when the asparagus became blue soup. We like your idea of pizza and movie," said Chedeng and Tina.

"The blue soup was hilarious. Was that a recipe?" asked Blanca.

"If I remember right, Bridget did not intend her soup to be blue. She did not have the time to buy kitchen ties to hold together the asparagus. She made do with the blue string from her sewing box. It bled during the steaming thus blue soup came into being," said Tina.

The three ladies burst into laughter.

"It would also be really nice if you could share with us your Netflix movies," said Chedeng.

"I am glad you like having a movie after dinner. I will check to see what is in my queue for next week. I will be happy to bring one if I am invited to your place next Saturday," Blanca asked.

"We are again inviting you for dinner next Saturday at 6 pm. See you. And thank you.

That was fun. Good night," said the sisters.

With the sisters gone, Blanca rushed back to her third floor condo to check what was next on her Netflix movies. Dr. Doolittle starring comedian Eddie Murphy was next. The summary says Eddie Murphy is a veterinarian who talked to animals since he was a child.

"This would be light and fun for everyone to enjoy. I learned my lesson from my boring movie choices. I do not like to disappoint them because Saturday night should be a relaxing one. Housekeeping is a backbreaking job. It would not be a good idea to watch a sad and and depressing one or read subtitles of foreign movies.I think Dr. Doolittle would be a perfect movie to watch next time." said a relieved Blanca.

Chedeng prepared a steak dinner the following Saturday at 22nd Street. It took Blanca by surprised because most Filipinos are not steak lovers. But Chedeng's looked good and juicy. Dusted only with salt, pepper and butter, Blanca could not believe what she was eating. The meat was well done but not burnt.

"It seems Chedeng knows the right time to get them out of the pan. This steak is far better than those served in many steak houses. How did you cook this? Blanca asked.

"Practice, I guess. I also cook with my heart my dear," replied Chedeng.

"I think you really do because your spices are no different from the best steak houses yet it is comparable," praised Blanca.

"Ladies, please eat slowly, take your time because our steak is not fillet mignon," Chedeng added.

"I hear you my dear sister. I will make a note of your reminder," smiled Tina.

The steak dinner of the ladies proved to be longer than the usual one hour. Blanca said steak was a lot for everyone to eat and felt heavy on the stomach. To relax, Chedeng then invited everyone for a chat. The break from the dining room gave Blanca an opportunity to ask the ladies questions she long wanted to ask but never had the chance to do so.

Blanca spoke with a smile on her face. "You've asked me how I got to America. Can you now talk about how you and your sister got here too?"

"No Problem! Allow me to speak for my sister and me," said Chedeng.

"You are so serious my dear. I am not *Tia Deli* (Filipino version of Ann Landers).

Do we need to turn off the lights so we could hear you better?" Blanca asked.

"No need. But you are really hilarious when you said *Tia Deli*. I was an avid listener of her radio program every 3 pm back in the days," Chedeng said.

While laughing and humming the theme song of *Tia Deli's* daily afternoon radio program, Blanca followed suit until Tina begged the two ladies to stop.

With a serious face, Chedeng talked about how she and Tina got to the States. "First, we took a boat from *Leyte* to *Manila*. "We were from the province *prom di* (slang term for someone born and raised in the province) as we love to say to separate the city folks from us. We found employment in one of the posh villages in *Makati, Urdaneta*. We all know that most of the employers in places like *Urdaneta*, *Magallanes* and *Forbes Park* are rich Filipinos and foreigners working for companies in the States. Some are diplomats and foreign businessmen. I was hired by an Italian businessman who happened to be married to a Filipina.

I knew early on that the Filipina wife would be the pain in my life. She was arrogant and looked down on people like me. You know our saying about the fly who got on top of the *kalabaw* (Philippine work animal – carabao) is like someone who feels on top of the world and that's how she was and her marriage to a foreigner made it worse. This was during the 80's. But I had to persevere at that time because I had no choice. Tina and I have children and family to support in *Leyte*," Chedeng said.

By 1982, my employer and I had moved to the States. The lady was hired by World Bank who gave us visas. They asked me if I want to go with them as their housekeeper. I did not refuse the job despite the wife's attitude. It was already an opportunity to leave the country to earn in US dollars. The equivalent of the US dollars back then was already three or four times more than our *peso* (Philippine currency). *Kapit sa patalim* (comparison of a chance to a sharp knife that can cut deep) was what I had in mind in my decision to go. Fear of my employer's wife will not get me anywhere. I mustered the courage and moved with them to the States.

The kindness of Mr. Antonini was also one factor in my decision to come to the States. He was a soft spoken man like a teacher. I think he could be one of those men who let their wives do all the *talak* (endless talking) to keep peace in the house? I think his formula worked because it kept his business going in peace. He sold lesson plans like Montessori schools to early childhood educators. That's all I know about his business.

So we ended up in Georgetown, in Washington DC. I am once again working in a place where rich people live. The Antoninis in the beginning rented a small house on Reservoir Road near Georgetown Hospital and university.

While in Georgetown, the lady socialized a lot. She would have frequent dinners at home. So frequent that I learned how to care for those expensive dinner plates, bowls, wine glasses, etc. The Madame told me that dishwashers ruin the designs of plates, cutlery and glassware. Handwashing was the way to keep them nice and shiny. The process takes forever, depriving me of my sleep.

After two years, my employer moved to another house then to another house. We must have moved four times in Georgetown until the Antonini's moved back to Italy in 1985.

Yes, I remember now. Their names are Marilou Arciaga and Simeon Antonini.

Looking back, Mrs. Antonini's business was buying and selling houses in Georgetown. Her customers were people who wanted to live and be amongst the people in Georgetown. One more thing, she was cunning in her real estate business. She would convince her friends to let her and the husband stay with them on the pretense that her place was being remodeled. Unfortunately, for me, I became the maid of the household hosting us temporarily.

I had to grin and bear the situation. My priority then was to bring Tina to the States through the diplomat friends of the Antoninis. I asked them to help me get a diplomat employer for Tina before they left for Italy in 1985. They found one who hired Tina on a diplomatic visa. Being part of a diplomatic staff was one of the ways to get Tina to the States. These ambassadors and international organization officials are the ones who can secure working visas for their household staff.

Back then she was already working in Bucharest. She was sad and lonely. Where is that country again Tina?" asked Chedeng. "It's the capital of Romania and located in Europe," replied Tina.

All the hard work of Chedeng paid off after working for the Antoninis for almost five years. Tina was able to join her in the United States on a diplomatic visa in 1986. "Having Tina moved to the States was my top priority at that time. But I would still shudder looking back at the treatment I got from her. "*Tratong alila talaga* (slave like). There is hardly any rest and hardly any day off. I guess she knew my visa depended on them, so she really took advantage of me.They still owe me in back wages. I had to let it go. They subjected me to a back and forth every time I come to collect my back wages. *Bahala na ang Diyos sa kanila* (I leave that to God)," lamented Chedeng.

After the Antoninis, the sisters vowed never to work as live in maid again when they got reunited in the States. As live out maids, they shared a small apartment with Chedeng's friend Naty.

They waited for a year to establish part time jobs around the Georgetown neighborhood then they moved to Dupont Circle. Still it was a group home arrangement.

"Did you not notice the location of Dupont Circle and Glover Park. Both places give us easy access to Georgetown.

You can also walk if you cannot wait for the bus. But most of all, Georgetown has lots of jobs for us. These could range from cleaning to cat sitting. All you have to do with the cat is keep company at night and make sure he or she is fed then you leave in the morning. Americans treat their pets like family. What is not to like working in Georgetown?" joked Chedeng.

"But renting an apartment in Washington DC is expensive. Everything has gone up since I moved here in 1993. My $475 dollar studio apartment in MacArthur Blvd. is a thing of the past. Why do you spend money on rent when living with an employer gives you free room and board?"Blanca wanted to know.

"Being a live out maid is worth it because you have more freedom and money. A live in maid is a 24/7 service. You are at the beck and call of your employer anytime. I have experienced this with the Antonini's and it was not fair. The job should be like any 8-5 office job but this often does not does not apply to a live-in maid. Don't' get me wrong. There are many good employers too. Not all of them are like Mrs. Antonini. You will understand what I am talking about till you meet Jelene. She is the live in maid of a World Bank employee," said Chedeng.

"Then how did you get this apartment? In my case, I had to submit a rental history and an annual income to the leasing office," asked Blanca.

"Well, since we had no rental history and required annual income to show for like you, I got a *padrino* (someone influential who pave the way to get things done) like in the Philippines.

I found a *ninang* (godmother) in the person of my Jewish employer Mrs. Leland. She is rich and in the real estate business. How could she be turned down? She went to the leasing office and completed the application for us. Mrs. Leland probably closed up or guaranteed for us. I did not care to know how it happened because her magic worked and so we've been living at 22nd for almost fifteen years," continued Chedeng.

"That was really nice and kind of Mrs. Leland. Some rules are bendable depending who is doing it in this country or someone with money could guarantee for you. By the way, where do you find an employer like her because I am looking for one too? Blanca joked. The ladies all laughed.

"I'm glad I can make you laugh but seriously I take my hats off to you ladies for your determination and independence. You've to got be to make it in this country. I'm sure I will hear more *kuwento* (stories) in the coming days. In in the meantime, I've got to go because it's getting late. Good night ladies," said Blanca.

On her way home, Blanca could not helped but wonder about the immigration status of the sisters. Recalling in her head conversation she had with the sisters, "Chedeng was never clear about their visas when the Antonini's left for Italy. Tina's diplomatic visa has expired after her diplomat's employer tour of duty ended. They talked about regular visits to the Philippines.

They were able to get out of the US and come back with no visa problem. What happens now that their diplomatic visas have expired? Everything looks alright for now.

They seem to be happy with the decision to work as freelance maids instead of being committed to one employer for years. This is the freedom the sisters are talking about. They go home every night to their apartment. They cook Filipino meals, relax and watch TV and enjoy their weekends. Chedeng for example could watch her favorite soap operas like "All My Children and "General Hospital" without being bothered. I am not sure what Tina does for relaxation. But let this friendship evolved first," Blanca joking herself.

The remaining days of the ladies in 2007 were filled with more dinners, pizza nights and Netflix Filipino movies. Saturday night at the movies became such a big hit, Blanca's Netflix subscription ran out of Filipino movies. However, that did not stop the ladies' from having a Saturday night event.

Jelene, one of the sisters' weekenders at 22nd Street promised she will get movies from the Filipino store.

"Not to worry ladies. We will have a movie next Saturday. My friend who is also friends of *Manang* Chedeng and *Ate* Tina (respect attached to ladies older but no blood relations) will come with a movie. She works for a Filipino store that also rents Filipino movies," assured Jelene.

"Oh! Are you talking about *Bahay* Kubo (bamboo house)? The owner calls the place *bahay kubo* to let the Filipinos know it's a Filipino store. I guess we are all set for next

Saturday's movie," said Blanca.

Over dinner, Blanca steered the conversation on Jelene. Blanca got the ball rolling with a recollection of her first meeting with Jelene.

"I remember you. I dropped by to 22nd one morning but can't remember why. We got introduced. You said you were staying with the sisters to recuperate from an operation. You also mentioned it was your *ninang*, (godmother) Tanya who requested Chedeng and Tina to let you stay in their apartment till you got better."

"How well you remember my situation back then *Ate* Blanca. I am really grateful to the sisters for letting me stay with them when I had surgery. This place gets to be very quiet when *Manang* Chedeng and *Ate* Tina leave for work. That silence really helped me recover faster than I expected. I got fully rested by sleeping all day.

You see my *alaga* (child Jelene is taking care of)) is a good girl but she can sometimes be *kulit* (nag). Also, I did not want her to see me walking slow and in pain. We are very close and she will cry when she sees me in that condition." said Jelene.

"That's understandable because sometimes the babysitter becomes the second mother. That little girl will feel sad to see you sick. So you live with your employer and come to 22nd on Saturdays?" asked Blanca.

Chedeng explained that Jelene is a live in maid of a World Bank employee. The lady employer is from Namibia married to an African American. Jelene's employment was facilitated by her *ninang* Tanya.

"By the way, Jelene and Tanya speak *Visaya* too. Jelene and her *ninang* Tanya are from Dumaguete City. Ladies, we still all know our Philippine geography right?" asked Chedeng.

"Are we about to review Philippine geography tonight," Tina asked.

Chedeng and Blanca winked at each other, laughed and said "*Bisaya tayo Day* (we are all from Visayan region). Do we need the review? Chedeng and Blanca asked.

They replied and said they know who is not from their province because of how they speak *Visaya*. They have a distinctive accent. They all laughed because it did not matter to them.

"Being a live-in maid, you become an all-around maid which means you not only do the house chores but babysitting as well. This is why Jelene comes to spend the weekend with us for a break. Is'nt that right Jelene," asked Chedeng.

"*Sinabi mo*! (you said it right), *Manang* (polite address to an unrelated older female).But this is still better than being in Cyprus. It's a beautiful place, but lonely because all you see is the blue sea and the tourists. So when I found out that *ninang* Tanya moved to the States, I did not hesitate to ask for help. I knew she had worked abroad for years. She started out in Hong Kong then she moved to the States. I knew she could help me get to the States because she has established connections, said Jelene.

Like *Manang* Chedeng and *Ate* Tina, I left *Dumaguete* and worked as a maid in Pasig.

My first employer was the famous opera singer Sylvia La Torre. They were kind to the help," explained Jelene.

"So did you learn to sing?" asked Chedeng. "Are you kidding me? Judge for yourself when I do Karaoke," replied Jelene. Everyone laughed.

After her employment with the singer, Jelene found herself working in a factory in *Pasig.* Working in the factory gave Jelene the idea of working overseas. The factory was abuzzed with stories of former workers who left to work abroad. She said their stories stirred her imagination.

So satisfy her curiosity about job overseas, Jelene decided to apply.

"If I remember right, POEA, the Philippine Overseas Employment Administration office was a short *jepney* (Filipino version of left over American jeeps used in the Philippines during the Second World War) ride from *Pasig*. POEA is the government office that regulates the hiring and management of Filipino Overseas Workers in the late 80s. It was under DOLE, the Department of Labor and Employment. These offices made sure I had a work contract with an employer before leaving the country," Jelene said.

After some months of waiting, Jelene found herself in a plane bound for Cypus. Her first employer was an elderly couple. Her dream of earning more money was becoming a reality. She said she was happy with her first employer who came to liked her a lot because she was able to free the old man of his big toe misery.

"How and what did you do?" asked Blanca.

"I already know how to do manicure and pedicure before I left for Cyprus. So I slowly pulled out an embedded ingrown nail from his big toe. You cannot imagine how relieved he was. I also taught them how to cut their toe nails so the ingrown nails would not grow back. The word got around about the toe cure and my manicure/pedicure clientele in the neighborhood grew. That meant extra money for me and that made me happy.

A part of me, however, knew that I could have done better if I had more education. Working as a maid is not bad. My wish really was to finish high school then go to college.

But my mother did not want to support me after my father died. She remarried and sold all the properties my father left us. Because of my mother's new family, it was best to stay with my grandmother. She did not have the money to support my schooling either. So when I got older, I took care of myself by working as a maid and later in a factory.

Everything in my life seems to be okay. I am here in America drinking and dining with you ladies. This is really something I never thought would happen to me. But going back to my mother, I have plans of recovering all the properties my mother sold. I am saving a part of my salary from here to slowly get them back but first I need to find a husband," said Jelene.

"That's a bold move in our culture but hilarious. Do you have any plan or strategy in mind on how you will get one?" Tina asked.

"Times have changed ladies. We can now discreetly pursue a man. There are not too many in the field," replied Jelene.

"My dear, where are all these ideas coming from? Chedeng asked.

No one had any answer but everyone laughed like crazy.

Blanca warned the ladies to tone down the noise because it was past ten o'clock in the evening. "Ladies, there is another floor above us, she said. We do not want the police to come here. We are in America now."

"*Paano ang* search for a husband? (How do you search for a husband).Will you go to the rice fields and hopefully find one? That might work," said Chedeng.

"Well, I met one the last time I went home. He comes from the same town and has been writing. If things work out, I might go home and check on him again. I have a working visa so I can check on him from time to time," said Jelene.

"The good old penpal writing still works. I love your story Jelene but I need to go home. Will I see you ladies next Saturday?" Blanca asked.

"Of course, but don't be late because Jelene promised us a movie," replied Tina.

On her way home, Blanca felt happy because she was getting to know the sisters more and more. She sensed that she had gained their trust. They talk more and with such ease.

"They seem to like my jokes, pizza, movies, and hopefully me. I need to find ways of reciprocating their kindness and hospitality. I thought we would never click. I am sure early on they knew my roots in the Philippines. But they did not seem to care about me being a city girl, college educated, etc. I also did not care if they are from the province and had been working as maids since they were young. They are very warm and caring folks," Blanca assuring herself.

The ladies were not disappointed the following Saturday. Movie night continued on as expected. Jelene's friend came with what they thought was a Filipino movie.

"Good evening. I'm Corina but in America they call me Corrine. I have a movie for us to watch tonight. I sneaked out one and nobody at *Bahay Kubo* (bamboo house) will notice. I work for the place every other weekend and sleep here once in a while," Corrine explained.

As t turned out, Corrine's movie was not a one time event. It was a *teleserye* (soap opera). Blanca knew that it would be a tearjerker because of the title – *Maging Sino Ka Man* (I love you and do not care about the pain you can cause me).

"This is going to be *bitin* (inconclusive). What guarantee do we have to get the next episode? "We will get hooked then what?" exclaimed Tina.

"But it would be nice to feel that way. It will keep us going and thinking what will happen next," replied Blanca.

"Look, this *teleserye* will introduce us to a new generation of actors in Philippine movies like John Lloyd, Bea Alonzo, Ann Curtis and Sam Milby. Can't we at least try the first episode," Chedeng suggested.

Everyone agreed to Chedeng's idea of watching the first episode of *Maging Sino Ka Man.*

The *teleserye* was good in the beginning until it got boring and time consuming. Like a prophet, Tina told the ladies the *teleserye* will take forever. "Did'nt you notice each episode takes two hours and we've watched it for six Saturday nights? Let's do a marathon watching.

We will finished it tonight and know the end. I bet it's going to be a happy one," suggested Tina.

The last episode of the *teleserye* lasted up to four o' clock in the morning. Everyone scrambled around for a spot to sleep when it was over.

Chedeng shared her queen size bed with Blanca who was too sleepy to go home. Tina slept on the bed across her sister's. Jelene and her friend slept on the sofa bed in the living room. Everyone woke up late to find Chedeng's breakfast of pancakes, bacon, scrambled eggs and coffee. No one mentioned church. Jelene and her friend left hurriedly. Both ladies are live-in maids and they did not want any trouble with their employers.

Over breakfast, Blanca and Chedeng talked about the new faces in Philippine cinema. Do you know John Lloyd is related to long time Visayan actress Caridad Sanchez?" asked Blanca.

"Oh! I remember her in the comedy skit *Tang Tarantang* (a father and son radio comedy program in the 50s who were always in trouble),"Chedeng replied.

Tina laughingly said, "You two should get a test on Filipino movies and stars."

Everyone laughed. "That's Blanca and Chedeng you know," said Jelene

"Thank you very much for the breakfast. Have a good week everyone," said Jelene as she and her friend headed out for the door.

Blanca also left and was grateful for the big breakfast of pan cakes, bacon and coffee. "The sisters would always have food for anyone who dropped by or sleep over at their 22nd apartment. Bless their hearts for doing it without having to request or ask. Everyone went home a happy camper."

Celebrating Birthdays

November 2007 came and Tina's invitation to celebrate her birthday was out. Blanca was invited for the first time. She did not know what gift to give Tina but she had to find something. Gift cards were not that popular with Filipinos so she decided to bring flowers.

Pretending not to be surprised but was nevertheless surprised, Blanca was overjoyed with Tina's birthday celebration. Food was just unbelievably plentiful. Guests kept coming then leaves after eating or singing. Part of what looked like an all- day event included Karaoke singing and card game called 49. Chedeng said these were Tina's favorite activities for her birthday.

The next weekend, Blanca raved about Tina's birthday celebration. Their Saturday night dinner for her was the best time to express her joy of having been invited.

"Tina's birthday was like those *fiestas* we have in the Philippines. There were lots of people coming and going some of whom did not know each other or were meeting for the first time like, me. I stayed longer to listen to the Karaoke singing. I also realized Tina can sing. Was it her Karaoke machine? Those *Visayan* songs like *Matudnila* (It is said So) and *Pobreng Alindahaw* (A little Bird) were sung with such gusto and feeling, I almost cried, even though I did not understand completely the meaning of the lyrics," commented Blanca.

Tina said the Karaoke machine is hers. She was quick to say that it came all the way from the Philippines because the country has the latest Karaoke technology.

"The newer ones project the lyrics on the TV screen. There is no need to hold song books like we used to do. The scoring game feature lets you know how well you did the song. Low scores should not be a problem because the purpose of Karaoke singing is to have fun. Don't you agree?

The forty one card game on the other hand, has been going on for years in our place.

I have friends who come to the party to play instead of Karaoke singing. Some of them go to the casinos on weekends they are off. I do not go to the casino. I think it's a waste of time and money. It could be addictive too because I know some who can't quit gambling. But that's their problem. The *41* card game we play at our place is just for fun. We have a five dollar limit when we play 41. Sometimes someone goes home with some money." explained Tina.

Excited to recall the past week, Blanca went back to 22nd for their usual Saturday night dinner. She wondered why the sisters retreated to the bedroom like there was a secret thing going on. Jelene told Blanca that the sisters would be counting the money gifts from Tina's birthday party. She also talked about her weekend arrangements with the sisters.

"What then is your arrangement with the sisters?" asked Blanca

"As someone who comes to 22nd on Saturday and leaves the following day, I give the sisters some money every month for my weekend stay. The extra money helps pay the rent and I have this ideal place to unwind during my off days. It's a place to go home to on a Saturday night after seeing other friends or shopping. I am relaxed and happy being with your group watching movies, talking, eating and sleeping in.

I do not like to spend my weekends in one of those apartments or houses rented to Filipinos. There could be five to ten people sharing the place to afford the rent. It's like a group home. One is in charge of the lease and sublet rooms to mostly live out Filipino maids. You cannot unwind with so many people around you. This place is quiet and spacious. The sisters like it this way," smiled Jelene.

"Guess what? We have collected $1,500 money gifts from Tina's birthday party," announced the sisters when they came out of the bedroom.

"That's great.It should be enough for *Manang Chedeng's* birthday party next month," said Jelene.

December came quick and the ladies were back at 22nd Street to celebrate Chedeng's birthday. Blanca was among the first to arrive at the party. "Living nearby has it good points. I get to eat the delicious food and warm soup prepared by Chedeng. They are all fresh and smell good. What is not to like?" said Blanca when the rest of the ladies arrived.

Chedeng's birthday celebration was no different from Tina's. It was a repeat of Tina's party—lots of Filipino dishes and guests who came also in trinkles. There was again the Karaoke machine and table for Tina's 41 card game. Not everyone knew the game but Tina explained they have friends who like to play it. "They usually come late in the afternoon when everyone had eaten and left," smiled Tina.

Blanca left the party around three o' clock in the afternoon. When the ladies asked why she was leaving early, she replied she came early. She whispered however that it was time to go home because Tina's card game was about to start. "The Karaoke singing has stopped too," added Blanca.

The ladies got the cue from Blanca that it was time to leave. The ladies did not talk about their gifts to Chedeng which worried Blanca. She wondered if she should speak with Jelene in private about right gifts to give when it is a Filipino party hosted by the sisters. She again ended up bringing flowers and a bottle of wine. "But this is not the way Filipinos do it, especially when it is a fiesta-like celebration of the sisters birthday," Blanca telling herself when she got home.

Blanca's wonderings about gifts to give to the next Filipino party like the sisters' ended when she bumped into Jelene while shopping in Friendship Heights. "Do you have the time for a snack or coffee? I just need to ask some questions about the parties at 22nd Street. You know the place I am talking about," asked Blanca.

"Of course, it would be great to have a one on one conversation with you. Feel free to ask me any question," replied Jelene.

"Then let's go to Mcdonald's unless you have another place in mind," suggested Blanca.

"McDonald's would be fine. We will see lots of Filipinos like us chatting and smiling," said Jelene.

Prompted by Blanca, the two ladies walked hurriedly to nearby McDonald's, ordered and got seated. Blanca could not hide her excitement over having Jelene alone.

"Are you ready for my first question?" asked Blanca.

"Just say it *Ate* Blanca. I'm here for you," replied Jelene.

"What are those envelopes coming from most of the guests at the party? Why are some guests in hurry to leave while some stayed up to late afternoon? Why do you have birthday parties on Sundays? Is'nt that supposed to be your day off?" asked Blanca.

"About the money gifts, those envelopes help buy the food and drinks in many of our parties. We also give money gifts whenever we go other people's birthday parties. In other words, we are helping each other celebrate occasions like birthdays. Please understand that most of us do not have families here in the States to celebrate important dates and events like birthdays. It always feels good to celebrate our birthday," Jelene explained.

"Then, what about other gifts like bags or something the celebrant wanted to have for his or her birthday?" Blanca asked.

"*Ate* Blanca, we've accumulated all kinds of gifts over the years. Most employers and friends give Christmas and birthday gifts. We do not know where to store them. So this is the joke among us, unless it is a house or a car, don't bother to bring in something for my birthday because it has no space in the basement or the little room I'm renting somewhere.

I'm lucky I have a room upstairs in my employer's house next to the daughter's room. But others live in the basement of their employers'house sharing space with the washer and dryer. Other live out maids could be bed spacers sharing a house with ten other folks. Bearing this in mind, we really have to think hard on what we should keep for our daily needs.

What do we do then with those unwanted gifts? The answer is simple, we insert them in those *balikbayan* boxes bound for the Philippines where they are welcome and can be put to good use," said Jelene.

The two ladies could not help but laughed at what they were talking about and Blanca's questions on what she thought were secretive and mysterious all along.

Jelene continued and said,"seem sad but like everybody else, we want to have fun too. We need it after a week's work of cleaning, cooking and taking care of children and sometimes adults. Did you not notice some are really dressed up for the party? We still love to dress up at least one day a week. We want to be away from the maid's attire of jeans and T-shirt. Don't you want to dress up once in a while? Dressing up brightens up my off days.

Why were some guests in a hurry to leave? It is because they are either on their way to another party or to a part time job. The point is that the ladies who left the party early had that taste of a fun weekend even only for a short time and make some money we can keep for ourselves. Our monthly salary is what most of us sends home. This practice spoils our loved ones in the Philippines

We send money right away every time they call. I heard one Filipino say we are like ATM machines and that her relatives think money grows on trees. But everyone have their reasons for sacrificing themselves for families left behind in the Philippines. I do not want to get into that because our love for our families is the main reason why we are here.

"Can I say the apartment at 22nd Street is the gathering place for friends of the sisters?"

Blanca asked. "In a way yes because there is no *amo* (employer) around. It is a private place where we can dance, sing, talk and laught to our hearts content. The 22nd Street apartment is like a refuge where we can be ourselves. Don't you agree?" asked Jelene.

"Yes. I have witnessed how the sisters' friends enjoyed their time with other friends in that apartment. It was fun to watch all the heckling, singing and eating like there is no tomorrow," replied Blanca.

"On another story, I heard November was also your birth month. Then let me wish you a belated Happy Birthday *Ate* Blanca. Don't be fooled by my looks. I am in my mid-40s too. Who knows, I might turn fifty and still be around doing housekeeping. But like I said before, I am looking for a husband. You know anyone?" teased Jelene.

"You are serious when you talk about this search for a husband. Good luck on that one. But let me ask more questions before you take the subway to Rockville. Why did Tina keep getting money from the ladies, in addition to the gift money?" asked Blanca.

"Oh! That is for the *paluwagan* (loosen the tightness of anything). It is a savings club meant to be used for rainy days or when money is tight among its members. Money collected from the participants is turned into a pool. If there are ten members each contributing one hundred dollars a month, the group would have one thousand dollars monthly for distribution.

This is how the word *paluwagan* (loosen up) applies in contrast to *mahigpit* (tight) meaning in dire need for money. I think you understand the idea.

Members take turns in receiving the money depending on the number one gets from a draw to determine who goes first to collect down the line. Once one gets her money, member contribution continues until everyone get their share from the pool. Then members can start over again.

The danger of the practice is when one runs away with the pot and stops contributing.

So far no one has done this bad act in *Ate* Tina's group. I heard it's been going on for years and *Ate Tina* has been the captain eversince. Trust factor is the key to the success of a *paluwagan*.

I am a regular member. I like it because it's like a forced savings. I will quit the club when *Ate* Tina and her friends put the monthly savings to five hundred dollars per month. I cannot do five hundred a month because I am a live in maid and can't do part time work. From what I know, the money for the *paluwagan* comes from part time jobs too.

I would rejoin when it's back to two hundred. The five hundred dollar contribution usually happens when a member requests a big pile of money to cover situations in the Philippines like sickness, house construction, or capital for a business.

Overall, the *paluwagan* has been a great help to its members and to the never ending financial needs of their families in the Philippines. I won't say anything more about our folks in the Philippines. I am not their mother," joked Jelene

They continued their walk to the subway. Jelene said she had to hurry because she had to prepare the Sunday dinner for her employer's family. "Sunday night is the best time to prepare for the week ahead. The little girl I am caring for takes a lot of my time during the day unless she is asleep. I can hardly wait when she starts school. That's one load off my back during the day. I will see you next Saturday," added Jelene.

Blanca's found her chat with Jelene helpful. She was happy to know from Jelene how she would blend in with the sisters and their friends. "I am glad that they did not treat me differently because I am not a housekeeper. I think I found new friends and I want it to last because they are nice and caring folks," Blanca smiling waiting for the bus.

The Saturday night dinner at 22nd Street was leftovers from Chedeng's December 10 birthday party. Chedeng reminded everyone that there was enough food to last for a whole week. Everyone laughed, except her sister Tina. Always outspoken, Tina asked her sister Chedeng to jazz up the left overs to give it a different taste.

"My dear we did not have *lechon* (roasted pig) that could be turned into another dish like like *paksiw* (chopped roasted pig flavored with vinegar, pepper, bay leaf and sugar),"explained Chedeng.

"Can we not just imagine the *lechon* while we are having dinner? Or can we focus on the *palitaw* (rounded boiled rice cake with shredded coconut, sesame seeds and sugar toppings) of Jelene? I have not eaten *palitaw* in a long time. Jelene make it sound so easy to make them. First, you have to have the right consistency of the rice dough and the right timing when dipping them into the boiling water.That's a hard one to perfect. Done wrong, they will get chewy and tough to eat," said Blanca.

"*Palitaw lulubog lilitaw, palitaw lulubog lilitaw*" (Filipino riddle on how it is cooked by dipping the dough into the boiling water and comes up when done)," sang the three ladies.

The song about *palitaw* made the three ladies laughed except Tina. "You two, pointing to Blanca and Chedeng would always find something to laugh about like the *palitaw*," complained Tina.

"Admit it sister, we never learn how to make *palitaw*," Chedeng added.

More laughter followed over Jelene's rice cake dessert. To appease Tina, Blanca then turned the conversation to the sisters' family and love life. Blanca volunteered to talk about her love life first. She knows most Filipinos are always within the boundaries of *hiya* (embarrassing) that it will take another thirty minutes of prodding and convincing to open up.

"Ladies since there is no movie tonight, allow me to be the starter. You know like our favorite line dancing, there is always a starter to get everybody to dance.

I just got dumped in 2005 when I met Tina the first time. We were both walking. Do you remember that now? I was on my way to see my hairdresser right after my then boyfriend left me to marry someone else. She lectured me on getting dumped only once. Second time she said is too much. She said always have a spare tire meaning another man in case it does not work out. Her last words were men do the same too.

She was right in many ways but I never learned. You see when we are in love, we get stupid. And everytime I fall in love, I fall hard. That's my sister's joke about me. You see maybe because I am part of that generation of devoted Filipinas who will stay through thick and thin. I heard that has changed over the years. Is this true?

Then let me continue, when the father of my daughter announced he won't be joining us, I let him go and moved on. Easier said but I had no choice. I had so much in my plate at that time. I had a kid in tow and for the third time needed to adjust to a new place which is America.

I think I made the right decision to forget him and the family I tried hard to put together despite our moves from Philippines to Hong Kong then Canada and finally United States. I'm here with you ladies and having fun. That's all that matters now. Life can sometimes be cruel and painful," smiled Blanca.

The ladies did not say a word. Jelene asked who would be next to talk about their story. "If I remember right, I already talked about mine early on when our Saturday night started," said Jelene staring at the sisters. Chedeng remembered what Jelene said and started talking.

"The family of my boyfriend already had their eyes on a teacher for their son. You know how it was way back then, we follow our parents so my boyfriend married the teacher and lived happily ever after. But now there is a new twist to my love story," smiled Chedeng.

Chedeng found out from her daughter that her ex recently got widowed. "Mama, *biyudo na si Papa* (Mother, my father is now a widower)," Chedeng's daughter said in message.

"My daughter encouraged me to get back with her father. I said that's a bad idea because he was never around when I needed money for milk. It's late and why I should I bring back memories of a lost fight? I only had an elementary education versus a college educated teacher. We were ten children of a policeman. That was ten mouths to feed. In other words, we were poor and did not dress well. It was best to let him go at that time", Chedeng sighed.

Before everyone got sad, Chedeng started laughing and said that Tina's was more fun and twisted.

"Oh! You know our saying about the "maaagap" (early birds) people. My competitor adopted that strategy even if that was not acceptable back then. She went right ahead and slept in my boyfriend's house. I lost and withdrew from a fight I will never win.

There was nothing I could do given the situation. Also, he did not fight for me. That's how simple it was or maybe sex was better with her," joked Tina.

"Oh! Oh! This is going to be an interesting night," interrupted Blanca.

Tina continued on to talk about men and how sex could be used to catch them. "*Buntis agad* (pregnant bomb)," Tina shouted about her competitor.

That really threw the ladies into laughter when Tina got graphic about the topic. Nevertheless, the ladies agreed when she quoted the Filipino saying *daig ng maagap ang masikap* (hardworking people oftentimes beaten by those more forward thinking or early brids). More laughter until Tina got serious.

"We have experienced not having money to buy milk for the baby. It will tear you apart to hear a hungry baby cry. This alone is a lesson to try our best to rise up. *Kung saan ka nadapa, doon babangon* (come back up from the spot where you fall) as we always say when we make a big mistake and there is no one else to help you. What would you do given our situation? We decided to work and make our own money instead of waiting for support from the men who did not have guts to do what was right. Child support was unheard of back then," said Tina.

With no help in sight from the men who got them pregnant, the sisters left Leyte and work as housemaids in the posh villages of Makati. With limited education, working as housemaids was the only job they could do. Tina barely had a high school education while Chedeng finished elementary, they got lucky and found good employers. Knowing some English Tina said also helped them with their work because it is the language of the Filipino elite and foreigners living in many exclusive areas of the city.

"I suppose you left your children with the family and send money regularly," said Blanca.

"Yes, we told our family that we would be sending money not only for the care of our children but for the family as well.

The same arrangement continued on when we moved to the States. My daughter is now a widow while Tina's son is married and with children of his own. We went home regularly when we were in the Philippines and did the same when we had diplomatic visas.

It was quite a sacrifice being away from the family. We did not see our children grow up like most parents do. We watched them through videos and listened to their messages via cassettes. It gets depressing and unbearable sometimes but Tina and I always have each other no matter what," Chedeng explained.

There was silence in the apartment after Chedeng's words on the sacrifice they had to do to keep the lives of their children going. Jelene knew how it felt because she is separated from her family too. Blanca was ready to cry but did not because she did want sadness to take over their Saturday night dinner at 22nd Street.

"By the way, how and where do you spend Christmas? It is just around the corner. This is my first Christmas with you ladies," said Blanca.

"Are we going to have the usual Christmas here with your old friends? Are we going to also have the fish and other sea foods from the Wharf for New Year?" asked Jelene.

"Oh, yes. Christmas is that time of the year that we reconnect with friends I met when I was starting out in this country. This was in the early 80's so you can guess how young I am. You must have met some them during one of my birthdays. So far no one had died yet but some have moved out of DC because their families have arrived. Some would still care to come for Christmas maybe for sentimental reasons. After all we were each other's family early on.

The same group comes for the New Year. It is also a tradition that we do not eat meat that day. Tanya and company would drive to the Wharf in South West DC to buy fish, shrimps and crabs. Everyone puts her share to cover the food. It is a very relaxing atmosphere. Some of us would eat with our hands because crabs can be messy. Of course, Karaoke singing is on the top of the list to do after a sumptuous lunch. While they sing, I watch football especially when the Redskins are playing. I've been a Redskins fan for years," said Chedeng.

"So you are a fan. Do you also have that pig nose while watching?" asked Blanca.

Everyone laughed at Blanca's question. Someone said that she was not a Redskins fan.

"Me, we are going to Montreal to spend the holidays with my sisters," said Blanca

"That's a very cold place in the winter time," said Tina.

"Yes, but we want to keep the Christmas tradition even if my mother is already gone. She was in a home in Montreal for more than ten years so we would visit whenever we can. But Christmas no matter how cold for us was always in Montreal when she was alive. We sang Christmas carols to her and ate even if she probably did not know what was going on.

My mother had a stroke but she had been sick with diabetes early on that caused her glaucoma. We were still in the Philippines when she lost one eye to glaucoma."

There was a pause. Blanca pulled herself together and bravely talked about the difficult decision of putting a sick aging parent in a home. "The idea is not yet accepted and well understood in our community," said Blanca. Filipinos of previous generations took care of their aging parents. "I saw my mother juggling the care for her mother and raising us. That was not easy for my mother," said Blanca.

She talked about how her family came to a decision to put their mother in a home.

"We had a family meeting and it was three in favor versus two. We were lucky because my oldest sister is a nurse so she knew how the system works. Although she found something to complain about in the home of our choice, my sister tried to make up for what is missing every time she comes to visit our mother. She would flip our mother in her bed so she won't have those bedsores. That was her main concern because bedsores cause so much discomfort to the elderly and death.

Given her loss of memory because of the stroke, the one thing hilarious about my mother was her vivid memory of her farm in Batangas. That was all she talked about during our visits but hey some things I guess stay with us even at our darkest hours," quipped Blanca.

"Let's greet everyone a Merry Christmas and Happy New Year in advance, shall we?" said Jelene.

"Wait a minute! Are you not coming here for the holidays?" Tina asked

"There are still two weeks to go before Christmas. My employer might not let me go out for the holidays because they have guests too. New Year maybe a lot easier take off but I do not want to commit right now. These are the uncertainties in the life of a live in maid. We all know these," said Jelene.

The holiday break gave Blanca a chance to sort out what 2007 had been for her and family. Her excitement of having new friends close by and being an empty nester went fast and unnoticed.

First, she never thought she would start missing her daughter who would be graduating in May of 2008. "I did not miss Miren since her freshman year but why am I missing her now? I guess she will be more independent and move away after graduation. Well she will have own life after school and this is how its' going to be from hereon. But God always sends me something to fill any void in my life like the sisters," Blanca joked herself.

Her newly found friends in Glover Park came as a surprise. Blanca had a hard time connecting with other people especially with her community. For one, she did not have the money and the car to attend Filipino community events. Babysitting is by the hour. Community events meant a lot of time spent something she could not spare as a single parent. She was also constantly looking for a more high paying job and professional growth.

As 2007 came to a close, Blanca felt that being friends with the sisters and seeing other people again was a blessing she did not expect that year. She knew it takes time to be friends with anyone.

"The sisters and their friends are very genuine, sincere folks who can put together an eclectic array of dishes for dinner, and joyously celebrate birthdays. How can I not like my life now?" Blanca asked herself.

The Friendship Grew In 2008

As the ladies hunkered down for the winter months of January, February up to March, they found it entertaining to talk about over dinner all the Filipino and foreign movies they had watched the past year. Bridget Jones was a favorite not only because the leading lady was on the round side, but was a self - deprecating character.

"You know there is always someone in elementary or high school that we had this secret liking or crush but was never aware of until you see each other again. I am talking about Darcy the lawyer and childhood friend of Bridget. He did not even care about Bridget's weight. I find that so endearing," said Blanca.

"What about the blue soup? I think that was the most hilarious part of the story. Bridget thought she had all the ingredients, followed instructions to the tee from the recipe book, but it turns out she missed the kitchen string to tie the asparagus. With no more time to run to the store, so she used a blue string from her sewing kit. So the blue soup was born. That was really cute and it was okay with Darcy. It also became Blanca's excuse not to cook and invite us for dinner," Chedeng said in her defense.

Blanca replied and said that only her daughter can tolerate her cooking probably because she had no choice. "All you ladies can cook and will be learning more maybe. I hope to learn too. Please don't get tired of feeding me," plead Blanca.

"Not to worry. We know you were a rich kid back home and maybe had someone cook for your family, but how did you manage when you got here?" Tina wanted to know

"It was best to recall how things were done back in the days in the Philippines. I also asked my sisters who were in the same boat like me. Comparing notes helped a lot. That's how it was for me when it comes to cooking.

You would not believe this, but I entertained my American friends with spring rolls, noodles and shrimps with coconut milk. I would serve *halo halo* (sweet mixture of beans, plantain, and jackfruit topped with milk and crashed ice) for dessert. Ladies, they love it so much that they look forward to it again and again. I am a little proud, but I would still have to eat *sako sako* (sacks) of rice to be at par with Chedeng's cooking," said Blanca.

"No! Mine comes from years of practice. You will be better than me one day and perhaps will invite us for dinner more often," said Chedeng.

"Oh! That will be the day when I can proudly invite you for dinner at my place," said Blanca.

"We know you have to go because it's getting late but we will see you next Saturday. I am assigning Jelene to continue our conversation about movies we've watched," laughed Tina.

"I will do it unless my employer has mission trip to somewhere then I cannot come next Saturday,"said Jelene.

"Have a good night and sleep ladies," said Blanca as she threw flying kisses to the ladies.

"You are here. I supposed your employer did not travel that could hold your day off? Let's have dinner first then we can continue with your favorite movie from Blanca's Netlfix subscription. Is everyone okay with my suggestion?" Chedeng asked.

Everyone said yes but Jelene in the middle of dinner started to talk about her favorite among their past movies.

"There were some really funny ones and *makabagbag damdamin* (very touching) ones. For example, the movie "So Happy Together" with Kris Aquino and Eric Quizon was really fun and wacky. I heard Eric is the gay son of Dolphy the king of Philippine comedy. I liked the theme which was about the friendship between two odd characters. One is a loud vendor of just about anything you can sell and a gay event planner.

They met in a *Santa Cruzan* (May procession in many provinces of the Philippines to honor Mary and other saints) where *sagalas* (ladies dressed in gowns representing the different saints) are gay men. They stayed friends until the gay man got sick and died. The ups and downs of their lives were funny, but really spoke of a deep friendship between the two main characters," said Jelene.

"What about you *Manang* Chedeng? Which one did you enjoy?" asked Jelene.

Chedeng said she liked the most *Mano Po One and Two* (a Filipino custom of holding the hand of an elderly person and putting it on one's forehead as a sign of respect). These two movies dealt with traditions and respect for the elderly. It was nostalgic of the good old days.

Mano Po also spoke of how women could be used by powerful men. It also showed how women can be clever when we revenge. These are very deep issues to talk about. What I like the most *Mano Po* was a star studded movies with the likes of Susan Roces, Vilma Santos, Kris Aquino and Christopher de Leon as the main protagonists. What are your thoughts ladies?" asked Chedeng.

Everyone laughed because actors old and new had been Blanca's and Chedeng's favorite topics. "Oh! Now, Tina is speaking Tagalog like the Chinese in the Philippines," joked Chedeng.

Blanca followed and began speaking in broken Tagalog too like the Chinese in the Philippines. "Well, no pun intended but when you pick up another language we are most likely to pick up the verb first then the noun. If you recall the dialogue in the movie, you will understand what I'm saying about learning another language other than your native tongue," explained Blanca.

"So, *tama ikaw* (right you are)," said Tina.

"Okay, I am going home before we start talking like those characters in the movie, "said Blanca. Good night ladies.

"Okay. We will watch you walk to your place until you get down the hill close to the front door of your building," said Tina.

2

The Graduation of 2008

"LADIES WE'VE BEEN INVITED TO A FILIPINO dance this Saturday at the Christ the King Church on East West Highgway. Most Filipinos know where it is because it is a major route of the L buses. Someone is driving us to the dance this time," said Tina.

"Good! I will not go if we have to take the bus although I know some Filipinos who take the bus just to go the dance. I can't blame them for taking the bus to a dance if there is really no one to take them. Saturday night is the perfect time to have fun and dance till you drop.

Who invited us? We have not gone to one in years. But I think it would be nice to check on those dance parties again. Words get around fast like a wild fire,"said Chedeng.

Tina smiled and asked if her sister still remembers Pacita from Georgetown. "Are you talking about the Filipina whose husband died of cancer years ago?' Chedeng replied.

"Yes, while I was cleaning a window at my part time job in Georgetown, someone was calling and making *sitsit* (Filipino way of hissing) across Mrs. Peterson's window. It took me a while to figure out what the woman was trying to say until she motioned me to drop what I was doing to meet outside.

It was the widow Cita! Remember now?" said Tina.

"Oh! Yes. She and her husband are one of the few husband and wife workers in Georgetown back then. It was really sad when her husband died because they had a young daughter. Is she still working in Georgetown? They have a very kind employer who let them live in the basement of their house. That's a great saver. They had a baby later on and were happy until the man got cancer and died. Like I said, they are known in the area because it's a husband and wife team. Did she invite us to the dance?" asked Chedeng.

"Yes, my dear sister. Cita volunteered to drive so we can go to the dance. Why would you not want to go? All she needed was a good navigator to give direction because she is not familiar with Maryland roads. Alright, then ladies, we are going to the dance next Saturday," said Tina.

"Yes, we are going to a *yugyugan* (non stop dancing). That's should be exciting," said Jelene.

Blanca was not at all surprised by the Filipino crowd when they stepped into Christ the King basement. "This is the same crowd I have seen in Hong Kong and Canada and I know why," Blanca observed as they look for an empty table for the group.

She went on to recall in her head an article she wrote for the Philippines'Daily that said," a majority of guests were women because they were the ones who left the country in the 80s and the rest followed. Unemployment was high and housekeeping did not require much education and skill. Anyone who has the physical and mental stamina can be employed as one. Kind of sad but most of these women are mothers and wives and if we pause for a moment, its social cost can run high. Let's think about its impact on their families."

Blanca quickly snapped out of her habit of overthinking and instead focused on the line dancing that was going on. The music reminded her of disco days. The only time she quit the dance floor was when the DJ switched to a slower music.

"Why did you leave the dance floor? I think you love to dance," asked Chedeng.

"Well, the music being played right now needs a partner. You know the oldies call a slow drag back in the days. Look, there are very few couples on the dance floor," Blanca replied.

"We used to come here when were younger and needed to have some fun. This is a good church to go to because it is situated along the bus line. I would sometimes drop by whenever I am in the area just to pray and enjoy the silence," Chedeng said.

"Who usually organizes events like this? Blanca asked Chedeng.

"It depends on the group like the *Visaya* group we usually go to in the past. They do it. We also get invited by other groups named after the province they came from. Their objective was mostly to raise funds for scholarships in the home province. A part of the funds tonight will go to the rent of this basement. This is not free but we're happy to work with the church Tickets are sold in advance at a very minimal price. You must have noticed food is rationed because the proceeds will be divided into three- rent, food and scholarship," said Chedeng.

For someone who did not frequent dance parties organized by Filipino Overseas Workers (OFWs), Blanca found the event very friendly and fun. She really enjoyed the night because the DJ had music from different eras. The 70' up to the 80's were her dancing days and so were many of the other ladies. Jelene also came to dance. "This is a big deal for me. It is my source of *tsismis,* get dressed and be pretty for a night. I don't feel isolated," said Jelene.

"Will there be a beauty contest tonight?" Blanca asked.

"I doubt it. I did not hear the emcee said anything about that. Look, there is no stage.

There is always a stage if there is one. Do you like beauty contests?" Tina asked Blanca.

"Yes. They are fun. I have seen lots of them in Hong Kong. It's amazing to see the transformation of a Filipina when she dresses up. We could be pretty too, you know like everybody else," replied Blanca.

"We have not been to one in a while. The next fun thing to do is Halloween. Georgetown is famous for their Halloween parade. All these young folks participate by walking up and down Wisconsin Avenue to show their off their costumes. It's a lovely event," said Tina.

"I'm looking forward to that one. My next question is what time are we going home? Please don't forget me please!" begged Blanca. "What do we have to worry about? We now have a driver happy to take us to the dance. All we have to do is check for the next one," said Tina.

On the way to the parking lot, Cita spoke with the ladies and said"Oh! By the way, I am inviting everyone to the graduation of my daughter Chloe this coming June 2008. I will let you know of the details through Tina. We are in close contact with each other. I see her every now and then in Georgetown. Please keep your June calendar open ladies,"

The ladies were happy to be invited to a different event – a graduation. The sisters said graduation reminds them of the graduation of their children in the Philippines. "Most of the money sent to the Philippines has been for the education of our children. Thus, when a child or grandchild graduates from high school or college, it validates our choice to leave our families behind. God almighty! Getting yourself educated in the Philippines cost a lot of money. You need tons of them. Let's be happy for Cita's daughter finishing high school," said Chedeng.

Blanca did not say yes to the invitation. Once again, she was not sure whether to go or not because she just met Pacita for the first time. "Am I included in the invitation? It does not mean I am too. Or can I say I am part of the group so *sama na rin ako* (I am also included)?" asked Blanca.

"Yes, of course, *Filipino tayo* (we are all Filipinos). Remember what she said, we are all invited to the after-graduation event. The graduation itself is only for family members," said Tina.

"What would be a good gift to give Cita's daughter?" asked Blanca.

"It is up to you. Chedeng and I will give her some cash as *baon* (something to bring) she will need for college," replied Tina.

"That's a good idea. I remember my daughter was happy to receive some money for her high school graduation back in 2003. It was a big help to buy dorm necessities like towels, bed sheets, kitchen utensils etc. including a new computer. I am sure Chloe will also be happy to receive some money gifts as well," said Blanca.

"I will let you know once Cita calls me with the details of Chloe's graduation party," said Tina.

The ladies wait on the details of Chloe's after graduation party did not take long. Through Tina, the ladies learned that the party would be held the first Sunday of June 2008. Tina took the lead in making sure they would get to the party on time. They took the ten o'clock bus.

"Ladies, this is how the morning will play out. First, it's Sunday so we will attend the 10:30 mass at Dumbarton Church on P Street in Georgetown. Since the party is at one o'clock, let's walk around M Street, do window shopping after mass to kill time. Another way to kill time is to attend the after mass coffee hour. Whatever we decide to do, the point is not to arrive so early at the restaurant because it is so close by. Cita already made a reservation at Hang Lung's in Georgetown. We all know where that is," said Tina.

"You are right my dear sister to go to coffee hour and walk around. Now we are ready to eat and we are just two stores away from the place. Let's go so we get the best seats before the other guests arrive. You know some of our *kababayans* are *makupad* (some of us are slow and late at events) and our parties can be disorganized too," said Tina.

Contrary to Tina's comments on Filipino parties, the Hang Lung reception lady ushered them to a section of the place where Chloe's lunch would be held. They were also asked to pick the name cards that had table number 5. Other guests also started coming in some of whom looked familiar said the sisters. Blanca on the other hand, could not help but introduce herself to guests who found themselves assigned to her table. "This is kind of embarrassing but it feels great to meet other folks from the Filipino community," smiled Blanca as she shook hands of the other guests assigned to her table.

Seated at their table was a lady who introduced herself as someone who works for a Clinique counter at Lord and Taylor store in Friendship Heights. "I'm Marie and I tell you Cita and Chloe have been my loyal customers for years".

Another lady who introduced herself as Lanie said she and Mel are neighbors in Georgetown. "I'm from *Iloilo* (a province in Visayan region) and course, Visaya," Lanie said.

The sisters knew Lanie so they started speaking in *Visayan* dialect. Marie is from *Bacolod, Negros Occidental* and spoke *Visayan* as well. They assured Blanca that they were not talking about her. Blanca told them that she could understand some *Visaya* because she has cousins who can speak the dialect. "I know when I am getting sold, ladies," smiled Blanca.

Once the food started to come, Blanca knew immediately that lunch would be *lauriat* style (Chinese banquet style service in the Philippines consisting of 21 different kinds of dishes). Tina's eyes kept moving and named each course as they came in. Blanca kept the names in her head so as not to spoil Tina's enthusiasm over the parade of dishes. She praised how organized Chloe's after graduation party was. "The name card assignments disciplined us because some of us could be impolite sometimes in events like this," Tina said.

After an enjoyable lunch, Cita stood up, tapped her glass and proposed a toast and said, "for Chloe and her success as she move on to college, *Mabuhay* (Cheers). Thank you for coming to celebrate not only a milsestone in my life but for Chloe who have been a good daughter. I am proud of her as you can see in the video how she bloomed from this little girl to a young woman that she has become."

"How come we did not see the video sooner?" Tina whispered to Chedeng.

"Well, we were busy eating and talking but Chloe's video has been on since we came in. Was I the only one watching the video?" laughed Chedeng.

"Wow, Cita's daughter graduated from Four Square Academy, a very exclusive school in Washington DC. That's great and no one ever told me about it until this video. Cita looked very happy with the other mothers from the school for a mother- and-daughter dance. It's their way of celebrating the graduation of their daughters.

She must be very proud not only because her daughter finished high school but also from the most exclusive school in the nation's capital. Am I the only one here who knows Four Square? It has been the school of the children of who's who in Washington DC.? I think most of the guests knew because they are friends of Cita. Whatever my views are, Chloe is a very lucky kid to have attended Four Square," Blanca said quietly.

Watching the exit of some guests, Blanca's mind again went into wonderings where Cita got the money to finance Chloe's schooling. "Tuition at Four Square is about seventeen to twenty thousand dollars a year. Chloe is what is often called in the private school parlance as a lifer meaning she been with Four Square since preschool. Maybe Cita had the money. I overheard her say that she has clients all over Georgetown and she is rent free, it is possible for her pull this off. She must have given everything she has to her only child. Who knows but this is not for me to pry,"Blanca telling herself to leave it alone.

As more and more guests started to leave Hang Lung, Tina told Blanca to wait. From a distance, Blanca saw Cita whispering something to Tina who was smiling. Chedeng on the other end was busy talking to the other ladies at our table. Tina came back immediately and told her sister that they've been invited to another after graduation party in

Georgetown. Blanca asked if the sisters were going to the party. They said yes, so Blanca asked if she could go.

"I really would not mind going home alone after this party," said Blanca.

"Just come with us. I am sure you will enjoy this get to-gether. This is going to be different from the restaurant atmosphere," insisted Tina.

Blanca adamantly went with the sisters and for the first time had the chance to walk in the Georgetown neighborhood from M Street. Except for Marie and Paco, no one else brought a car, so the sisters, Lanie, Blanca and Cita, walked back to Mel's employer's house in Georgetown. Blanca noticed that most of the ladies were familiar with the neighborhood. Lanie lived and worked in the area and the sisters too. She told the ladies she learned about Georgetown because she takes the D6 bus that passes through the neighborhood.

"The bus riders from Georgetown are always well dressed. The men are in suits while the ladies' dresses I could tell they come from those boutiques in Georgetown and Wisconsin Avenue. They all look like lawyers or lobbyists," said Blanca.

Chedeng said she and Tina also ride the D buses, "so we ride with them too. That's how it is and Georgetown folks are not uppity like some other rich folks you know. They don't care who we are. It is about being courteous to everyone," said Chedeng.

"That's good to know. Are you sure those security alarms will not beep when there is a stranger in the neighborhood," Blanca said jokingly.

When the group finally arrived at Cita's employer's house, the ladies went up to a circular deck. There was a big round table with matching swivel chairs. Aquamarine seemed to be the color of the day, to match the napkins and plates.

"I am allowed to bring guests so do not worry. Mrs. Robinson already left for the summer to visit her children in Switzerland," said Cita.

When everyone got themselves comfortable, Cita and Paco started bringing in food from the kitchen of the main house. A bridge connects the kitchen to the deck.

As a first timer in Georgetown, Blanca looked around the neighborhood from the circular deck and began to understand why the place is such a fabled one.

"I have not been to something like this in a while. So this is the grandeur of Georgetown. It is like being transported to Europe. Imagine being in London with its cobblestone streets and well-tended little gardens. Every house has a back alley for the cars and garbage. Some houses even have gazebos and swimming pools. It's amazing how some small federal and Victorian houses have everything while the big ones like Cita's employer is three floors up. This is still DC without the hustle and bustle of the city. It is so quiet and peaceful," murmured Blanca.

Cita as hostess moved around like she owned the place. Food was plentiful, as if we had not just come out from a sumptous restaurant meal.

The flow of another batch of food and drinks kept everyone entertained and talking. Blanca had the chance to know the host, her daughter and of course her gentleman friend. She also joked about changing her province to any of the Visayan provinces. Cita and Paco objected.

"We are from *Tarlac* (a province in the Luzon Region) and speak *Kapangpangan* like the people from the province of *Pampanga*,"the couple said.

Everyone's eyebrows went up. *Uy uy* (Hey, hey) the ladies cried. "Ladies, hear this! They speak the same dialect. Is that not a good sign?" Tina joked.

Chedeng then sat down and spoke, "I am sorry for not getting in touch with you for a while. We've been busy and maybe you were too. But time went by but here we are eating and joking again after all these years. You look pretty and happy. Maybe someone is making you happy again?

"Well, I had to stay positive after my husband died. There was nothing I could do about his drinking. I did not make it an issue because he was a caring and loving man. His cancer ran quick and spread all over his body. Nothing more could be done to stop it. To keep his memory, Chloe and I would go visit him at Gate of Heaven Cemetery on his birthday and *Todos Los Santos*. (All Saints Day November 1). She was five when he died so she remembers her father," Cita said.

Lanie interrupted and asked "How are your sales going at Lord and Taylor these days Marie?"

"So far so good but I have to make sure I protect my turf because there is one woman on the other side of the Clinique counter trying to steal my customers. To stop that, I told her point blank to stop it or we will see each other in the parking lot," said Marie.

Day Pinoy ka talaga (Hey lady you are really a Filipino). When I ask to see you in the parking lot, beware, because I am going to get you," said Tina.

"But you cannot do this in America. There is the rule of law here," emphasized Chedeng.

'Yes, we can no longer have the *patay kung patay* (like a duel) mentality here in the US," Paco added.

"Well, I had the same problem like Marie's in the workplace. It was'nt stealing customers but making me look bad. So I confronted a Hispanic manager who kept complaining to management about callers' complaints against me. This was before I left for my Christmas vacation. So what I did was to give her all the thank you cards from my callers to negate her claims. She was embarrassed in front of the employees in her division. I told her we should start with a clean slate in the coming New Year. Then I left. I think she got my warning.

Sometimes we need to speak for ourselves ladies like Marie. This is what America taught me. Most Filipinos take in stuff for most of the time then we explode. Our solution is then I will see you in the parking lot scenario," said Blanca.

That drew quite a laugh from the ladies. "Seriously, we need to keep our cool," said Paco.

"Oh! *Kodakan na* (Filipino word for picture taking synonymous to the brand when Kodak Company was popular in the country years ago). There is still some good light," cried Tina.

"Okay, let's have a group picture first, then one solo with each of you ladies. I want to thank everyone for coming again and of course for your money gift. So who goes first?" asked Chloe.

The *kodakan* took a while but, in the meantime, Paco started clearing dishes and left over food. He told Cita to wrap the left overs for the ladies to take home. He said, "we cannot eat all the left overs so feel free to get a Ziploc bag and take whatever you like. I will drive the sisters and Blanca back to Glover Park while the rest could walk home like *Manang* Lanie.

"This has been quite an afternoon to remember. Our next get-together should be at my house ladies. Please plan to visit. I live in Laurel, Maryland. Everyone is welcome. I will let you know ASAP. Let's keep in touch please," said Marie.

"Sure, just let us know. Laurel is a little bit far but we have a driver. Thank you very much for having us. Chedeng and I will not have dinner tonight. We ate a lot today," said Tina.

"Thank you very much for having me too. It's been a lovely afternoon. Congratulations from one single parent to another," said Blanca

"So we will be seeing each other soon," said Marie.

It did not take long for the ladies to have a reunion. Packed in Paco's small jeep, the ladies went to Laurel one bright Saturday afternoon in July for another get together and eating. Cita sat at the front while the sisters and Blanca inched their way to the back of the small jeep. The sisters asked Blanca to sit in the middle so they could stretch their arthritic legs a little bit. This drew a bit of laughter but the sisters did not take offense.

Marie's house was big and well decorated like something out of a magazine. The living room has a winding stair to the second floor of the house where all the bedrooms are located. It has a formal dining room with a table set for eight to twelve sit- down guests. The kitchen has the latest appliances and an island counter that could also double as a dining table. It has that Georgetown feel, Tina opined after a tour of Marie's house.

"The table is all set. Feel free to warm your food in the microwave. I know our food is always served warm but I do not do it that way. I do not like the stress of keeping it hot while waiting for the guests to arrive. I have not seen *Manang* Lanie yet," asked Marie.

"Lanie will be coming with two other ladies from Georgetown. Let's wait for a little bit then, let's eat. It looks like everyone is getting hungry," said Cita.

"I think someone just parked. Ah, they are finally here. Relax ladies, we will finally eat. It is good to have some room in your tummy. Marie's food looks delicious," said Paco.

Lanie was the first to come into the living room. She greeted Marie in *Visaya* and introduced the other ladies.

"This is Clara, and this is Lulu, and her friend Natalie. Lulu and Clara are both from *La Union* province while Natalie is a long-time friend of Lulu's," said Lanie.

"Lulu and I met in Saudi Arabia. I did not expect to see her again after Saudi. Who knew we would both end up in America, "explained Natalie.

"Now that everyone is here, let's eat before food gets cold," suggested Marie.

Food was served on fine china. It was like a formal dinner. Marie used her collection of dinner ware and cutlery. The ladies joked about what it feels like to have some fine things once in a while regardless of your station in life. "We serve our employers in fine china so why not experience it ourselves?

I really dreamt of a house after years of rooming in. My ex-husband and I did not agree on having one. He did not care for the trouble of mowing the lawn, checking the gutters and all the work that comes with the upkeep of a house. I wanted to enjoy home ownership. Is that not the American dream? I will show you my garden later on ladies and one gentleman. But let's eat first," said Marie.

After the early dinner, Marie asked her guests to go to the family room for dessert. Tina suggested playing truth or consequence. "Maybe something true will come out. Please be ready with your questions," Tina teased with a big smile.

Like many truth or consequence games, Cita finally got hit. The ladies were excited to ask about the status of her relationship with Paco. She hesitated, but Paco came to the rescue. He admitted that he and Cita became couple after Chloe's graduation."I had to wait for the Italian guy to leave to make my move," said Paco.

"Oh! You are such a gentleman. How did you meet? I never saw you in Georgetown. Maybe you should give us a little background on how you guys became a couple. We will deliberate on it to see if you are a suitable match to our dear friend here," said Chedeng.

"I knew her uncle back in the Philippines. We belong to the same club and we got reconnected here in the US recently. He kind of made the match. I really liked her the day I saw her from a distance," said Paco.

The ladies burst into laughter when the relationship between Cita and Paco was unraveled. "Truth and consequence game always works wonder when it comes to knowing the truth in a silly and fun way. It is always good to hear it from the horses' mouth otherwise we might burst into flames speculating about whether you guys are a couple or not. So it is now confirmed," said Tina.

The game lasted for another hour until Marie asked the ladies to stay a little bit more so she could show her house. "Let me give you a tour of my house before you drive back to DC. It is getting late. It will take about forty five minutes to go back.

"Oh! Do you like a tour of the house, ladies? Tina asked.

"Of course, another five or ten minutes won't hurt," said Lanie and Chedeng.

Marie obliged and started going up the steps to the second floor. "As you can see on your left wall are pictures of my children and my ex. I did that on purpose. It's a good deterrent against anyone who plans on harming or robbing me. Look at him closely, his face is serious and means business. He is a big handsome African American male strong like Incredible Hulk.

Let's have a quick look at the bedrooms then we will go to the basement. I had this finished three years ago in time for the arrival of my children from the Phillipines. Their petition got approved but they all left after a year.

We just can't seem to get along, maybe because we have been away from each other for so long. I told them that I will no longer support them like I used to when they were in the Philippines. Maybe it was for the good of everybody that they moved out and free from me. It's a long story. I don't want to talk about right now because it is still painful," said Marie.

Th ladies did not say anything and instead steered the conversation back to the house.

"Wow! Your house is beautiful and nicely decorated, like those houses in Georgetown. We will be happy to come back," joked Tina on their way out.

"Oh! Why are there so many houses for sale in your area?" asked Blanca.

"Well, some of my neighbors I think overspent, then the housing bubble burst in 2008. Buying a house and a Mercedes at the same is tough to manage even on a two income family. You have to earn a lot of money to keep up. I, for one, still work part time whenever former employers call. It takes some juggling of funds to keep this house going," explained Marie.

Paco started the jeep to let the ladies know that it was time to go home. Cita took the front seat while Blanca and the sisters sat at the back. Lanie, Clara, and Natalie also said goodbye to Marie while Lulu started her car too.

The ladies were quiet on their way home. Paco teased the ladies everytime they go on a silent mode." Ha! I thought you never get tired of talking and laughing but you do. I like it.

I can drive in peace. You over there *Manang* Chedeng, *gising* (wake up)," shouted Paco.

"So now that I am awake, I will be talking all the way to DC," said Chedeng.

True to what Chedeng said, the ladies talked and laughed on their way home.

As usual, the sisters were dropped off first at their 22nd Street apartment then Blanca at nearby Benson Street. When she got home, Blanca sat down and reminisced what happened after her get-together with the ladies. This time was at Marie's house.

"It was another fun day with the sisters and couple Cita and Paco. It looks like my Saturday group is gaining ground and membership. But Marie's house is a revelation. She had a dream and fulfilled it through hard work. I must say she is also very smart. She figured out how the banking system works in order to get a home loan. But some of these OFWs are college educated so it should not be a surprise that Marie got herself a house," smiled Blanca.

To satisfy her curiosity about the other ladies at Marie's house, Blanca called for a middle of the week get together with the sisters. "Let's have pizza at my condo. It would be a good break from the Filipino food we've been eating the previous weeks. Let me know if you are amenable to my request. I do not mind if you are late. I really have a craving for pizza this time," speaking with Tina over the phone.

"Chedeng are you free on Wednesday night for pizza?" Tina asked her sister.

"Yes," replied Chedeng.

"So let's have the usual pepperoni and cheese pizza and one Hawaiian for Chedeng.

"Don't forget the Coca Cola please," said Tina

"You're the best ladies. See you this Wednesday," sighed Blanca.

3

The Ladies and Pet Duty

ON PIZZA NIGHT, BLANCA WENT STRAIGHT to the point on why she called for a get- together in the middle of the week. She wanted to know more about the ladies Lanie, Lulu and Clara. She said she did not have a chance to talk with them at Marie's house.

She remembered Lanie and Marie from Chloe's after-graduation party, but was curious how Clare and Lulu came into the picture.

"So this is what it is all about. From what I know, Cita, Clara, Lanie and Lulu met at Montrose Park. They walk the dogs of their employers every morning or late afternoon. That's how these ladies became close friends. Remember, dogs do not talk, but their walkers do. Dog walking is part of their job. It is done religiously, rain or shine, unless the weather is really bad. That's how much dog owners love their dogs.

Pets are like their children such that when they get sick, thousands of dollars are spent on them by their owners. Dogs are part of the family. Check the holiday pictures of the friends of your employers. There is a smiling dog somewhere in the picture.

Cat lovers give the same treatment to their cats. I must have told you that I do cat sitting for a lady in Georgetown.

She would never *entrega* (deposit) her cat to an animal day-care if she can help it. She would call me to take care of her cat when she has a business trip. Her cat needs company at night," said Tina

"Lanie and Marie, from what I know are from *Bacolod*, *Negros Occidental* province. I am not sure if they are related, but I could tell that they've been friends. They love to share stories days back in Bacolod in the *Visayan* dialect of course. So I'm able to pick up what they are talking about," added Chedeng.

She went to say that she and Lanie both started in Georgetown in the late eighties.

"We were already in Georgetown when CVS was still People's Drug Store in M Street.

"Lanie is a widow. Her first work abroad was Rome. Her first employer was a lady who works for Food and Agricultural Organization (FAO) of the United Nations. Ms. Sandra was the regional head of FAO in Europe. That was a very high position. I bumped into Lanie on my way home and the rest was history. I was sharing a small apartment on top of a deli store in Georgetown when the Antonini's went back to Italy. Lanie spoke *Tagalog*, with a Visayan accent. I knew that she was from the Visayan region. Speaking the same dialect and working in the same area, we got along immediately. So, we became friends. I would often see her walking one or two dogs. Oh! Lanie has always been a live in maid.

Ms. Sandra has three dogs that needed to be walked daily. Lanie said that this is her top priority. Lanie said those dogs are Ms. Sandra's children. She even hires part time workers to help keep the house because her dogs could be a handful. Ms. Sandra's house by the way is a three story one surrounded by small gardens. That's a lot of upkeep. But Ms.

Sandra loves to cook. That's one less chore for Lanie to do every now and then.

Lanie is friends with Cita. I think she was already around when Cita got widowed. Chloe knows her well too. Being a widow herself probably created some bond between the two women. Who knows? But Lanie could be fun. Why? Lanie knows all the songs they sing at Dumbarton Church. So, whenever the choir director is absent she leads the singing. Everyone follows because she knows all the appropriate songs to every part of mass. Do you know or remember all the songs when you attend a mass?" asked Chedeng.

Blanca and Tina laughed at Chedeng's story. "We believe your story Lanie leading the singing of mass hymns at Dumbarton Church," agreed the two ladies.

"I was attending the anticipated mass for Sunday when it happened. Lanie was at the back and from out of the blue she started the tune loud so you can't help but follow her. After the mass, the Korean parish priest thanked Lanie for leading the singing. The Korean pastor said it kept the mass alive," Blanca said.

Chedeng continues,"Clara and Lulu are from *Pangasinan* which is in the *Luzon* region. They are probably new to Georgetown because we met them for the first time at Marie's dinner. I remember they said they are from *Pangasinan* when they got introduced at the same party. I heard Lulu talking to *Manang* Clara or Clare in *Ilocano* (a dialect of Ilocos region). The late President Marcos spoke that way.

"Clara is a live in maid. She lives closer to Mel and Lanie in Georgetown. Her employer is an ambassador from New Hampshire. We do not know if she is a widow but I am sure Lanie would know," said Chedeng.

Do you have any more questions?" asked Tina.

"I still do if you would allow me another fifteen minutes of your time," replied Blanca.

"Well, I know you by now when you have more questions. You look like a lost kid, a bit embarrassed but ready to ask. I love you observations and comments after our get-togethers. My sister does not like us gossiping or talking about what we heard or saw at our get-together with our friends from Georgetown. Don't be deceived by my sister's apparent indifference to our talks. Her ears are wide open and is listening too," Chedeng addeds.

"Here is another one I caught when everyone got quiet at Marie's. Lulu said her husband got killed in *Mindanao*. So, is she is a widow of a soldier?" asked Blanca.

"Well, you are the teacher in the group so do the research," replied Tina.

"That's what happens when we speculate. Remember, the truth has a funny way of coming out," said Chedeng

"Yes, we believe you Madame Chedeng," said Tina and Blanca.

Celebrating the 4th of July, 2008

"Are you going anywhere for the 4th of July?" Blanca asked.

"We have not planned on anything," replied Tina.

Blanca said she had not heard yet from her brother in Springhill. "They usually have a cookout. I am not so keen to go this time because their friends are not my type of folks."

After a couple of days, Blanca got a word that Cita would be hosting a July 4th get together in Georgetown. Tina passed the word around and said that all those at Marie's dinner are invited which included Blanca. She was happy about it and could'nt wait to tell her brother she would be celebrating July 4th in Georgetown.

Cita's July 4th cookout was held at the back driveway of her employer's home. The space was huge and decorated with American flags and red, white and blue ribbons. Paco was in command of the grill doing barbecue and hotdogs. Except for Mrs. Robinson's nephew, Cita's guests were her Filipino friends who work in Georgetown. They all know each other. They came in red, white and blue shirts, headbands and necklaces. Cita also had some red, white and blue trinkets for her guests.

"This is such a joy to see how Filipinos participate in the July 4th celebration. Cita is very generous sponsoring the event considering the expenses in hosting one" whispered Blanca to Tina.

"July 4th is not complete without potato salad. Please don't forget to taste my potato salad. My salad did not come from Penny Saver," said Lulu. That caused laughter among the few male guests. Someone asked if the salad was made from scratch. Tina smiled and asked who has the time to make everything from scratch. She did not get any reply from the men.

Lanie stood up and reminded the guests not to forget her fruit salad, Filipino-style.

"Listen, this is not so sweet. I'm aware that some of us are already borderline diabetic. It has less condensed milk but more Nestle cream. I am not taking this home. Feel free to take some home," said Lanie.

The July 4th event at Cita's lasted till 8 in the evening. Some of the guests left earlier because they had other parties to go to. Some of the ladies stayed another hour to clean up.

Blanca also helped in the clean up. Embarrassed about always being fed, she felt she owed it to the group to at least to help in the clean up.

Once Blanca got home, she did her usual recollection of what she did with her newly found friends.

"That was one July 4th I would always remember. I like the red, white and blue *burloloys* (hanging decorations) initated by Cita, Paco and Chloe. They really know how to make a get- together fun and colorful, *feel na feel ko* (joyous feeling) *ang* July 4th. I hope to get invited again to any upcoming events with the ladies," wished Blanca.

Blanca's wish indeed came true.The ladies got another invitation to a dance. This time however was the All Filipino Ball to celebrate Philippines Independence Day.

"Is this not kind of late? Our Independence is on June 12," asked Chedeng.

"Ladies and gentleman, the following is what I picked up from the column of *Makabayan* (a Patriot) of Filipino News. *Makabayan* said that the hosting of the All Filipino Ball in August by its organizers was a compromise. He said "there can't be two Independence Day Balls on the weekend of June 12. It will diffuse the sale of the tickets of an already divided community. That's not good."

"But here is my take on the issue. The entrance of the All Filipino Ball concept in the mix of the annual Independence Day events broke the long held celebration by the elites in our community. Their tickets are really priced a bit high to cover the expensive hotel venue. The All Filipino Ball tickets on the other hand are affordable. I bet you it would be the same *yugyugan* (nonstop dancing).

"You are right again Blanca Samonte," said Tina.

"If there is one thing I am happy about the All Filipino Ball is its inclusiveness. True to what the organizers envisioned the night to be, everyone is welcome regardless of what your job is or where you come from in the Philippines. It is the night to celebrate Philippine Independence Day without the long speeches and parade of wealth by the Filipino elite of Metropolitan Washington. Have fun ladies and do not forget the *Kodakan*," said Blanca.

Their smile was from ear to ear as they posed for group and solo pictures. Lanie and Chedeng who either has hip or foot problem stood up and danced like everybody else. Rissa was, of course the star of the dance floor. Not anymore a surprise, everyone knew she's been taking dance lessons at the Archie's Dance Studio. Rissa was happy to teach the basics of the Cha Cha, Rumba as well as the Tango. "This is where the fun of dancing really begins, when I am able to teach others or find a partner who can dance with me like a pro," she once said.

Summer 2008

The ladies did not stop at the night of the All Flipino Ball. Cita told the ladies that they've invited to a picnic the last week of August. "Let's enjoy the last hurrah of summer ladies and go to Virginia," Cita said.

Like the All Filipino Ball, lots of Filipinos came to the picnic. They were spread out in the big park with games for children and adults. The Hula Hoop caught the fancy of the ladies. They tried their hula hoop skills and Blanca was the most proud. She had the longest time keeping the hoop from falling to the ground. She admitted to the ladies that she bowed down a little bit to keep the hula hoop stuck to her waist.

After summer, the sisters and Blanca resumed their Saturday night dinners at 22nd. Tina mentioned Cita's invitation to have mass at the Basilica in Washington DC to celebrate her birthday. Lulu and Paco would drive everyone to the church.

"Is this the last of the birthdays for 2008?" asked Blanca.

"No. November would be mine, and December is Chedeng's. Have you forgotten? You were here last year for our birthdays," said Tina.

"Can I celebrate mine next November? I don't usually celebrate it because no one made a big fuss over it when I was growing up," said Blanca.

"It's up to you," replied Tina.

It was Blanca's first time attending a mass at the Basilica. The place was huge and located on the campus of the Catholic University of America. Dubbed as the center of Catholicism in the nation's capital, the service had a professional choir and altar servers from the nearby seminary.

Blanca realized the solemnity of the place. She reminded herself to behave and that she is still a Catholic and will die as one. "I need to be quiet and pray while my friends are in their silent moment with God. They pray with their eyes close. I'm reminded of my mother. She prays that way," smiled Blanca.

After mass, Cita, Paco and the ladies joined other tourists checking every nook and cranny of the place. The Basilica happens to be in the list of tourist destination in Washington DC.

They paused for a bit and knelt before images of saints in every corners of the church. Some lit candles to their favorite saints like St. Jude, St. Anthony including the Mother of Perpetual Help. Filipinos believe St. Jude is the saint to go when you are desperately looking for a husband or wants him back. While the belief has become a joke in the community, St. Jude remains popular among Filipinos. They swear their request had been granted.

The round up of saints took almost forty minutes. Tina asked about lunch because it was already twelve thirty. "Ladies, Filipinos are used to taking lunch at twelve not the usual one o' clock in America," said Tina.

The ladies were not disappointed. "Now that we have prayed and toured the place, it is now time to eat. Paco and I discovered a reasonably priced cafeteria downstairs where we could go for lunch. Let's go and check out what they have today," announced Cita.

"Good! This is something different from the usual birthday celebrations we've been having the past months," said Tina.

The cafeteria was already full when the group came down from the main church. Cita told the ladies to join the line to get food and pick whatever they wanted for lunch. "It's on me so I will be by the cashier to pay for whatever you have on your tray. I have also asked Paco to look for a long table so we could seat together. I am sure he will find one," said Cita.

Following Cita's request, Paco found a long table with a bench on both sides of the table. The ladies got surprised when Lulu stood up and spoke after everyone got seated.

"This place looks familiar and I remember now why. I was here one Thanksgiving day for lunch. I came down following a bunch of immigrants after mass.I was new in the area and like them, I did not have anyone to celebrate the holiday with. I found the food reasonably priced and still is served in tune with the occasion. Please note their turkey is good. It's minus the hassle of preparing it yourself. Places like these are great. They could bring overseas Catholics together," said Lulu.

"I agree. I remember the time I was in Bucharest. I am talking about the early 80s.There were very few Filipinos in the area. I remember this one *madre* (a nun) who would care to see us in a Catholic church every Sunday. She would have a Filipino movie for us to watch in the rectory. That really made my weekend otherwise I would have felt so alone,"added Tina.

"I would say the same thing. The Catholic Church does a good job of reaching out to many overseas workers, regardless of their nationality. I met Jelene's *Ninang* Tanya back in Hong Kong that way. She was active in one of those church organizations. I was delighted to see her again in Georgetown. The world is really small. Who would ever think I will see her again after my stint in Hong Kong.

But before we all go home, I want to thank Cita for inviting us to the Basilica. It's a special place for Catholics. Also, I find there is always something new to discover in the city like what just happened today," said Blanca.

"You are welcome. Cita and I would come here any day of the week or when both of us are free just to pray," said Paco. All the ladies could say was "Amen."

Cita's birthday celebration like many others by the ladies would not be complete without *Kodakan*. For fun, the ladies outdid each other with their poses. They all wanted a solo picture with the celebrant leaving Paco holding five to six cameras to use.

Chedeng said, "Say cheese to my camera."

Blanca said, "repeat after me, say sex s e x." Everyone burst into laughter. Lanie said, "Ladies, we are in front of the Basilica."

"Who cares?" Tina butted in. More laughter followed and more Kodakan.

"Now the time has come for us to leave the couple alone. Let's take our time going back to Georgetown but enough *beso-beso* (kissing and hugging) for now," said Tina.

The ladies kept laughing as they headed to the cars. In keeping with the agreement to leave the couple alone, Paco was spared from driving the ladies home. Lulu took Lanie and Clara back to Georgetown while Blanca, Tina and Che-deng asked Paco to drop them off near the Catholic University metro stop.

"Enjoy your day guys. Don't do anything I wouldn't do," said Tina.

Cita's Basilica birthday celebration was followed by something the ladies did not expect. It was not a birthday celebration but a two night stay at a hotel in Virginia. "How?" asked Tina.

November weekend fun for the ladies began with a pajama party hosted by Lanie at the Marriot Hotel in Crystal City, Virginia.

"It's the only accommodation my Time Share could give me at this point. Come on ladies, I know it is strange that a weekend at a hotel is all I got from my Time Share. Just come with me and have a fun weekend in a hotel for two nights. Let's take advantage of the opportunity to explore Virginia. All we know is Washington DC, so let's go for it," said Lanie.

By Saturday afternoon, the ladies packed their bags for a two-night stay at the Marriot Hotel. Paco drove Mel, Lulu, the sisters and Blanca in a van. He stayed for a while but since it was an all girls' night out he went home. With Paco gone, the ladies' night got started.

The focus of the night was Lanie. The ladies asked why she bought a Time Share at a time when time share reputation was going down. "Well, the company that sold me my Time Share promised I could enjoy vacation places all over the world. As it turns out, those places are never available. We all know their scheme. Let's not talk about that anymore so we can enjoy the night," pleaded Lanie.

"Then tell us more about you and your younger days," said Lulu.

"Well, I was a virgin when I got married. I lived and breathed the Catholic religion all my life. I went to Catholic schools and worked for a seminary for years until I met my late husband.

The *ligawan* (courtship) back then was the old way. *Aakyat siya ng ligaw* (home visits to start courtship). It was customary that Sunday afternoon is the best time to do it. If the man is liked or approved of by the family, he may get dinner. If not, then *ilalatag ang banig* (spread sleeping mat) in the living room meaning it is time for him to leave. The family is getting ready for bed," said Lanie.

The ladies jumped up and down the bed, laughing and joking. "Ladies, we are in a hotel.

You remember those out towners while we were checking in. They are mostly old folks from other states who will be touring around Washington DC tomorrow. They need their sleep," Cita warned.

"It is good to know that you had the *Maria Clara* (Filipino female role model of propriety) style of courtship. Virginity was a deal breaker during the 50's. Weddings could be cancelled back then if the bride broke that unwritten law. I

81

heard so many stories about that while growing up. Pre-marital sex is a sin in the Catholic Church. I've also heard that attitudes have changed. But let's get back to Lanie's story," smiled Blanca.

"Did you hold hands, go dancing or see a movie? That was the time to do those things. I am sure holding hands were not possible during the Sunday visits. I've heard stories of fathers or an elder member of the family going back and forth in the living room to check for holding hands or kissing," Lulu said.

Again, the ladies got boisterous, talking and laughing. Chedeng asked them to calm down. "Someone can call the front desk and complain about us. The hotel knows our room number. I am not ready to go home tonight," said Chedeng.

The ladies got quiet and Lanie continued. "I thought I would get pregnant when we started holding hands. That's how naïve I was during that time,"Lanie admitted to the ladies.

"Did you love him enough to marry him?" Mel asked.

"What do you think? We have two boys. Times were different back then. We stayed married come hell or high water. Remember those words, to have and to hold until death do us part? That meant a lot to me. I was with him to the end as he battled cancer. After a few years of being a widow, I left for Italy and never looked back," said Lanie.

"How is Ms. Sandra as an employer?" Lulu asked.

"I never got a raise, considering I am a live in housekeeper which is pretty much 24 hour work. I have lived with it, but it still hurts to know that I am way behind the going rate in Georgetown. I choose to stay, so I take my low pay with a grain of salt. I owe her my green card. What I asked her instead was to help me bring my son Benito to the States. That took a while. I look at those visas being dangled at me after all these years of service to Ms. Sandra. What can I do? I guess I have to pray to St. Jude," said Lanie with a shrug.

The ladies broke into laughter again. Lanie found herself in an impossible situation. They assured that her that prayers would be answered one day with the help of St. Jude. "That said, let's end the night with a good thought because it's been fun," said Cita.

"Virgin ha!," whispered Lulu.

Blanca said good night for the last time while Chedeng asked everyone to be quiet and go to sleep.

"Our agenda for tomorrow is to explore Virginia," Chedeng reminded the ladies.

The next morning, while preparing for the Sunday walk in Old Town Alexandria, Virginia, Lanie told the ladies that she had to drop by the satellite office of the Time Share. She wanted to let them know that she had used her privileges. When the ladies walked into the office, a couple of sales people were again pitching to those they had booked in different hotels across Northern Virginia They became a captured audience but, had to be polite and left.

The arrival of Paco at the Time share office saved the ladies from another boring sales pitch. He saw what was happening when he walked to the Time Share office.

Pretending to be a driver for a tour company, he asked if he could talk to the ladies outside. Once the ladies got out of the office, they all left and toured Old Town. Paco knew the scheme of the company. "You ladies are new recruits through Lanie. It's a pyramid," said Paco.

"Well, my relatives in Virginia are in the same boat. They are smart people but even so, they were taken and had a hard time selling their shares. I do not know if they got back their money," added Cita.

"Aren't we supposed to move on and make the most of the day? Ladies, there are nice places to eat in Old Town, like I know of any. I am just joking. Let's find a place everyone would like, but no pizza please," begged Tina.

"You are damn right Tina. Let's leave it to Paco to talk and explain to Lanie what just happened," said Cita.

"All right, we are not going to talk about it today but we want to know what went wrong with Lanie's time share later on," said Tina.

The sister got the explanation from Blanca at the following Saturday's dinner at 22nd Street.

Blanca explained that their weekend stay at the Marriot was already a plan by the Lanie's time share sales group to recruit more buyers. "The truth is Lanie never got to vacation to any of the places promised by the company even though she has paid the monthly payments everytime they are due.

"It's a rip off. Lanie could have been a victim of one of those over- the phone- sellers. They usually target seniors who are always ready with their credit cards. Let's hope that she will be able to sell her share. The worst scenario is for her to lose her investment," said Blanca.

"I told you Chedeng. You're one of those who always answer the phone even when caller ID says it's not someone you know. Please be aware," Tina exclaimed.

"Will she ever get back her down payment, at least?" asked Chedeng. "I doubt it. Did you see the frustration of those men in suits? They could not make a sale because most of the folks in the room were their victims like Lanie. We were gathered and booked in a hotel to sell Time Share to friends of Lanie which happen to be us.

There was one woman who told me that she will help my daughter get a job if I buy one Time Share from her. That's when I realized Paco was right about the pyramid scheme. Buy a share but you have to sell another to a friend and to another friend, one on top of another like a pyramid. That's how it works." Blanca said.

After listening to Paco and Blanca's explanation of Lanie's time share fiasco, the ladies went on their merry ways and enjoyed the rest of the afternoon in Old Town. It was also their way of diverting Lanie's pain coming from her bad Time share deal. Cita and the ladies heckled Lanie about being courted the old way. "It felt good to go back and reminisce those days," said Lulu.

Lanie laughed and said in her usual forgiving ways,"*bahala na ang Diyos sa kanila* (God will take care of them). I cannot wish them evil because I agreed to their proposal. I just want to leave the matter that way."

"Let's now move on to my birthday. I will have at 22nd Street the Sunday before Thanksgiving. We will have the usual Sunday lunch, catered by my sister. All the ladies are invited, including long-time friends," said Tina.

Cita asked the ladies to come early so they could talk privately about her plans for the coming Thanksgiving. The ladies came early enough before the arrival of other guests.

"I will be hosting our first Thanksgiving together. Lulu, Manang Clara and Lanie have been coming to my place every Thanksgiving since we met at Montrose Park. They do not have families or friends nearby to celebrate it with. Lulu said her sister is not into cooking for Thanksgiving. She does not want to be cooking either because it had happened in past years. Lanie does not have friends in Georgetown except me. Ms. Sandra will spend it at her sister's. She also lives in Georgetown. So it will be her and the dogs Thanksgiving night. That sucks!

Chedeng, Tina, and Blanca will be the new additions to my Thanksgiving dinner. Chloe, might bring her current boy-friend, but I am not sure about that. I am sure *Manang Clara* who lives down the road will be late.

Ladies, that's my guest list this Thanksgiving. Why I am taking all the trouble of gathering folks? I believe in the saying no one should be alone Thanksgiving night. I almost experienced this when I was single but someone invited me for a Thanksgiving dinner. That was something I've treasured over time," said Cita.

"Thank you very much for inviting me. It's been a while since I cooked for Thanksgiving. I did it for my daughter. I guess it all started in the school and talked about over and over again why it's a big celebration in America. I like the thank you part of it. We often-times forget what we should be thankful for and Thanksgiving gives us that kind of reflection," said Blanca.

"Thank you for inviting us too. If you do not mind, my sister and I will be coming late but you can go ahead and eat. You do not have to wait for us. Thanksgiving is the time our Jewish employers ask us to be servers at their big family dinners. This includes all their grandchildren. Freeing themselves from the clean up gives them more time with the family.

We have been doing it for years and they pay well. We did not have the heart to turn them down. They have been very kind to us, just to let you know," Tina explained.

"Don't worry. Others might also come late too because their employers are celebrating an early Thanksgiving dinner as well. I know Filipinos are not crazy about the turkey so we will have our own way of celebrating the occasion, minus the bird," said Cita.

Blanca was the first to arrive for Cita's Thanksgiving dinner. She came in at six.

"The bus service from Glover Park is on a holiday schedule. It runs every forty five minutes. I hope I'm not too early. Wow! Your place is all decorated in fall colors of orange, brown and yellow. It gives you that Thanksgiving feel, "Blanca complimented Cita.

"Well, I've been doing this seasonal decoration for Chloe. This is what we do when her father was still alive. I want to keep the tradition going. You can see it in some of the pictures on the wall. I am glad you like it. Make yourself comfortable. I'm sure the others will be coming soon," said Cita.

"Oh! Here they come. I could hear someone speaking in *Visaya*," said Blanca.

It was Lanie. She came with her friend Yaya who did not have any place to go for Thanksgiving. Cita knew her too because she works in Georgetown. The sisters called and were expected by seven forty five. Cita had to call Clara to remind her that they were waiting for her. She said that she was on her way. Lanie asked what was slowing her down. "*Sus ginoo* (Jesus Christ) all she has to do is cross the street," laments Lanie said.

The sisters finally arrived with Clara right behind them. Lanie led the prayer over the food and urged everyone to say what they were thankful for. One by one, the ladies said they are grateful for their health. Chedeng said she is grateful for having found new friends which everyone agreed. "Let's be thankful for having Cita as the host. Bless the hand that prepared the food like Paco's and Chloe's,"said Lanie.

"Oh! Are you talking about me? Thank you to *Tia Maria's* (Auntie Maria). She supplied most of our food tonight," said Paco.

"Oh! By the way, Chloe made some Mac and Cheese. She will not be with us tonight because she's been invited by the family of her boyfriend," said Cita.

Half way through their meal, Tina asked for coffee. She also offered to make it for anyone else wanting coffee. Blanca sat where she could see everyone and commenced the conversation for the night.

"There is someone here I do not know," said Blanca.

"That's me. Hi! I am *Yaya* (babysitter) and I work for a British businessman here in Georgetown. We came from London and I've been their daughter's babysitter since she was born. I want to thank Cita for inviting me otherwise I would be alone in the house. My employer's family went to the Bahamas for Thanksgiving. The wife is from the place," she said.

Blanca encouraged the ladies to greet *Yaya* even if most of them already know her. Then she got them to focus on Lulu and Clara. She said the sisters and she did not know the two ladies. Blanca remembered and said that the two ladies are from *Pangasinan* province. "They were at Marie's dinner. This stayed in my head because the province of *Pangasinan* was famous for having a strong team in the *Tour of Luzon* (Filipino version Tour the France but not as grueling) bicycling contest when I was growing up," said Blanca.

Only Chedeng and Paco remembered what Blanca was talking about. It made everyone laughed. Lulu said, "Guys you are really from a different generation."

More laughter and Clara said, "I was born in *Pangasinan* I spent my growing years in the city of *Manila*, selling vegetables in *Santa Mesa* to help my family."

"What part of *Santa Mesa*, because if I remember right, there was a junction called *Altura* that forked out to *Mandaluyong* and *Cubao*. By the way, I am familiar with the place because my growing years were spent first in *San Juan* then *Cubao, Quezon City*, "replied Blanca.

"I worked as an extra at *LVN* Pictures. Are you familiar with that place?" asked Clara.

"Yes, my sister and I would walk to that compound and be at the gate around four in the afternoon hoping to have a glimpse of *artistas* (actors) on their way home. Why did I not see you?" asked Blanca.

Everyone laughed and were curious to know what the two ladies were talking about. Blanca asked the ladies to take a close look at Clara. "Look, you can still see that Clara was a beauty back then and still is," said Blanca

"We agree with you Blanca."

"I did audition once and got a non - speaking part," said Clara.

"Did you get another part in any other movies?" asked Tina.

"No. But that was just one part of my life story. Ask me how I got to the States," said Clara.

"That would be interesting story. I've been working in Georgetown for years but I never saw you walking up and down the place, like most Filipinos do," said Chedeng.

"That is why I need to tell my story. My life in the States began in New Hampshire in the 80's. I was hired by a businessman who owned a chain of hotels in the Northeast area. I took care of his household and his clothes. He liked the way I ironed his shirts. Then he was appointed as an ambassador so his family moved to Georgetown. That's what I was told. He asked me to move with his family to Georgetown because I already know how to keep his household going. This is what he said when he asked me to move with them to Goergetown,

"I want to save myself time from training another person to take care of our new place."

Would you turn down an employer who likes you? I figured it would be good to join him and his family. He knows a lot of people in the government. They come to his house during parties. In fact, I met Hilary in person when she came to one of his parties. His present wife is his second marriage. She is younger and a lawyer. They have two children.

The benefits I got when I joined them were enormous. The ambassador helped me get my children to join me in the States. My husband came with them but we separated after a couple of months. He left me for another woman. That was alright because my children are with me now.

My two sons are working for the ambassador's hotel in New Hampshire. My only daughter is now married and has two children. She is also expecting another one. It is a joy to have them around after a long separation. I stopped counting those years to lessen the pain.

As for my parents, they had something to keep the family going. That's should have been enough if you stay in the province but I had the ambition for a better life. So, early on I started a small business selling vegetables, spices and everyday household items like plastic buckets to *walis tinting* (stick broom made from bamboo cuttings). I do not have much in terms of schooling but I know math like a pro," said Clara.

"Of course, we all are? *Pera Yan*, (that's money) ladies," Tina said.

She made everyone laughed and said, "you're right, dear sister." In response. Tina reminded the ladies that quick math thinking is important when you send money to the Philippines. "The exchange rate changes at the blink of an eye.

Beauty na, smart pa (Tagalog English combination meaning pretty and smart). "That's *Manang* Clara everyone," added Tina.

"Now ladies the night would not be complete without a little story from the other lady who is also a beauty like *Manang* Clara. If I remember right at Marie's dinner last summer she is from the province of *Pangasinan*." said Chedeng.

"Okay, I will make mine short because it is getting late. Allow me to say I am Lulu Santos from the province of *Pangasinan*. I am currently living at 31st Street in Georgetown. I am single and I have been in this country for ten years. I won't tell you my age because I want you to guess, "Lulu smiled.

"That's not a story about you. I remember that was your opening speech when you joined the *Miss Pangasinan* beauty contest," said Clara.

"Oh you did. Look at you, a beauty queen. You have the height maybe in the vicinity of five four or five feet five inches in height with pearly skin, what do you say Ms. Lulu," added Blanca.

Lulu immediately began strutting around like a beauty queen to the delight and enjoyment of the ladies. Everyone followed her line dancing way. Paco could not believe what the ladies were doing. "Walking like beauty queens must have been your dreams, only in your dreams.

You really do not know someone until fun night comes and with a little drink you get all these surprises," said Paco.

"Let's do the beauty queen walk again, only this time with the Miss America song," urged Blanca.

Tina led the second walk while Blanca hummed the Miss America pageant song. Blanca could not believe what she had started with the ladies.

"Thank you. I want to thank Cita for hosting tonight's Thanksgiving celebration. I think Mrs. Robinson is already sleeping upstairs," Blanca, thinking it was time to call it a night.

The ladies quietly said good night to Cita and Paco. Not to be missed in the good night wishes was Cita's cat Millie. Paco offered to take the sisters, Blanca and Lulu home.

"Good night ladies. We will also be on our way. Let's keep our fingers crossed that these oldies will safely get home in this darkness," Lanie referring to herself

"Do not worry. All you need to do is call me to say that you got home. Can you please do that for me? Imagine two oldies lost after a Thanksgiving party," Cita joked

"By the way, do not forget my birthday party. It will be at my place on the first Sunday of December. You are all welcome," said Chedeng as she said goodbye to the Lanie and Clara.

Blanca as soon as she got home took time and mulled over what she learned from her first Thanksgiving with the ladies. She remembered the saying no man is an island." Human connection could be part of our daily life in America too. All we have to do is find the time to have fun with folks we encounter along the way. Who would ever think that I would have Thanksgiving with folks I met just met months ago. It's good to be out there,"smiled Blanca.

December 2008

Chedeng's December birthday party was the last of the ladies' get together in 2008. Like what Jelene told Blanca early on, guests come and go depending on what their friends have scheduled for their weekend. Chedeng of course did all the cooking. On top of her famous *lumpia* (spring rolls), she had a pot of *monggo* (green beans soup). *Tama yan* (right) for winter," shouted a guest.

"Chopped spinach mixed with *monggo*. Chedeng could really be creative," added Cely. "Who is that lady beside Lanie?" Blanca whispered to Tina.

"Oh, that's Cely, Minnie's mother. You've met Minnie and the boyfriend one Saturday night dinners. Her daughter works for a bank and she comes once in a while to help us with our accounts, remember? She used to come here like our weekender Jelene. She lives with her employer in Bethesda. Don't just sit there, go around and talk to other people. Everyone is friendly here. Look at Lanie, talking to fellow *Visaya*," said Tina.

Like a kid told by her mother to socialize, Blanca heeded Tina's advice. First, she talked to someone she remembered seeing in TJ Max at Friendship Heights. "So you are friends with Chedeng and Tina?" asked Blanca.

"Yes. Like Tina and Chedeng, I also have a sister in the States. My sister Norma asked for me to come like what Chedeng did when she worked a way for Tina to join her. We've been here for years. In fact, we are thinking of going home to retire. By the way, I'm Marcia and you?' the lady asked.

"Oh, I'm Blanca and I am a neighbor of the sisters. I've been coming to 22nd S Street since I met Tina in 2007. You know they cook big dinners every Saturday to start their weekend fun. They've been feeding me since then. I live alone since my daughter left for college in 2003.

I really welcome their company." Blanca replied.

"Most of the guests you see around here are about the same age as the sisters. My sister and I are one of them. You will get to know some of them when you come to birthday parties like this one. Tina will be setting up the Karaoke soon and the fun of the afternoon begins. If you will excuse me, I want to check the song book and pick my song," said Marcia.

"Sure, I will pick mine later. Most of the ladies are very good Karaoke singers. I like Tina when she sings. It is really with gusto and smile. She gets a lot of kick in the scoring system of the machine. "Don't feel bad if you get a low score. Honestly, I am not a good singet but

Karaoke singing can probably make a good singer out of anyone, through practice," said Blanca.

"*Sinabi mo* (you are correct). In fact, I'm going to sing right now," added Marcia.

Realizing that Karaoke got most of the guests' attention, Blanca moved around the apartment to meet the other friends of the sisters. Like in previous parties at 22nd Street, the crowd got bigger then smaller depending on what part of the afternoon or early evening. Blanca wondered how they all fit in the barely 550 square feet apartment but, they do. Some were seated in kitchen, bedroom and small hallway. Space did not matter because most of the guests know the sisters and every nook and cranny of their apartment.

Lulu for instance, would move everytime she finds an empty seat. She knew some of the guests. Someone said that she looked familiar." Were you not in the Miss *Pangasinan* beauty contest?" a guest asked.

"Yes, but I was only the runner up," Lulu replied. She walked around the small living room, bowed and curtsied to the delight of the guests. "Lulu, Lulu," the guests cheered.

"This is really one hundred per cent fun. It can't get any better than this," Blanca said talking to a guest she did not even know.

Lanie who was seated near the TV set found camaraderie with fellow *Visayan* workers.

Like Marcia, she also picked a song from the Karaoke song book.

"Ladies and gentlemen, hear ye, the lead singer of Dumbarton Church, Lanie Balbao also known as Lanie Dion," shouted Blanca.

"Does the Karaoke have my favorite Visaya song *Matudnila* (It is said so)," Lanie asked.

"Don't worry. We will search for it once the current singer is finished," replied Tina.

In the middle of the frenzy over the Karaoke song book, Chedeng left the ladies and went to the kitchen. She found Clara and her daughter Sherrie talking. "I am looking for a ladle so I can replenish the food on the table," Chedeng explained.

"This is embarrassing but I have to and eat and run, *Manang* Chedeng. My *mag-aama ko* (husband and children) went to the mall for a while and will be coming for me at four. My mother wanted to be dropped off to be with you before going back to work at Georgetown," said Sherrie.

Chedeng held Sherri's hand and told her not to worry. She said she cooked a lot and that it was okay to eat and run. Sherrie in turn said, "*Salamat Po* (thank you). I'm sure the children would be all tired and sleeping in the car when they come for me."

After an hour, there was a knock at the door and it was Sherrie's husband sticking his head in the door telling her to hurry.

By early evening, Blanca signaled the ladies she was ready to go home. Lulu also joined Blanca in saying good bye. She told Tina that she would be driving Lanie and Clara back to Georgetown. Paco and Cita also said their good bye. An early evening commitment in Virginia was a good excuse.

On their way to their cars, they chatted about the need to leave the place before there is no more space to move around in the sisters' apartment.

"Thanks for getting my cue to leave. Guests kept coming and they are already all over the place," said Blanca.

"Oh yes! That was a lot of fun for me. Imagine someone remembering me in that Miss *Pangasinan* beauty contest of years ago, "added Lulu.

"Who will forget your beauty and you are still beautiful after all these years," said Lanie.

Lulu again strutted in her beauty queen walk as they moved back to their parked cars.

Blanca did the same as she climbed the hill to Benson Street.

"Go Blanca, go," cheered Paco and Cita.

"Don't forget 2008 will soon be over and Christmas is just around the corner" shouted Blanca.

"We heard you lady. Let's call each other about plans for the coming holiday," said Cita.

"Okay, I got it," Blanca replied.

On her return for the usual Saturday night dinner at 22nd Street apartment Blanca asked the sisters about their holiday plans.

"We've not figured out any plan yet because of our work. We have two long weekends during the holidays depending on what weekday it falls. We are entitled to a day off before and after. The holidays are days off our employers won't have help. Short of making up for our absence, their houses just the same need to be ready for the holidays. What does the preparation entail? We do deep cleaning of the house, especially bathrooms, pull out those extra beds and dress up the guest rooms. It will be a lot of work for us, but hopefully lots of gifts too," said Tina.

"By the way, I forgot to introduce you to our half – hearted, undecided weekender, Cely. *Waray din yan* (meaning she is from Leyte too). We grew up in the same neighborhood in *Leyte* and met up again in the US after her stint in Melbourne, Australia. She also happens to be the mother of Minnie, the young lady you met one Saturday night," said Chedeng.

"Hi, I'm Blanca. You are Minnie's mother. Were you at Chedeng's party last Sunday?"

Blanca asked.

"*Oo, Day*, (Yes my dear). You surprised me because you knew Visayan songs like *Pobreng Alindahaw* (a little bird) and *Matudnila* (It is said so). How come?" asked Cely.

"Those were the favorite Visayan songs of Pilita Corrales ladies," replied Blanca

Chedeng laughed like crazy when she heard Blanca say the name Pilita Corrales.

"As far as I can remember, Pilita is the only singer in history of the Philippines who can bend backward while singing. Look at me, I can copy her when she sings "The Day You Came Along," Blanca singing as she bent backward.

"Blanca you are really something else," said the three ladies, laughing and clapping.

"Seriously, my favorite part in *Pobreng Alindahaw* was the *tigadog, tigadong, tigadong* (stumping) that comes when you sing it. That's really the fun part of the song. Pilita could really wow her audience every time she would get to that part. She must be in her eighties now," Blanca said.

"Do you still remember those scenes when Elizabeth Ramsey, another famous *Visayan* singer joins her on stage as a guest?

That usually turns out like a competition between two *Visayan* singers. How much *Visayan* can you get?" Chedeng laughed.

"Here we go again with Blanca and Chedeng getting nostalgic over show biz personalities," laughed Tina.

Almost in tears from laughter, Blanca turned her focus on Cely. She asked if she planned to be a regular weekender at the sisters' place. Cely said it depends on her employer's out of country schedule. "I am a live maid in Kesington, Maryland. Coming to 22nd is my way of taking a break from the lady of the house. It gets worst whenever they go for their holidays.

She resents the fact that I will be free from work and gets paid. But I stay home to guard the house and keep it clean. But actually I clean a week before their return. Why? The house does not get dirty but dusty. It's a long story. Who knows maybe we can have a get together one of these days and talk more about it," Cely said.

"Oh! I'll look forward to that day. Lastly, I have one final question for Tina,"said Blanca.

"What is it Blanca?" asked Tina.

"I'm just curious about Ninang Tanya's choice of song - *Usahay* a not so popular *Visayan* song. I haven't heard sang by anyone in past Karaoke. She sang it with such feeling that your guests sang with her. Was that also popular *Visayan song* you know growing up?" asked Blanca.

"Well, it was amazing that Tanya still remembers the lyrics of *Usahay* (Sometimes I Dream of You). It is one of those songs that remind us of home. That's why some of the guests sang with her. All it took was someone to take the lead and the rest will follow. It was also their way of not shedding a tear or two because it is really sad to be away from your family. *Usahay* really touched everyone's heart," smiled Tina.

"Thank you but let me wish you and your families a very Merry Christmas. I am getting ready to leave," said Blanca as she slowly headed out the door.

"Likewise, by now our families have received our Christmas gifts. We send our *balikbayan box* as early as October. You know it is Christmas back home when the month of the year ends in the letters "ER" like September but officially ends in January 6 to honor the Three Kings. *Ang haba* (long season),"moaned Tina.

"Oh! Don't go yet. Where will you be spending Christmas? You can come to 22nd for Christmas," asked Tina.

"Thank you but we are going to Montreal. My oldest sister in Montreal wants to keep our Christmas tradition going even if our mother is long gone. My daughter and I will meet up in Montreal. She'll be coming from Vermont. I will come back for the New Year to keep another tradition going. I am sure you also have your own rituals to welcome in the coming year.

"So what is your New Year's tradition to welcome the coming year?" asked Tina.

"Well, I grew up seeing my parents opening all the windows, doors, cabinets, closets, etc. on New Year's Eve. The belief is by opening the windows etc, luck comes into your home at the same time letting go of whatever was bad in the past year. Instead of dangerous firecrackers, we would also bang pots and pans for noise. Lastly, we would wear polka dot clothes and buy round fruits also for luck. Those circles are symbolical because it has no end," Blanca smiled.

The Ladies celebrate the 2009 New Year

When Blanca returned home after Christmas, she immediately got a call. "Hello, yes this is Blanca, Tina. It's great to hear from you. I came back the 29th but it takes me a while to recover from the trip. Montreal to DC is a 14 hour bus ride with a stopover in New York. But, I am fine now and looking forward to the New Year. How about you? Blanca asked, "Listen, I got a call from Cita. She said she will be happy to host a New Year's Eve party at her apartment. She is inviting us and her neighbors in Georgetown like Lulu, Clara and Lanie.

You can bring other friends too," said Tina over the phone.

"What happens now to my New Year's Eve ritual?" Blanca asked Tina.

Tina replied laughing and told her to come in her polka dot dress. "Can you not skip your New Year's eve ritual this time?" asked Tina.

"Okay but I hope all the ladies will come. New Year merriment would be nice with lots of people around," Blanca replied.

"So let's go together around eleven pm New Year's eve," said Tina.

New Year's Eve came and Cita as a host did not disappoint the ladies. They were greeted at the door by Millie the cat. No fuss like she knew the ladies. Then Chloe came, giving each of the ladies a hug and Happy New Year greeting.

"Please put this Happy New Year 2009 headbands on and these long necklaces and one *torotot* (noisemaker)," said Chloe.

Tina could not help but blow the *torotot* on her sister's ear. "Sis, do you still know how to use this?" asked Tina.

"Honestly, I haven't seen this thing in a while. Where did you get this Chloe?"Chedeng asked

"We got them from a party place in Wisconsin Avenue near Penny Saver," replied Chloe.

Blanca interrrupted when she saw a new face. "Hi, I am Blanca and this is Chedeng and Tina,

"I'm Sharon. Chloe and I go to the same college."

"This place is ready to welcome in 2009. Cita really knows how to decorate this place. Her fresh Christmas tree smells good like the season is still very much around. The white lights around it look bright yet not cluttered like some trees I have seen," said Blanca.

"Yes, the place looks really *Pasko pa rin at* now *Bagong Taon* (ambiance of Christmas and New Year). This is our first time to come here on New Year's Eve. Like most Filipinos, Cita's Christmas and New Year should be with a bang. She's got everything done and put to together.

I'm talking about her décor to noisemakers. This is really heartwarming," said Chedeng

"I heard you have this series of early dawn masses before Christmas day in the Philippines. I also learned you have these overpowering firecrackers to welcome the New Year. Please tell me more about those Filipino traditions," asked Sharon

"Oh, I will let my sister Tina answer your questions. Tina could you please enlighten Sharon about some of our customs and traditions during the Christmas holidays," smiled Chedeng.

"I can't tell you its historical background but Filipino Catholics grew up attending *Misa de Gallo or Simbang Gabi* (early dawn mass) one time or another in their lives. It is so ingrained that the tradition is replicated by Filipinos in the States too. It starts in the morning of December 16 and runs through Christmas Eve.

"The early dawn mass is a fun activity too because the weather is a bit cool in December. Philippine weather you know is like summer forever – always hot and humid. After mass, people converge in the plaza of the church. It is like a fiesta with lots of traditional Christmas food to buy like *puto bumbong* (tubular shape steamed rice cake) and *bibingka* (round rice cake). Hot *salabat* (warm ginger juice) drink helps water down those rice cakes. The drink is believed to be good for the throat. It is said that most opera singers in the country take the *salabat* to protect their vocal chords. I for one take *salabat* drink whenever my throat is itchy.

There is also that socialization aspect attached to the early dawn masses. I remember those early dawn masses as the meeting place or rendezvous for teenagers which parents are not supposed to know ha! It's either they are still asleep or have joined the mass too.

I know a couple from Leyte who met each other in one of these dawn masses. Is that not worth waking up so early?

How is the early dawn mass done here? I have been to one in Alexandria, Virginia. Mass is celebrated at seven in the evening instead of dawn followed by a reception in the church's basement. As always, it's like a fiesta with lots of food. Regardless of the weather, some of us have gone to the extreme like celebrating it at four in the morning. I guess they want to experience the real deal. Imagine the freezing cold weather in some places in the US like Chicago or New York.

Some of us challenge oursleves by attending the dawn masses from the 16th of December to the 24th.

To quote the pastor of Dumbarton Church in Georgetown when he learned about the four o'clock dawn Christmas masses, "I am glad I am not assigned to the Philippines and have to get up three or four in the morning for the early dawn mass from December 16 to the 24th. What have I done to be punished that way?" Of course, he was joking.

"New Year on the other hand, follows a different ritual too. It would not be complete without firecrackers. It's ironic because we know we could lose a finger or two but still we do it because its fun. That's how it was and has been since I can remember,"Chedeng explained.

Blanca interrupted and said,"see these black lines below my right knee, it was not from firecrackers but from hitting a step as I ran away from a lighted *triangulo* (triangle shaped) firecracker. That was the kind my brothers and I could afford while growing up."

"That was interesting. I guess each culture had different ways to celebrate their holidays. I don't remember rituals in my family except we try our best not to fall asleep.

We should not miss the dropping of the ball at Times Square in New York. I guess that's what we are doing now. Why don't we start Karaoke singing while waiting for the 2009?" suggested Sharon.

"Perfect!" shouted Cita while putting the final touches on the food and drinks.

Chloe jumped in and said "my Mom right now is into My Heart Will Go On by Celine Dion from Titanic. You can't beat that? This would be followed by Killing Me Softly by Roberta Flack. Since we are welcoming the New Year, I will let it go Mom," said Chloe as she handed the mike to her mother.

Cita went on to sing My Heart Will Go On followed by Killing Me Softly. Everyone was in awe. Blanca said,"Cita may not be the best singer but she has this cunning ability to follow the ups and down of the song. We all knew she can hit those notes like Celine Dion".

Everyone agreed with Blanca and for the first time Mrs. Robinson's nephew Allen volunteered to sing. His choice was not the Christmas song but the other Joy to the World.

"Oh! I know Allen's song. I remember there is something about Jeremiah the bullfrog. Let' get on with it and see if my guess is right," Blanca said.

Allen's choice of song got everybody singing. Everyone waited for the Joy to the World part of the song. Like Allen, everyone was out of tune but laughing.

At the stroke of midnight, the ladies took turn in hugging each other. Blanca hesitated to hug. It was her first time to celebrate New Year's Eve with the ladies. Instead she picked a pot from Cita's kitchen and banged it as loud as she can.

"You are really serious about this practice," smiled Tina.

"Don't you like it? It adds to the fun and noise. I want to keep this ritual even if I am away from home. Next year, everyone should wear polka dot shirt or dress, if Cita invites us again," said Blanca.

"Since we are talking about luck, in *Tarlac* where Paco and I are from, we do not prepare any dish calling for chicken. It is bad luck. Feathers fly thus drive luck away," said Cita.

"Yes, those chicken feathers are not good for New Year. Paco then popped the champagne and proposed a toast. Cheers and *Mabuhay* (long live). *Manigong Bagong Taon* (Happy New Year)," said Paco.

Blanca got emotional the minute when the singing of *Ang Pasko Ay SumapitI* (Christmas is Here) began. She realized only Paco and she could sing the song. The rest hummed and guessed the words of one of the most loved Filipino Christmas song.

"Ladies this is embarrassing. *Ang Pasko ay Sumapit* is the closest to our national anthem. How can you not know the lyrics by heart?" Paco laughed.

"Of course, the oldies were already born when the song was written," joked Tina.

"Oh! Wait everyone. Where is Mrs. Robinson? Is she upstairs? We are getting loud," asked Chedeng.

"Oh, she went to celebrate New Year with one of her book club friends. Do not worry. But hold it, Paco has a surprise gift for you ladies," said Cita

Paco handed each of the ladies a DVD compilation of the activities Cita and Chloe had with the ladies in 2008. "It's a bit amateur but I hope everyone likes it," said Paco

"Thanks a lot Paco. This will make our families back home happy. Our photos here are fairly recent and a far cry from those cassete tapes we've been sending for years. It would be nice if we could talk to them everyday? Long distance calls are expensive. This video will bring joy to our families back home. Again, thank you so much," Tina exclaimed.

"This is a really a nice and unique gift – a DVD of 2008 with the group," Blanca agreed.

"Can we give Paco a round of applause?" said Cita.

"Of course, let's clapped our hands for Paco," said Tina

"Let's not forget Sharon and Allen. They've been very tolerant and respectful of our New Year frolics.

"It was nice meeting you," said Blanca.

"We are happy to be here. You are a fun group," said Allen and Sharon.

"Allen, we did not know you could sing," teased Lulu

"He just wants to have fun like us," Clara said.

Allen smiled and said he was ready to go home which was upstairs. Sharon said it would be a sleep over for her.

The ladies left using Mrs. Robinson's front gate. "So this is the front of the house. It's good to know that we could also go to this way from the basement. We've been using the back entrance ever since I've been coming to Mrs. Ronbinson's house," said Blanca

Lulu who lives on Wisconsin Avenue drove instead of walking. She said she felt safer in her car than walking home at two o'clock in the morning. Lanie and Clara walked home as they always do.

Cita, implored the two walkers to call as soon as they got home.

"Do not worry. If you two ladies get lost then Georgetown will have something to talk about. It would be in the headline in the Georgetown Gazette. Two seniors missing after attending a New Year's Eve party close by," teased Paco.

"That could happen you know. I am a little bit tipsy from the champagne," said Lanie

"*Manang* Lanie, we drank sparkling apple cider. I will serve real champagne next time," added Cita.

To cut the long goodbyes and usual after party talks, Tina yawned loudly and told everyone it was time to go.

Chedeng asked everyone to keep in touch. She suggested it would be nice to continue seeing each other in 2009. "Let us know what you have in mind like where to go or what we can do together besides eating," said Chedeng.

"That was great,"said Blanca as she sat down in her sofa to relax. It's been a long time and I can't remember anymore my last New Year's Eve party? I am glad I did not hesitate to come to the party. Do I have new friends now? Time will tell," said Blanca as she gets ready for bed.

By January 20, 2009, they were again at Cita's apartment to join in the celebration and inauguration of the first African American and 44th president of the United States, Barack Obama.

Cita suggested walking to the US Capitol for the swearing. "Be ready to walk from Georgetown to as far as our feet could go or where security will allow us to go. There will be portable toilets along the way if you need to go but I would not encourage using them. It is a test of being able to hold back. You know what I mean? We will be walking back because it's the only way to go. This is not going to be for the faint of heart but it will be fun and an experience to remember. So let's all go," urged Cita.

Most of the ladies joined her for the walk to the Capitol to witness the historic event. Blanca and Clara did not go because of bathroom and leg issues. Paco who had always been critical of Obama came and joined the walk with Cita. Another surprise was Tina. "Walking slow will be good for my aching legs and toes,"Tina justifying her effort.

"Ladies, I will be watching on TV. Let's have a recap of everybody's experience when we get together again in the near future. Thanks you for suggesting the inaugural walk," said Blanca.

To make up for her absence on the inaugural walk, Blanca invited the ladies for an after work pizza at her apartment. "I've want to hear it from the horses' mouth this time," she told Cita over the phone.

Pizza night in the middle of the week worked well for the ladies. It was quick and yet their conversation went on till eleven. Cita started off by talking about how slow some of the ladies walked.

"I was like their mother egging them to walk faster when the crowd was starting to pile up. I am happy that Clara was not with us. I am afraid she could get lost in the cowd. You see *Manang* Clara never learned the roads of Washington DC even after all these years. One thing though, she does not get lost when walking the dog," said Cita.

"Oh! Losing a dog while you are walking is not acceptable in Georgetown.You will be in big trouble with the owner because that is like losing a kid," quipped Tina.

"Folks, let's not focus on Clara's ignorance of Washington DC places. Please understand she never learned to move around DC because she gets picked up every weekend and dropped Sunday afternoon by family. I doubt if she has taken any of those buses that goes to Dupont Circle. She takes the taxi for short trips around Georgetown if she needs to. At least, Clara never lost the ambassador's dog, "said Chedeng.

"You are right so let's stop talking about Clara. Chedeng might cry," said Tina.

"Walking with our group not knowing the route to take to get close to the Capitol was hilarious. There was no pushing. All we could do was go with the flow of the crowd. A million people probably came to Washington, DC to witness President Obama's rise to the presidency. The crowd was bigger compared to the one of Bill Cinton," added Chedeng.

"I agree. I got in here in 1992 when Bill Clinton got elected. He was inaugurated 1993. It was our first time to see an American president got elected. I was not an American citizen yet but I already wanted to participate in the celebration because my daughter received a letter from him. He encouraged her to do well in school. I am not sure if it was a formed letter but for a kid newcomer in the DC public schools, it meant a lot to receive one from a president of the United States.

We went to the Mall to check on most of the festivities surrounding his inauguration. There were games and entertainment before and after the innauguration. But the Obama crowd was much larger and a mix. There were blacks, whites, Latinos, and Asians from different parts of the country and the world.Though I did not join you, the aerial view covering the event for TV was spectacular. It was like a sea of people ascending to Washington like *parang di mahulugan ng karayom* (so many and so tight one can drop a needle that won't go in or be felt)," commented Blanca.

Tama Ka! (you are damn right) Blanca. Let's see how Obama administration plays out over the first four years," added Cita.

"Moving away from politics, have you watched Paco's DVD for 2008 ladies," asked Chedeng.

Everyone said yes with a smile from ear to ear." Someone for the first time cared to capture our get together since June of 2008," said Tina.

"Paco's DVD recording of our activities for 2008 is a brilliant idea. Oftentimes, events in our lives just come and go but to see them like a diary or journal is really sweet and endearing. It is also easy to keep compared to those bulky photo albums," said Blanca.

Tina's take on Paco's 2008 DVD had a different twist to it. Really happy and over-joyed seeing herself and her sisters dressed for the Independence Day Ball, she roasted Cita as being special in most of the photos.

Oy! *Oy*! *Oy*! (Hey, Hey,), "shouted the ladies as they ate the extra slices of pizza.

"That DVD almost made me cry. Does it mean we will have more DVDs if we keep seeing each other," asked Lanie

"That will probably depend on how long the courtship would last. We have no idea how far along is Paco. Has he won Cita's heart? But you see we believe in the saying, however long is the procession, it always ends at the altar," joked Chedeng.

"*Galing talaga ni Manang Chedeng*" (Chedeng is smart). That was a word for word translation of that famous Filipino saying about courtship. Is that what happens when the English language becomes second nature to us?" asked Blanca.

"*Siguro* (maybe) but, *waray pa rin Day* (still the lady from Leyte province),"Chedeng replied.

"Ladies, have you met our friend Erlinda? She asked me one time about ways to improve her English because the mother of her employer complained about her children starting to speak bad grammar. So this is how she replied to her employer.

"Madame, I am sorry but it is hard for me to keep changing channels – Filipino to English and back to Filipino. There are times I do not know the words in English so the kids help my English."

"Is that how it's been with your friend Erlinda and the employer? Lulu asked.

The story caused a round of laughter. Luckily, Blanca's condo had a sisal carpeting to absorb their stumping and clapping.

"Erlinda is one lady who also comes to our birthday parties but she is always late. She leaves right away to pick up her *alagas* (wards). She drives around town like crazy. You will be surprised but she serves the kids "sinigang" (sour soup) and no complain. Again, her excuse is she does not have the time and energy to change channels like Filipino dishes to Italian dishes," said Tina.

"I think the employer just lets it go to save herself from the demands of her kids. Erlinda's technique in running the household reduces stress, so everybody is happy," declared Chedeng.

"You are probably right. There's always a way for us to simplfy situations in order to get things done. It's getting late. My cat Millie is probably waiting for me by the door. She does not stray around the neighborhood like some cats do. Millie just goes up and down the main house and my place in the basement or garden. She knows when Chloe and I are home because of the light. In the meantime, she would patiently wait by the door to greet us.

Millie, by the way, is adopted. She used to be the cat of Mrs. Robinson's lady landscaper. She gets free rent for a room upstairs in exchange for taking care of the garden. I really do not know the deal between these two white folks of mine.

So, shall we go ladies?" Cita asked.

"Thanks for the pizza Blanca. We should do this pizza get together again. It's fun to do in the middle of the week. Somehow it shortens the long work week. Good night everybody," said Tina.

"By the way, I am parked below the hill. We could walk together. I'm taking Lanie with me ladies. Don't forget us. Georgetown is just around the corner," Cita requested.

By February, Chedeng and Tina volunteered to host lunch at their apartment. She said it would be a good way to lessen the boredom of winter.

"I prepared *sinigang buto buto* (sour beef bone stew) and *lumpia* (spring rolls). The purpose is to perk up our aching *kaso kasuan* (joints)," said Chedeng.

Chedeng's aching joints comment threw everyone into gales of laughter, as always.

"Is this *bulalo* (bone marrow) soup?" Lanie asked.

"Somewhat I guess. Penny Saver has the best beef bone in town because they sell bones with some meat on it. I am after the flavor from the bone that blends with the veggies. I made sure it's not so sour such that you scream," Chedeng assured the ladies.

"If you don't mind, I brought my famous fruit salad. I also made sure it's not too sweet but enough to wear off the sour pangs of the *sinigang*, said Lanie.

"Anything you bring is always welcome. The more the merrier, as we all love to say ladies," added Tina.

After all the talks and heckling over *sinigang* and desserts, Tina asked when the group would be seeing each other again.

"I don't know any dance party anytime soon. We are just getting back into the loop.

I am sure something is in the offing we just don't know about it yet. Who knows one day I'll bumped into someone at the bus station in Friendship Heights. It's like a hub to pick up coming events in our community. We do not know what has happened to the *Waray* organization too. It used to be our source of news and *tsismis* (gossip). Are we getting old that we've lost track of people?" Chedeng asked.

"*Oy!* "*kalabaw lang ang tumatanda*" (referring the working water buffalo of the Philippines that gets slower as it gets older)," said Lulu.

The ladies danced around the apartment after hearing Lulu's comment. Nearly in tears, "you are right. We need to keep ourselves young and active. Why don't we have a monthly lunch?

"We seem to be a good group – meaning we like each other. That being the case, we can accommodate our quirks here and there and everything else that comes in between. It would be unfair for Chedeng and Tina to host us all the time. Also, I cannot be doing it often because Mrs. Robinson and her friends are a handful to care for. While my other jobs are just around the Georgetown neighborhood, going around to different houses can be exhausting," said Cita.

Everyone agreed to Cita's suggestion of having a once a month lunch.

"Let's start 2009 and go from there," suggested Blanca.

"How are we going to do this?" Lanied asked.

The sisters asked for the Sunday lunch to work around their off days which was every third Sunday of the month. The rest of the ladies said their Sundays were free and would be happy to accommodate the sisters' schedule. Lanie, however, reminded everyone to be open to changes in schedules due to unexpected emergencies in their employers' household. To keep expenses low, they also agreed there would be no lunch hosting if someone is celebrating a birthday.

"Let's start our schedule by drawing from a basket that has names of each month of the year. This is not written in stone but feel free to swap if you are not available in the month you picked. Is that fair enough?" asked Tina.

"Wow! This is democracy in action ladies," cried Blanca.

"So far there is no objection to the monthly lunch. Could we go into our birthdays?" asked Lanie.

Everyone gave the month and day they were born. Paco, the only gentleman was born in February. The month of September had three celebrants – Cita, Lulu and Clara while November had Tina and Blanca. Chedeng was the only December celebrant.

Siyempre (of course), I am the star because I am the oldest among you ladies," said Chedeng in her self-deprecating humor.

"It's great that we agreed on having monthly lunches and celebrate our birthdays. I'm looking forward to it, "said Blanca

4

Once a Month Lunch Hosting and Birthdays

Blanca Samonte did not expect her friendship with the ladies of Georgetown to develop and grow. From being a *sabit lang* (a tag along friend) of sisters' Tina and Chedeng, she immediately blended in with the ladies of Georgetown by the end of 2008.

"After so many years of not socializing at all, now I have a group to have Sunday lunch with, celebrate birthdays and the holidays and long weekends. My world changed," smiled Blanca. It was something to look forward to aside from shopping, said one member. It's a fun and productive way to spend a day off, said another.

The first to host in 2009 were sisters, Tina and Chedeng. They volunteered to serve lunch in February to celebrate the groups' successful walk to attend Obama's inauguration. "It was a long walk," said Tina. But they all agreed that it was worth it.

"The dead winter months of January and February are the best times to have Chedeng's *monggo* soup (dried green beans like lentils, boiled until soft, mashed and sautéed in garlic and onion and water or chicken stock) and spring rolls. It gives you that warm feeling.

Let's eat slowly and take our time. I'm glad we started early so we can talk about anything under the sun," said Blanca.

"The monggo soup of Chedeng is delicious. I hope I can invite everyone to lunch so you will taste my version of *monggo* and other Filipino favorites," said Clara.

"Don't worry Clara. We will keep you in mind on that one. Right ladies?" said Blanca.

"Yes, we are all looking forward to having lunch with you Clara. But since we started early today, how about giving our group a name? Why? I found out our other friends have been calling us the Golden Girls. I am not comfortable being called that way.

"On the first one, is that a compliment or not?" Lulu asked.

"I think it's a joke coming from our other friends. We used to hang out with them before we started seeing each other more often. Maybe they noticed the similarities between our group and the TV show ladies. Like our age range is the same as the Golden Girls and most of all the camaraderie and fun we are having," said Chedeng.

"That's great," added Cita.

Nevertheless, Cita expressed her discomfort them using that name. She said the entire nation knows the name "Golden Girls is synonymous with the characters in the popular TV show.

"Please tell your friends to stop calling us the Golden Girls," said Cita emphatically.

"What name do you have in mind? The old ladies group maybe?" said Chedeng.

"Please do not be mean to yourself *Manang* Chedeng!" Tina said to her older sister.

"What about the Filipino Group? It is generic and would not offend certain groups in the community who love to be identified with their provinces such as *Batangas or Cagayan*,"said Blanca.

"Why don't we call ourselves Golden Group or maybe Sunday Group? Either one would be safe. Let's not run into a legal issue just to have a name," added Cita.

Everyone laughed at that very safe name.

"I like the word golden. It connotes maturity and let's face it some of us are getting there in age," joked Rissa.

"You are right, so let us not worry about a name. We already have a group and that's what really matters," said Clara.

"I think being call the Golden Group for the sake of being a collective one sounds alright to me. This will save us from explaining to other friends what we've been doing or where we've been in the past months. Some folks are really nosy. Can we just agree on this one?" Lulu asked.

"That sounds good, "Tina said.

"Is Paco included in the hosting rotation and birthdays?" Blanca asked.

"Can we exempt Paco from hosting lunch? Please consider us as one," requested Cita.

The ladies looked at each other and smiled hearing Cita's request.

"It's good to know that you are now one with Paco,"Tina smiled.

Paco's face turned red, he smiled and held Cita's hand.

"Can my sister and I be also one like Cita and Paco?" Tina added.

"That's shouldn't be a problem," said Lulu

"Let's rally behind Tina's request. We all love their cooking don't we?" Blanca said.

"Of course, you have our support Blanca. Lanie said.

"In the meantime, I need to go home because Sunday is the best day to do laundry in my building," said Blanca.

"Wait," whispered Cita. She called everyone to the bedroom while Paco and Chedeng ws glued to the TV watching football. Both have been Washington Redskins fans for years.

"What is this all about ladies?" asked Lanie

"I have plans to give Paco a surprise birthday party. This is rather late because his birthday is also in February. It does not matter. Chloe and I can put together a party for him. Please keep your schedule open next month," Cita whispered.

"What's happening? Is there any problem? Redskins just did a touch down," said Paco.

"Great! We should get ready to get back to Georgetown. I promised Chloe we would watch a seven pm movie," said Cita.

"Well, it's time for us to leave too. We have work tomorrow. I'm parked in front of the building. I will not complain about the difficult parking this time. I got one right in front of the building," said Lulu.

"Paco and I are parked down the hill. I will take my neighbors, Clara and Lanie with us. Let's keep in touch and have a good week everyone," Cita said.

Cita's surprise birthday party for Paco turned out to be real surprise not only for him but for the ladies as well. She had it in an undisclosed place in Clarendon, Virginia. Lulu drove and took the ladies with her. Four of the ladies squizzed themselves on the backseat whileTina sat beside Lulu to serve as a guide. Rissa came from work and drove herself to the place.

"Chloe will meet you at the back of the place. I will call her to signal to let you come in as soon as *Irog* (sweetheart) and I get in," said Cita.

The surprise party worked. Paco thought Cita was arranging a party for one of her employers. Chloe and the ladies came in and sang happy birthday to the lone male member of the Golden Group. Cita gave the ladies an introduction to Silly Times. She asked the ladies to check out the place and its offerings.

"This is an adult version of Chuck E. Cheese. There is a Karaoke area, pinball machines, games like put the tail on the donkey and a small dance hall. This is reserved for three hours. Enjoy while I check on the food and drinks. I also have some goodie bags for everyone to take home.

Like little children with goodie bags, the ladies went home happy to have found an adult version of Chuck E. Cheese. They cheered on Cita for hosting a surprise birthday party for Paco.

"But before we all go home ladies, take note of how Cita calls Paco. *Irog* means sweethearts so they are now sweethearts," said Tina.

"Yes of course. I like to call him *Irog* for two reasons. First, we're now a couple. Second, the name Paco is from *Pacundo* which sounds like an old uncle in the Philippines and he is not. Take a look. He is still young. You all understand what I mean," Cita explained laughing.

The ladies' eyes sparked which turned into laughter and cheers.

"Are you stretching our imagination Cita?" Tina asked.

"Oh! I know what you're thinking but our time is almost up in this place, Cita said.

"Okay, this conversation will cost Cita extra if we do not leave now," said Lanie.

On their way home, the ladies talked about the new place they found and things learned like playing pinball machines. Now I have something to tell my daughter like I learned to play pinball,"laughed Blanca.

"Who would have thought that there is a Chuck E. Cheese for *bagets* (Filipino slang for older people)? I wonder what would be Cita's idea next time to celebrate Paco's or her birthday. Do you remember Cita's birthday at the Basilica cafeteria? That was not lavish but we all enjoyed it. It was an experience going to a different church with an attached cafeteria. We prayed then ate in the house of the Lord. It does not get any holier than that," joked Lanie.

"You are committing the sin of gluttony with that statement," said Tina.

The ladies burst into laughter as Lanie tried to explain her point about praying and eating afterwards. "Sorry about that. Eating after praying in a big church are new to me," joked Blanca.

"Let's get back to Silly Times. The place gave us an idea about where we could host or spend our birthdays. Of course, we could always go to a restaurant where we can eat, sing happy birthday, blow your candle then go home. Don't you think it's boring to do it that way? Let's get creative once in a while ladies," said Blanca.

"You are right Blanca. So the next celebrant or host should think of something different," said Lulu.

"Is that a challenge?" Tina asked.

"No. What I want to say is we are stressed enough because of our work. But we have not lost our creativity, have we? Like for example, have we forgotten we have our own version of the Spanish Piñata called *pabitin* except we do not have the candies stashed in a paper maché animal to be beaten by kids with a baseball bat or stick until all the candies and chocolates comes out. Mayhem follows because everyone wants those candies and chocolates.

Our *pabitin* is the meshed bamboo, in the shape of a square, laden with candies and tied to a tree in the backyard. An adult pushes it up and down for the kids to reach for the candies. The up and down creates the excitement for everyone," explained Blanca.

"So, are we going to have that kind of fun too?" asked Lanie.

"It is really up to us to think of something different to celebrate our birthday?" said Lulu.

"Ladies, this is not to pressure you. All we want is to have fun and sometimes it comes from something random and spontaneous like Paco's birthday at Silly Times," added Blanca.

Cita's idea of a different birthday celebration was followed by her own when she celebrated at the Karaoke Idol Restaurant in Virginia. Named after the famous TV show American Idol minus the competition, everyone had a good time singing Karaoke especially the celebrant. Cita sang "My Heart Will Go On" from the movie Titanic. She sang with gusto amidst the surprise of the mostly Filipino patrons.

To cut the gawking of some of the guests surprised by Cita's audacity because Filipinos are modest people, Lulu whispered to the ladies that their singing drove away some of the customers. "On the contrary, we encouraged them to sing regardless whether one is in tune or not. Did it not turn to be more fun?" asked Lanie.

"Yes," agreed the ladies.

Blanca did not say a word. It was her first time watching Karaoke singing in a restaurant. "I have not been really out in places like this one or a bar with anyone for years. But start getting used to Karaoke and whatever else would come along the way. This is your group now and enjoy yourself," giving herself a silent pep talk.

After a week, Blanca got a call from Tina inviting her to a joint birthday celebration party for Clara, Lulu and Cita the following month of September. "But Cita already had her birthday last week at the Karaoke place," she told Tina over the phone.

"Cita said she does not mind having another birthday celebration with Lulu and Clara. Her employer, Mrs. Dana Robinson, will throw a party for her this weekend. That's how much of a birthday lady she had become. And do not forget the party would be at our apartment this coming Labor Day weekend. It falls on a Sunday so no work the following day. This give us time to relax, linger and enjoy the weekend," added Tina.

"Do I need to bring anything like soda and chips?" Blanca asked.

"You do not have to bring anything. Chedeng will be cooking. The birthday celebrants gave Chedeng money to buy all ingredients she needed to prepare whatever she could cook. Chedeng can pull this off even on a short notice. Her cooking is not only good but healthy as well. You know this because you've been coming to our Saturday dinners for months now. So, we will see you Sunday at one," Tina replied.

"I will be at your place bright and early with some flowers for the celebrants," added Blanca.

The joint birthday celebration of Clara, Lulu and Cita was a lot of fun. Everyone agreed that Filipino dishes cooked by

Chedeng were delicious as always. Her *monggo* soup with lots of spinach was divine. They've wondered how Chedeng makes that soup with such consistency you sweat in the middle of winter or airconditioning.

"My *monggo* soup recipe ladies is a secret," Chedeng joked.

"Just like the age of our birthday celebrants," quipped Paco.

That threw everyone into laughter until Blanca suggested that it was time to cut the cake and sing the Happy Birthday song. Chedeng cleared the middle part of the buffet table to make way for the three small cakes.

Jelene, Lanie and Tina came into the dining room each with a lighted cake for Lulu, Clara and Cita. They blew out their candles together. Blanca started the singing of the Happy Birthday then shouted "how old are you?"

No one among the celebrants answered the age question. "Oh! Did I just ask a sensitive question," murmured Blanca.

Lulu then requested to blow the candle on her cake again so she can send a picture to her family in the Philippines. "You know my children oftentimes forget to greet me on my birthday but I never forget theirs. They will apologize and send me the cheapest card you can find at the bookstore. It hurts but it is what it is," lamented Lulu.

Blanca immediately diverted Lulu's complaint about her children by asking Clara to blow her candle again so Paco could take her picture. "Oh! Lulu should not cry. Let's cheer on Lulu ladies. Did you not say that you want to show your grandkids that *Lola Clare* (grandmother) could blow all her birthday candles too?" asked Blanca.

"Yes, my dear. Thank you for reminding me. My *apos* (grandchildren) will be happy see me blow my candles. I love it every time they call me *Lola Clare.*" smiled Clara.

Cita compared their candle blowing like a race. "Let's see who can blow their candle first?"

"Now I know who is the oldest. It's Clara!" said Tina

"Not me. Blowing my birthday candle with Lulu and Cita came as a surprise. I got excited when the birthday cakes came in. That got me out of breathe," Clara explained.

"It's alright Clara. Age is just a number. I am sure everyone was also surprised how this triple celebration came to be. We never had this kind of birthday party. Three birthday candles lit on three cakes blown at the same time is quite a feat," Chedeng said to Clara.

Chedeng reminded everyone to get thee slices – one carrot, one chocolate and one yellow cake.

"This is a lot of cake. We will be bouncing around all over the place like my *alagas* (kids she is taking care of) after trick or treat," said Rissa.

"Do not worry about the calories. It will get burnt after a week of work," Tina added.

"Can the October celebrants also have a double celebration? I'm talking about Lanie and me,"asked Rissa.

"It might be too much for Tina and Chedeng. They will also be celebrating their birthdays in November and December. It's just a month apart and I suppose you and Lanie will have your joint celebration at 22nd Street," opined Cita.

"You are right Cita. Maybe Rissa and I should find another place to celebrate our birthdays," replied Lanie

Pressed for time and no place to host, Lanie for her birthday invited the ladies for dinner at Dish Thai in Georgetown. Blanca was happy about Lanie's choice. She finds Lanie's apartment in the basement suffocating, furnished with Ms. Sandy's old furniture.

Lanie's choice of Dish Thai was perfect. Located near the Georgetown Park overlooking the Kennedy Center, Dish Thai was really nice with fancy plates and cloth napkins. The crispy fall season blends well with what we are about to do – eat spicy Thai food on fancy plates. "Take a look at the *Pad Thai* dish across our table. It is served in a cave like plate but the noodles do not fall off. Ha! How neat. Bon appetite," said Clara.

"Dig in," said Lanie the minute all the orders finally arrived.

When dinner was over, Chedeng asked Lanie if the ladies could have dessert.

Lanie said yes. The only problem was no one was familiar with Thai desserts. Tina got a solution. She volunteered to discreetly check the dessert of the other guests across their table.

"That was a quick look. I think they are having something similar to our *halo-halo* (a mix of sweetened banana, yam, black or pink beans with fine crushed ice and milk and sometimes topped with flan). Would you like us to try what they are having?" Tina suggested.

"Please wait. Can we have something that has no milk? It does not go well with my stomach. Yes, my problem is lactose intolerance. I hope you don't mind," said Blanca.

So as not to confuse the servers who spoke English, the ladies agreed on the familiar looking *biko* (sweet rice cake) for dessert.

"I swear to God, this is *biko*. *Ang galing* (brilliant)! It is the same *biko* we all knew except they serve it fancy round plate sprinkled with shredded coconut and strips of yellow mangoes around it. Let's eat this new version of *biko*," joked Blanca.

The ladies smiled, laughed, joked about the transformation of the familiar Filipino favorite rice cake. "Ladies, I would love to tell other Filipinos about this *biko*," Chedeng said.

After dinner, Cita suggested to have ice cream at a nearby shop. Lanie again offered to pay for the ice cream that cost so much in Georgetown.

While everyone wondered off with their two scoops of ice cream on a cone, Lanie was left at the counter to get her ice cream and pay for everyone. Blanca saw her rushing out of the store like a lost child wondering where everyone had gone. Cita stood up and directed her to join them.

"You are a bunch of ungrateful people. How much was a scoop of ice cream in that place?" asked Clara.

"It was two dollars a scoop," replied Chedeng.

"Of course, it would be expensive. We could have gotten this ice cream cheaper from the other ice cream shops but we are in Georgetown. If you look there is the Kennedy Center. It is nice and it's a full moon too. Eating ice cream under a full moon, it does not get any better than this. We look like we do not have any worries and smiling from ear to ear," said Paco.

To keep the fun going, Blanca came up with a question and answer game.

"This is not like that TV show Jeopardy but a test of how well we know each other," said Blanca.

As she took out a piece of paper from her bag, Cita enjoined everyone to join the game.

"Look ladies, she came prepared, so watch out," shouted Cita.

"Your game is really fun but it is getting late," said Lanie after five rounds of Blanca's question and answer game.

Lanie said she was worried about Ms. Sandy's dogs. "They are not used to me coming home late. *Parang mga bata din yan sila* (they are like children too). They miss me because I rarely go out on Sunday nights. Also, there is work the following day," explained Lanie.

Blanca had fun and wished that they could have stayed longer. "This is such a lovely night by the light of the silvery moon for strolling alongside the Potomac," said Blanca.

"We should do this more often," said Clara.

"Now that you know this place *Manang* Clara, you might want to bring your family here too," said Cita.

"This is too far from Maryland. Maybe when they come to pick me up one weekend," replied Clara.

"Just a suggestion *Manang* Clara," Cita added.

Rissa's birthday followed Lanie's in the same month of October. She invited the ladies to a buffet restaurant on Rockville Pike. The sisters were delighted to find out Rissa's choice to celebrate her birthday.

"Buffets are great. You want pasta and salad, buffet has them. Seafood like shrimps, crabs, clams and fish, they've got it. Anything your heart probably desires. Check out the variety and you will find one or two dishes you like. For picky eaters, if nothing else takes their fancy, this place has pizza, mac n' chesse, fries on stand by," said Chedeng.

On their second trip to a buffett, Blanca concluded eating at a buffett was an alternative to a restaurant. A majority of the ladies like it and those who did not just went along for the fun of it. "Aha! Buffett is a good place to have lunch and birthday celebration. There is a variety of food to please everyone's palette.

This coming November, I am inviting you to another buffett to celebrate my birthday except we are going to downtown Springhills," announced Blanca.

Bluemoon buffett was packed when the ladies came one Sunday for Blanca's birthday. "*Sus Ginoo* (Jesus Christ). It looks like the entire population of Maryland has descended on Silver City," said Chedeng

Located in the basement of Silver City mall in Spring Hills, Maryland, "this place was highly recommended by my brother when my *Kuya* (older brother) from the Philippines came to visit us two years ago," said Blanca.

"Oh, well it should be worth the wait. We've been here before and I tell you this buffet serves the best *lomi* (Chinese noodles) compared to others Chedeng and I had before," said Tina.

That assurance from Tina kept the ladies smiling as they stood behind a long line of people waiting to get in. The wait staff told the ladies they can put together three tables to accomodate the group. In the meantime, the ladies watched with envy how groups of two or three customers got seated quickly.

To console the ladies because of the wait, Blanca joked and said "they also serve those who stand and wait." It made everyone laughed until finally a wait staff joked and said "that by the grace of God finally you have a table."

"See! I told you they really serve those who stand and wait," said Blanca.

"You really have a way of cushioning things when something goes a little inconvenient," Paco said.

Blanca replied and said,"I don't remember where I got that quotation but it made sense today. Besides, it's my birthday and I want to be upbeat. I want to celebrate in different place minus the wait but it did not happen that way. I apologize," said Blanca

Despite the wait, the ladies enjoyed Blanca's birthday at the buffet. Tina once again talked about the convenience of going to a buffet. She said the dishes at Silver City were delicious. "I told you their *lomi* soup is the best".

"Are we doing another buffet in the near future?" asked Lulu.

"I don't think so because I am celebrating my birthday next Sunday. Don't forget I am also a November celebrant. That will give us a break from restaurant food. My sister Chedeng will be celebrating her birthday too in December. So we can forget the restaurants for now. By the way, everyone is invited at 22nd Street," said Tina.

As expected, the birthday celebrations of the two sisters were always fun because of the food, the Karaoke and their guests. The arrival of their other friends to celebrate their day plus the Golden Group was always a riot. Their fun and laughter could turn their apartment upside down but in a good way.

By 2010, Tina and Chedeng announced that they will start the hosting cycle early. Fresh from Chedeng's birthday, the sisters hosted lunch by the second week of February to start their cycle of lunches and birthdays. They served the usual fare that everybody loved like *sinigang, lumpia, adobo*, steamed fish and desserts.

Over lunch Cita told the ladies quietly about her plan to throw a get together by the end of February. "I want it in time for *Irog's* birthday and promotion. I have not figured out a venue yet but I will keep Tina posted," said Cita.

It did not take long for Cita to arrange a celebration for Paco. It was again a surprise but the arrangement this time was through Tina. She was asked to make a reservation for twenty people at the famous La Cocina on Wisconsin Avenue. Tina happened to be working in the area on certain days. She already knew the menu.

"Let's order the *plato gordo* (Spanish for big plate) because you won't go wrong. It has little bit of everything from tacos to tamales. Each tray can feed three to four people. I think it's great that way," Tina smiled.

"Then as soon as everyone has eaten, the servers will gather around the table of the celebrant and sing Happy Birthday," Chedeng added.

Everyone laughed. "It's true. The singing makes you happy, excited. Someone leads the singing and everyone else follows along. How much birthday can you get?" Tina said.

Cita tapped her glass after the singing and told the guests the celebration was a double one. First, she said Paco got a promotion at work, and second she wished the man in her life the best of health. She also introduced her uncle responsible for her meeting Paco. There was a lot of clapping and cheers for the couple. The ladies then looked at Cita's daughter Chloe to check if she was okay with the new man in her mother's life.

Blanca on the other hand smiled and murmured about the snubby relatives of Cita.

"It's good to know that they have names. We've met them many times but never engaged the ladies to a conversation. Who do they think they are," smirked Blanca.

The months of March, April and June passed until a reluctant Blanca invited the ladies to her first lunch hosting at her new house in Silver City. Since it was her turn to host, she concluded what would be more fitting but to have lunch with the ladies at her new place.

To free herself from the usual non-stop cooking common at Filipino parties, Blanca ordered from the nearby Salad Fresh place in Wheaton Mall. She felt this would give her time to talk to the ladies. She laid the food on the kitchen counter and told the ladies to help themselves and feel free to come back for more helpings. She was worried because the tacos and the wraps came in finger food sizes.

"I'm done with cooking after almost twenty years of doing it," she told the ladies.

"Don't apologize because eating to go food is fun and relaxing. No one stayed in the kitchen all night to feed a group like us. This will give us time to talk like we are right now,"

Lanie said.

While binging on tacos, salad, salsa and chips, Lulu asked the ladies if they were ready to play Bingo. It took everyone by surprise. They admitted they had not played the game in years.

"Bingo is played in senior centers, ladies," said Tina

"Oh, this is only a game for old ladies now," said Chedeng

"Aren't we," Lanie asked.

"Is that hard to admit?" Cita asked

"Let's ask Paco this time," said Blanca

Paco did not say a word. He instead checked the Bingo kit Lulu brought. He said,"its a complete set ladies. There's even a small *tambiolo* (lottery drum). Let's play Bingo ladies," said Paco.

"But first let me tell you how I got the set. I was surprised when I got it in the mail. This was not given to me by some Avon lady you encountered in the past but as a bonus for buying Avon products. You see Avon has products I like. It's like a small prize for patronizing their products over the years. I kept it even if I have no one to play with in my apartment. Because this could be gambling for some folks, I also did not dare to play Bingo with my *alagas* (wards). So let's play and enjoy an old time Filipino favorite.

"Thank God, this Bingo will keep the ladies entertained," Blanca murmured on her quick run to the kitchen to heat some water for tea.

"How are we going to go about the game ladies?" asked Paco "Well, why don't we partner, like you and Cita could be one. The sisters can partner with each other while Blanca and Lanie can be partners. I will be the caller and have my own cards to keep track of the game. What do you think ladies?" asked Lulu.

"I think everyone now remembers the game. So let's play Bingo," said Blanca.

The ladies' Bingo lasted for three hours. They had so much fun that they forgot the passing of time. Cita was first in filling in all her cards. She won a total of fifteen dollars. Blanca lost while Lulu and Lanie had fifty three dollars split between them. The sisters said they will donate their winning to the church. Lanie and Lulu said they are looking forward to another Bingo day.

There was laughter on their way out of the house to the driveway. To appease Lanie's frustration over not winning anything, Lulu promised she will be the next caller in case another Bingo day or night happens in the future. The sister said they would be on the lookout for signs of *daya* (cheating).

Blanca's drew a sigh of relief when the ladies left. "That Bingo game saved me. It kept the fun and conversation going until everyone got tired and was ready to go home. I guess this is the essence and beauty of why we have the group," Blanca talking to herself while relaxing on her sofa.

Clara's absence at Blanca's party was noticed by the ladies. That was not the first time it happened. Since Cita is her neighbor, she could not help but come to Clara's rescue. She explained that Clara gets confused the minute she gets a call from her daughter about her pick up time for the weekend. "That's why she sometimes forgets we are having lunch or a birthday party," Lanie further said.

"Speaking of *Manang* Clara, I was told she would be hosting lunch in September. So, ladies please keep your calendar open," said Cita.

"Oh! Clara has resurfaced. I am not surprise. You are neighbors so you probably bumped into each other somewhere in Georgetown. What are her plans for her birthday?" asked Tina.

"Well, she asked if *Irog* could rent a van to take us to a place. She did not say where she plans to take us. I told her that it shouldn't be a problem. A week's notice is all that is needed before the trip. Most rental companies do not keep vans in their fleet. So, we are still waiting for *Manang* Clara's call to finalize the reservation?" said Cita.

"*Manang* Clara is probably thinking of something different and enjoyable for us to do. Please keep us posted so we can prepare something like Chedeng's banana cake," said Tina.

For her lunch hosting and birthday, Clara had a day of prayer and lunch. She invited the ladies to the National Shrine of Our Lady of Lourdes in Emmitsburg, Maryland. Clara said she had a personal request to ask to the Virgin Mary.

Blanca called Tina the following day to know how how the trip went. Tina gave her a vivid account of what happened during the trip.

"*Manang* Clara was a little bit embarrassed when she saw what the ladies brought to the grotto. We had *adobo* (sautéed pork cuts or chicken marinated in vinegar, garlic, whole peppers and bay leaf), *pansit* (noodles), tomatoes, rice and mangoes, corn and spaghetti. We assured her that we are always ready to share whatever we can prepare on short notice.

Her plan was to take us to a nearby restaurant but there was really none in the area. But just the same, we had a blast like we always do. The grotto has a big garden where devotees like us could eat picnic style. We met other folks from *Visaya* so it was fun talking with each other. I think the place was meant not only to be a religious site but has areas to gather after your conversation with God," joked Tina.

"I agree but we are really very religious. We as a people are always grateful and happy that another year was added to our life. That's what probably she had in mind," said Blanca.

By the way, do you know how old *Manang* Clara is?" asked Tina.

"She is more or less in the vicinity or age range of Lanie and your sister. And don't forget

Paco too," replied Blanca.

"We are bad because we are talking about very sensitive issue among ladies," said Tina.

"You know we'll get there someday and hopefully we stay the same sharp and quick witted ladies. We shouldn't be sensitive about it. Let's say goodbye for now before we end up laughing all day," said Blanca.

Clara's birthday celebration in September was followed by Cita's. She announced that the ladies were going back to the grotto for her birthday. Blanca was happy to join the trip this time.

"Although, I've been to one in Vermont, it would be nice to visit the famous one in Maryland," said Blanca over the phone.

Unlike Clara'apparent lack of planning, Paco and Cita took care of everything from the ride to the grotto and food. They got to the shrine around ten in the morning. By arriving early, the ladies had enough time to explore the huge place. Blanca was excited about the ample time they had to explore the grotto. She told the ladies she would like go alone to check out the place since everyone have been to the grotto in the past.

"What time and where should I meet everyone for lunch?" asked Blanca.

"Why don't we meet you for the mass in the open air chapel at twelve?" asked Paco.

"That sounds good! I have a map to guide me around and a cell phone to call in case I get lost," replied Blanca.

"This is not something new but it's been a while since I've been to one so, let's go Blanca," she said to herself as she separated from the ladies.

Blanca was glad to be on her own touring the grotto. She could not tell her friends she was not into the pilgrimage type of birthday celebrations. That all she wanted was to see the place and not much on the the praying. "I do not want the ladies to know my take on prayers and other aspect of the Catholic religion at this point of my life. Me and my big mouth could offend the ladies," smiled Blanca.

While walking and exploring every nook and cranny of the grotto, Blanca realized it was good to have joined her friends. "Visiting this religious site is a good one for now until maybe the group can organize a trip to other Filipino favorites like Lourdes in France or Fatima in Portugal. OnlyTina had been to Lourdes during a trip to Europe with her Swiss boyfriend. Cita had been to the Vatican in Rome with her then Italian boyfriend. Will see if I could convince the ladies to take an overseas trip to check on other grottos?

But come to think of it, a place to pray is immaterial. We can pray anywhere," Blanca smiled as she passed by every little versions of the teary eyed Virgin Mary holding Jesus's lifeless body after being taken down from the cross.

Blanca continued on exploring the grotto until she finally found the place to meet the rest of the ladies. It was an open church on the hill with an altar below it. It's a perfect spot for visitors to gather and cap their visit to the grotto with a mass and communion.

"What a nice spot to end my tour," said Blanca.

"We're glad you found us. We will have a little party in the garden after the mass," Cita said.

They held hands praying the Our Father during the mass. Everyone received communion except for Blanca.

Like any tourist spot, the grotto has its souvenir shop, as its last stop for visitors. Blanca could not help and said," Wow, merchandising is really everywhere even in a place like this."

"Could this be one of the branches of the Smithsonian Museum except they sell religious things?" asked Lanie.

"Aren't you being silly? Find something you like. Pray over it when you are in trouble,"

Lulu said.

"St. Jude if that's what you mean," replied Lanie.

"The ladies burst into laughter. Lanie told Lulu that St. Jude had already given her a husband and she did not want to ask for another one.

Lanie's reply drew more laughter from the ladies while the ladies were looking for spot in the garden to eat.

"I was just joking Lanie," said Lulu.

"I think this corner with two big trees is a good spot to eat. It has more shade compared to that one accross," said Cita.

The ladies agreed and gathered around Cita's find to celebrate her birthday. Paco asked the ladies to open their *baon* (bagged food) from Georgetown to start a late lunch.

"Ladies, we are not bringing this food back to Georgetown. We will finish it and if not, some of you will have to bring some home," said Paco.

"Yes, commander," said Tina as the ladies stood in salute.

"Was he in the army?' one lady asked

"Yes, but that was a long time ago," replied Cita.

"He never got out of it I guess," said Chedeng.

At the garden, the ladies met other Filipinos. Those short exchanges among the Filipinos in the garden led to more conversation. First, they ask where you are from in the Philippines. Then next how long have been in the country. Once they find out you share something in common, like same province, the conversation turns into some kind of probing.

On the way home, Blanca talked about the Filipinos at the grotto. It kept everyone in the van awake. She kept laughing while trying to keep a straight face as she exaggerated and even made up part of her story.

"Wasn't it fun to see throngs of Filipinos at the shrine? Did you know that they had *dinuguan* with *puto* (blood soup from the blood of pig eaten with rice cake)? We exchanged pleasantries so I got an update on the latest *tisismis* (gossip) and other issues back home. I do not have a Filipino channel and I could tell they have it. Their *balita* (news) seemed fresh compared to mine. *Visaya din sila* (they are from the Visayan region too)," said Blanca.

Everyone got wide awake and broke into laughter.

"They really thought I am a *Visaya*. I told them I grew up in *Camotes Island* in Cebu.

Asked me how I passed as someone from *Cebu*. I'd been to *Cebu* in the late 70's so I just played around with what I knew about the place and they believed me. It worked ladies," said Blanca.

"You are really a trip Blanca," said Lanie

"Listen, what are the chances that we will ever meet them again. *Nada* (means nothing in Spanish). At least they have something to remember us by," said Blanca.

"I am sure you pull this trick again. Are you going to pretend to be an *Ilocano* (from Ilocos province) next time? "Paco asked.

"Maybe but I don't know if I could pull that off. Let's see next time," said Blanca.

The next birthday celebration was Lanie's and Rissa's. Lanie's choice for the second time was Dish Thai in Georgetown. "We understand" as the ladies love to say.

"Let's be happy at Dish Thai with Lanie. It would be unkind to force her to celebrate her birthday in some faraway place when she barely has time for herself. We've been there before so maybe we can order the same dish or try something else. It would be probably fun to try something different. The servers at Dish Thai are very accommodating and would be happy to explain the dishes. You want some heat, they'll give it to you," said Cita.

"Here comes the birthday lady," said Tina as Lanie joined them.

"Thank you all for coming. The place doesn't matter. What's important is we are together and you will sing the Happy Birthday song. I will be delighted to hear it," said Lanie.

Tina was quite animated during the dinner. Her sister Chedeng said she probably got a dish that was a bit spicy. "She loves spicy food. We always have Tabasco at home and she is the sole consumer of that because I'm happy with pepper in my food,"Chedeng said.

"Do we get the same fancy *biko* (rice cake) like we had last year?" asked Tina.

"Can we try Donna's Ice Cream in Wisconsin Avenue for dessert? It's homemade so it must be good," suggested Lulu.

"That should be fun and cheaper. Can you believe this? Three blocks away from the shopping and restaurant areas, a scoop of ice cream cost less than Georgetown," Paco joked.

"Look, there is a long line to get the cheaper ice cream ladies," said Tina as they joined the line.

The ladies waited patiently for their turn to get the ice cream. Lulu and Tina asked for three scoops while the rest asked for two. Blanca suggested they should all pay for their ice cream. Lanie said no but the ladies insisted and paid for their own.

"Aren't we cheap?" asked Chedeng as she laughed.

As always, the laughter that followed made the wait bearable and fun.

The ladies walked back to Georgetown after their trip to the ice shop. "Thank you for taking me home. It's always fun walking in Georgetown minus the dogs," Lanie exclaimed.

Everyone said yes but muted. Something Blanca understood because it's true. Filipino maids in Georgetown are always seen walking dogs.

"You won't miss Lanie's house. It's the only blue painted house on P Street. We hope you had fun because this is not the last one for October," said Chedeng.

"Well, Rissa is yet to confirm where we're going for her birthday. She will be calling us soon about that, right Rissa?" Cita asked.

"I am thinking of Red Lobster in downtown Silver Spring," replied Rissa.

Tina and Blanca got excited with Rissa's choice.

"This is what we've been waiting for. Everybody is talking about Red Lobster's biscuits but I never got the chance to travel all the way to the place. Finally, I will have a taste of it to confirm what everybody was talking about," said Blanca.

"The place is not only about the biscuit but their sea food too. It would be a break from Filipino, Chinese and Thai food we've been eating the past few months. It should be another fun afternoon," said Tina.

Without a reservation, the ladies had to wait to get a table at Red Lobster. Rissa also invited two friends from her dance class so the group got bigger. The servers apologized for the wait but promised to find a way to accommodate a group of ten in one long table.

Tina accepted the apology and said they did not mind the fifteen minute wait but was ready to order once they got seated. "May I suggest for each one of us to order a different seafood combo to share. This way will have a taste a variety of their seafood preparation. I hope this is alright with you?

You know if my sister has those grilling equipment like what they use here, I bet you Chedeng can prepare some of this combo from the menu," said Tina after reading the menu.

"We need to wait not only because we are a group but they still catching the shrimps and lobster?" said Paco.

The bantering over the long wait lasted for ten to fifteen minutes until they were finally served.

"Oh, here comes the food. I can smell it from afar," said Rissa's friend.

When everyone had their order, silence followed as the ladies started to eat.

"*Sus Ginoo* (Jesus Christ) ladies aren't we all hungry?" said Chedeng.

"But can we trade our orders with one another so we can taste the different dishes in their menu?" Tina asked.

Three of the ladies obliged but the rest were almost done with theirs and there was little to share. Blanca, on the other end, had a ball with the biscuits. She was happy the servers put a lot on their table. The servers also started singing the Happy Birthday song for Rissa.

Everyone followed suit and made Rissa smile and blush.

Rissa's party was over by four o'clock. Paco and Rissa drove the ladies home while Blanca got a ride from Rissa's friend.

"I can take Blanca home. I can drop her off because her place is close to where I live," said Rissa's friend.

Blanca followed Emmy to the parking garage and saw she has a mini Cooper. She held her breath on the way home because it was her first time to ride in such small but power-ful car.

"That was one hell of a ride Tina. Never underestimate a small looking car like a mini Cooper. It has a powerful engine like those big cars. Oh, about Rissa's friend Emmy and Lorrie, they said Rissa is the best dancer in their group," said Blanca over the phone.

"I am not surprise. Rissa was teaching everybody during the Independence Day Ball. Do you have plans for your coming birthday on November?" Tina asked.

"I am turning sixty this year. I want to have a party in a restaurant and invite the ladies, my family, and other friends to celebrate with me. I do not know if I can keep my promise that this will be my last birthday party since I am turning sixty. I hope everybody can come," said Blanca.

"We are both November celebrants and my sister's day comes after a month. I am sure we will have the same get together at 22nd Street because it's been like that for years. Our other friends look forward to it not only because it is our birthday but as an end of the year activity before we all head out for the holidays. They feel good that another year will soon be over and a couple days off during the holidays will give them a big break from work,"

Tina added.

"Turning sixty for me was something I did not take seriously until I realized it is another milestone in my life. I am nearing retirement. I could see in the mirror a sixty year old woman and I think I would like to celebrate it. There is still time to make a reservation but I would like to have it on a Saturday," Blanca told her sister in Montreal.

"I will come and I hope your daughter will come. I do not know your friends but it would be really nice to have a party for your 60th birthday. You did not celebrate your 50th birthday because you did not have the money. Have one this time," Blanca's sister Sara said.

Blanca agreed and had her 60th birthday in a Chinese restaurant in Bethesda. Her brother and sister came including her daughter and fiancée. The ladies from her babysitting group in DC also came. She was dressed in a pink suit looking like Hilary Clinton said her sister in law. Her invitation said no gifts please but two of her relatives brought gifts as a tradition.

"First of all, I want to thank one or two relatives who kept the tradition of giving gift money. I am happy that my family and friends are around to celebrate a milestone in my life. I already have what I need but they probably accept cash in heaven," said Blanca in her short speech.

It made everyone laughed. They wished her long life during the toast. But she missed the ladies during the picture taking. Blanca had a crown on her head to celebrate her 60th birthday. The crown came all the way from Canada. It was her sister's idea to wear one.

"I think it would be a good idea for the ladies to wear one too when they celebrate their birthdays. This would look good on Tina on her coming birthday next week. I could lend her mine then pass it on to the next one," Blanca thought as she cut and passed her cake.

The ladies could not make it to her party. Saturday afternoon had never been a good day for her friends to come because of work. This she understood, and had to be happy with whoever could make it to the Saturday lunch she planned. She hoped that Cita and Paco would care to come. "I do not understand. They do not work on Saturdays," sighed Blanca.

Tina's birthday party was a week after her 60th birthday. It was like nothing happened a week ago. No one among the ladies ever asked how her party went.

She was hurt, but kept her cool and rushed to put her crown on Tina's head to indicate she was the celebrant and queen for the day. Everyone was delighted with Blanca's gestures of crowning Tina. She told Tina's guests it was a gift from her sister to celebrate her 60th birthday. They were surprised to find out that Blanca was also a November celebrant. She replied and said that it would be fun and pretty for Tina to wear a crown on her 61st birthday.

"I do not want the ladies and other guests to focus on me but instead on Tina. So let her have my crown, Blanca murmured.

Cita said she loved the idea of the birthday celebrant wearing a crown. She said it looked cute and very celebratory. Everyone agreed.

"That's all I cared about even if the ladies gave me a hard time and fifty million excuses why they could not come to mine," murmured Blanca as she watched everyone admiring her crown on Tina's head.

As always, Tina's November birthday party was lots of fun. She led the Karaoke singing while the guest chose their song from the songbook. Tina loves to say singing was not mandatory but she would appreciate it if they could sing too as a gift.

"Who could turn down the birthday lady? I will sing even if I'm out of tune. Singing I guess would be fun," said a guest.

Karaoke singing lasted for hours while guests kept coming and going. Again, the card game 41 started around five in the afternoon. Tina told everyone that their game with regular card players would last maybe till nine in the evening. "Remember we are in America now so ten is like a curfew when it comes to noise. We also have work the following day," joked Tina.

Cita asked the ladies if it was okay to leave once the card table had been set up. Lulu and Clara said that it should be alright. Lanie said not knowing the game would be a good excuse to politely leave. "Don't forget, I will be going home to Rockville, Maryland. Remember *Manang* Chedeng's birthday is next month, so we will be seeing each other again," said Jelene.

Chedeng's December 2010 birthday party celebration, turned out to be the same as in previous years. Their other friends came with gift money and had fun all afternoon singing Karaoke, playing a favorite 41 card game and eating Filipino food they could not cook in their employers' home.

"It's always a sight to see the sisters' friends come over in November and December. I am really happy to see them because they've been friends for years. I am pretty sure they miss their families so much now that their diplomatic visas have long been expired. I gathered they've not gone back to the Philippines in years, is that right?" asked Paco.

The ladies' conversation stopped. No one replied to confirm the sisters' immigration status. Blanca on the other hand, had known their immigration statues ever since she started having dinner with the sisters. "Their visas have expired but avoided talking about it. Anyone's immigration status in the United States is a private matter," Blanca said to tone down the conversation on a sensitive question.

Paco realized the sensitivity of his question, backtracked and instead talked about how he could make the sisters happy. "Ladies, a compilation of our 2010 activities is now in progress. I'm waiting for the sisters' photos to complete the year. Again, you will each have a copy to keep or send to your families in the Philippines. Chedeng and Tina will have the 2010 DVD activities of the Golden Group ready for their next *balikbayan* (care package) box," said Paco.

"Yes, the sisters regularly send those care packages up to now. Thanks God my children are already here otherwise, I will be like the sisters. I heard they buy most of the stuff from bulk stores like Costco or Sam's Club, "Clara whispered to Jelene.

"You know what, those care packages have spoiled a lot of Filipinos back home," Jelene whispered back.

No one cared to add to Jelene's little comment. "That's another sensitive issue. We sometimes love our families to a fault," Blanca smiled at Jelene.

Paco's announcement of a 2010 DVD of the Golden Group in the making got the ladies' attention diverted from another sensitive They all went home happy and were looking forward seeing their activities in DVD. Lanie said another year was about to end and was just glad to have the group around for another year. "*Sabi nga ni* Dean Martin (as Dean Martin said in his song) "thanks for the memories"," said Lanie.

"So when are we going to see each other again?" asked Blanca.

"I will let you know but I plan to host the New Year's Eve party," said Cita.

The Fun Continues

On her way to a New Year's Eve get together at Cita's, Blanca could not help but think about the transformation of the ladies of Georgetown to the Golden Group. "It's been two years of rollicking outings, lunches and birthday parties. We finally got it together. This is really great. Everyone cared enough to find the time to invest in it, given their busy lives," said Blanca while waiting for the bus to get to Cita's place in Georgetown.

At the New Year's Event at Cita's, sisters Tina and Chedeng announced that they will be the first one to host lunch to start 2011's round of fun and get together. "We are looking forward to it," said the ladies.

Everyone got excited the minute the ladies got into their first party of 2011. They saw a pot of piping hot *mongo* soup and spring rolls on the table. "For lunch, I think it would be okay to prepare your *mongo soup at lumpia* (green bean soup and spring rolls) and nothing else. What do you think ladies?" asked Lulu.

"We agree but I want the steamed fish and *adobo* with rice," said Lanie.

It sparked the conversation about ways to prepare *adobo*. Blanca listened intently and admitted that her *adobo* needed improvement. To cover up her lack of cooking skills, she asked the ladies if they wanted to taste her blue soup.

The ladies wondered what Blanca was talking about while Chedeng explained what was the blue soup?

"The origin of the blue soup to say it again dates back to the movie Bridget Jones we watched in the past. Bridget Jones invited her childhood friend Darcy for dinner one night. She did not know how to cook and depended on a cookbook. While cooking she found out that she did not have the kitchen rope or thread to keep her asparagus together. There was no time to run to the store so, she used a blue thread from her sewing box. It bled and the dish turned blue. But Bridget Jones and Darcy had fun just the same," said Chedeng.

Paco interrupted and said, "That's a fun story but listen, I agree with Lulu's opinion about the spring rolls and *mongo* soup make us happy. The combination had been a good break from the monotony of the boring days of winter," added Paco.

"*Manang* Clara is not around again. Did you miss calling her Cita?" Lanie asked.

"No, I did not but maybe her daughter picked her up early yesterday. I don't know.

What's going on with her?" said Cita.

"I'm just asking because we are neighbors here in Georgetown. We are just a stone throw away from each other but she's been quiet," chimed in Lanie.

"So what's next for us this year?" Tina asked.

"Let's see because it's too early to plan or commit. Winter is still very much around. Remember the saying spring is not far behind. Did I say that right?" Lulu asked.

"It doesn't matter. I like the poetic *dating* (nice rhyming) that's sounds hopeful," said Blanca.

"I think it is best to keep us dazed and in cloud nine until one of us calls and say "she has an idea for a get together," said Jelene.

"But before we all go back to work tomorrow, let's thank the sisters for their patience in hosting us during the winter months of January and February," said Paco.

Cita and the rest of the ladies seconded Paco's gesture of thanks. Blanca also thanked Chedeng for putting together extra food to take home.

"Let's now all go home but keep in touch. Someone might decide to host lunch next month or early summer. "I'm inviting you to a 4th of July weekend. I will be hosting," said Cita.

While on the bus, Jelene and Blanca wondered who would be the next host.

"I think this is going to be a free-wheeling random hosting from now on. I mean whoever likes it and has the time," said Blanca.

"Why do you think that way *Ate* (a word of respect to an older sister)?" Jelene asked.

"Well, the friendship among the ladies is now entrenched so whoever wants to host can freely do so to keep the fun going. Yes, we have a schedule to follow but Cita takes the lead most of the time then the rest of us follow. Haven't you notice this? I bet you *Manang* Clara will resurface to host," said Blanca again.

Jelene and Blanca could not help but laugh about Clara. "Is she back from somewhere?"

Jelene asked,

"You see, they heard what you just said. This is the fun of riding the bus on Sunday. We see other folks don't we?" Blanca asked.

"You're really fun to be with *Ate* Blanca. This laughter will keep me going for the coming week," said Jelene.

Blanca was right about Clara's return to the group. Cita called everyone and said Clara will be hosting lunch at her daughter's house in Hyattsville. "It's the fifth birthday of Clara's grandson. She would be cooking for the party. *Manang* Clara, found the occasion to host and invite the Golden Group," said Cita.

In two separate cars, the ladies headed out to Clara's daughter's house for lunch one late spring Sunday. Lanie, Lulu and couple Cita and Paco the ladies had gifts for Clara's grandson like clothes and toys but sisters Chedeng and Tina including Blanca gave money gifts.

"We will be opening a bank account for our son starting with all the money gifts he's been getting for a while," said Sherrie and her husband.

Beaming with pride and joy, Clara introduced her daughter's family and other guests. Clara whispered to the ladies

149

that her son-in-law is a good man. He's got a steady job with the metro system as an engineer. I could not ask for anything more," said Clara.

Everyone could not help but agree to a point that her son in law got somewhat uncomfortable. He immediately expressed his gratitude to Clara and said "my mother in law did all the cooking."

The occasion really showcased Clara's cooking. Like most typical Filipino parties, the amount of food and variety was amazing. There were about two to three Filipino vegetable dishes Blanca identified. "My favorite among them was *chop suey* (Chinese Filipino dish with Napa cabbage, button mush-rooms, snow peas, and pork or chicken strips), and *pakbet* (veg-etable dish consisting of bitter melons, squash, long green beans, sautéed with lots of tomatoes flavored with fish sauce). Her *chop suey* was cooked the way the Chinese cooks in the Philippines would prepare it – vegetables so crispy drenched in white sauce," described Blanca.

"I think *Manang* Clara also served *diningding*. It is a veg-etable dish from the *Ilocos* region of the country," said Lulu.

"As long as the food will not give me stomach problem, I am fine with that dish. "*Masarap lahat* (everything is deli-cious). So that was Clara's cooking prowess," said Lanie.

"To continue our usual talk about after our lunch or birthday get together, did you notice Sherrie's cold attitude towards her mother. She did not hide her anger about Clara's mistake in ordering the birthday cake. Instead of a 5th birth-day icing on the cake, 4th was put on it. Clara ignored Sherrie and asked everyone to join in the in the singing of the Happy Birthday song so the little celebrant would blow his candles without help," said Cita.

"Sherrie however, remained stoic and looked at her mother with a warning. She was not the Sherrie we know who would drop by 22nd to pick Clara for the weekend. But we do not know about that mother and daughter relationship. Let's not be nosy ladies," Lulu said with a smile.

"You are right Lulu. Our friendship with Clara does not give us the right to get into her private life. She seems to get it all together after a long separation from her children," said Cita.

"So what's next after Clara's return to the fold?" Paco asked.

"Oh! We don't know what Clara is up to. Let's be glad she invited us," Lanie replied.

"Well, she's been out of the loop and we do not know what is going on. Her invitation came as a surprise disrupting our hosting schedule. It looks like we will be having surprise lunches hosting from now on. Is our hosting schedule out of the window?" asked Blanca for the nth time

Since the ladies didn't say a word about their monthly schedule, Blanca smiled and assumed the fun continues.

By summer of 2011, Rissa invited the ladies to one of the most expensive Chinese restaurant at Friendship Heights in Chevy Chase, Maryland. The lunch was to celebrate the first death anniversary of her husband who died in July of 2010. Cita thinks it was probably meant to end her period of mourning. "Please remember it's still our tradition," added Cita.

The ladies got dressed, a break from the casual Sunday jeans and blouse and went with no gifts or flowers. Rissa also invited her other long-time friends who also came in their Sunday's best.

"Gee! Rissa reserved five big round tables, it's like a banquet," "whispered Lanie.

"Yes, the servers said we have this room to ourselves," said one of the guests.

There were no table assignments. Cita suggested to the Golden Group to spread out and be with other guests. It was taken so seriously by the ladies they found themselves seated with complete strangers. Blanca did not know anyone at her table.

"So what is the best move here without feeling like an orphan?" Blanca asked herself. "My pretend older sisters Tina and Chedeng are on the other side of the room. I think the time has come for me to introduce myself to everyone and hopefully the rest will do the same," Blanca said as she figured out how to start the round of introduction at her table.

All of Rissa's guests gave their names and a little story on how they came to know Rissa. Some said they've been friends with her for a while. Others said they are also *Visayans* like her while others said they met Rissa at parties where she'd been invited to dance.

Blanca was happy to hear from other guests how they met Rissa except one unusual guest at her table. A lady with the knee length hair caught her attention. She introduced herself then talked about her business of reselling things her employers had given away such as furniture and other household items and décor. She went on to say that she gives free fortune telling for every purchase. "I'm like the famous *manghuhula* (fortune teller) Madame *Auring* in the Philippines. That is the draw of my business. Also, my husband and I have a truck and will deliver for a fee," said the lady.

"Oh! You are well received by Rissa's friends. Are'nt you surprised with the clapping? Blanca asked.

"Yes, because I know most of the guests here. They also know my husband over there," replied the lady.

Blanca did not say a word after their short conversation for two reasons. She was never into fortune telling because it is a scam. Secondly, she had an eerie feeling that some of the lady's hair could go to the food. Blanca noticed she fixed her hair often then would swing it left to right in a way it could land on the food. "Crazy but I could be imagining things here with this long haired lady beside me," Blanca thought nervously.

But the place got quiet once the Chinese dishes started coming out of the kitchen. There was like a parade of food served by some very experienced servers. They placed the food on top of a big lazy Susan spinner. Everyone got busy reaching out for the dish they wanted once the lazy Susan stopped on their side. Blanca could not get the dish she wanted so she decided to wait until the spinning slowed down. Not surprised, she saw a strand of hair in one of the dishes. She didn't say a word smiled instead and focused on Rissa's speech. "There is no point upsetting this crowd," thought Blanca.

By three pm, Rissa's hosting was over. Other guests left the party earlier because they had other parties to go to said one guest. "That's the best way to maximize a day off," said another one of Rissa's guests.

Jelene and Blanca joined the rush of ladies saying good-bye to each other some of which they really did not know. They joked about being from the *bukid* (farmlands) of Rockville, Maryland and needed to run for the next bus.

On the way out, Blanca asked Jelene to wait. She needed to drop by the ladies room. While Blanca was in one of the stalls, she heard a conversation between Rissa and another lady. She knew it was the long haired lady because she saw her long hair coming out of the stall divider. Blanca decided to linger in the stall and heard a conversation.

"Why did you treat us to this place? Are'nt you aware this Chinese place right in the heart of Friendship Heights near Bloomingdales, Neiman Marcus etc. is very expensive?" the woman asked Rissa.

"I am not worried about the expenses. Most of the guests gave me money gifts even if it is not my birthday. It will cover a big part of the expenses," replied Rissa.

"But you could have kept the money gifts and treated us to lunch in a cheaper place. That was a complete waste of money," added the woman.

"It does not matter Shirley. They are my friends.I also think it would be nice to have a little bit of luxury like eating in a fancy Chinese restaurant instead of the usual take out. This is not a crime. Aren't you tired of eating on styrofoams?" Rissa replied.

So as not to embarrass the two ladies, Blanca did not come out of the stall until the two ladies were gone. "So her name is Shirley. That's her name and good to know. What a feisty woman."

"Let's go my dear, buses on weekends come every forty five minutes," Jelene said.

Blanca never mentioned to the ladies the conversation she heard between Rissa and Shirley regarding the Chinese lunch treat. "It would not do any good. The lady is Rissa's friend not ours. There will be other similar lunch hostings in the coming year," smiled Blanca.

The rest of the lunch hosting and birthday celebrations for 2011 was done either in restaurant or at home like the sisters. Going to a buffet was one of those that caught the ladies' fancy until their favorite one got closed due to sanitary violation.

"Would you believe the unsanitary issue about our favorite place? Only Blanca knew about it because it was in the news. Look ladies, it has the closed sign by the county. Please don't worry! There is another Chinese restaurant nearby. It is not a buffet but serves good Chinese food too," said Jelene the volunteered to host.

"Thank you for picking up the hosting for August. *Manang* Clara and Lulu went home to the Philippines together. Lulu's son is getting married and *Manang* Clara would be the *ninang* (sponsor) at the wedding," said Cita.

"Then their friendship would be cemented and cannot be broken," added Paco.

"Why did you say that Paco?" asked Lanie.

"We call this in the Philippines *magkumare*.The newlyweds become Clara's godchildren.

One could be your godchild because you were chosen to be a godmother at baptism. This time Clara was picked by Lulu to be the wedding sponsor,"Paco reminding the ladies of the custom.

"That's great. Their trip to the Philippines is not only a vacation but a big event too. I am sure Lulu will come home with a DVD of the wedding. Remember ladies, Jelene also came back from the Philippines with a DVD of her wedding," said Lanie.

The ladies focus then turned to Jelene who was hosting the lunch. Tina wished the wedding entourage cared to practice the entire process to avoid what happened at Jelene's wedding.

"So what were the mistakes again at Jelene's wedding?" Chedeng asked.

Blanca burst into laughter. "First, the ring bearers and the flower girls did not want to walk. They were crying as their mothers pacified and prodded them to keep going. They cause the march to slow down and delayed Jelene's walk to the altar."

Jelene just laughed as the ladies recalled her wedding. Tina told everyone that when her turn comes, a rehearsal is a must. Chedeng echoed her sister's joke.

"I wonder when that day will come but there is nothing wrong with having a rehearsal before a wedding. Crying ring bearers and flower girls are not new in wedding scenes ladies. Their mothers would beg the bride to consider the son or daughter," said Chedeng.

For more fun, the ladies hummed "Here Comes the Bride". They all laughed but expressed their gratitude to Jelene for hosting lunch at the height of Metropolitan Washington's punishing summer. Jelene replied and said she felt it was the best time to do so. "I haven't heard my employer talk about any vacation plans or out of the business trip so far and summer is almost over. My Sunday days off also seem to be going great.There's been no cancellation so far, "smiled Jelene.

The next volunteer to host lunch or dinner surprised everyone. Cita got a call from Lanie one Wednesday evening and said that an unofficial member of the group whom the ladies came to know as *Yaya* (babysitter) would be hosting.

"She would like to host the ladies this first Wednesday of September. It would be in the evening and her choice is everyone's - the Cheese Cake Factory in Chevy Chase mall. I guess we all know the place I am talking about," said Lanie.

Tina was so happy when she heard about the invitation from Yaya. "How come no one among the ladies thought of the place? It is not that expensive but the wait time to get seated is long. We will see how this dinner will play out. This is exciting – a dinner at Cheese Cake Factory," said Tina over the phone.

Clara did not come to *Yaya's* dinner. No one cared to ask why she could not come. The ladies instead focused on the host. The wait to get seated gave the ladies time to talk to *Yaya.* "Wait ladies, one at a time, "she said. She felt besieged by the ladies' barrage of questions.

"Oh! We just wanted to know you. I think Lanie and Cita know you but not us," explained Tina.

"Let's stop calling her *Yaya* and instead used her real name or *palayaw* (nickname). So, how do you want us to call you? I am not comfortable calling you *Yaya* because you are not taking care of us. The word *Yaya* in *Tagalog* (national language) is a babysitter. But *Salvacion Dimaano* sounds so formal, right ladies?" said Chedeng.

"I prefer to be called *Yaya* in the States and England. Foreign employers easily remember the name *Yaya.* Imagine them saying Salvacion then put my last name Dimaano. That's like tongue twister, "Yaya replied.

Tina whispered to Blanca she felt relieved knowing *Yaya's* real name.

"I feel the same. Lanie is the only one who knows your real name but never told us," wondered Blanca.

On their way home, the ladies could not help but asked questions again.

"So, what was *Yaya's* dinner all about? Will she be joining our group?" Lulu asked as she drove the sisters back to their 22nd Street apartment.

"Yaya never said she wants to be part of our group. She just wanted to reciprocate Cita's kindness for inviting her during holidays and long weekends," said Lanie.

"Let's forget Yaya. She is such a chicken and a fickle. It's too Filipino you know what I mean. She made up her mind so she is not joininig us ladies. That was the verdict," laughed Blanca.

Yaya's surprise hosting at Cheese Cake was followed by Cita's. "Let's be patriotic for once and check out this Filipino restaurant in Rockville our community is talking about," she suggested while making her round of calls to the ladies.

The service was ala carte with astronomical prices. They ranged from fourteen to fifteen dollars per combo – two dishes and rice. Blanca was comfortable with the cost and estimated Cita's bill would be over a hundred dollars. The rest of the ladies were not. They settled for the combo and avoided extras like fried fish or vegetable dish.

At the cashier, Cita said not to worry because her part time jobs will take care of the bill. "It's important we enjoy the afternoon and not to worry about money all the time," said Cita.

"That's great so I am inviting everyone to a buffet place in Silver Spring. I thought about it since we've never been to Silver Spring for any birthday celebration or hosting," said Blanca.

She told them they were free to choose if they have other places in mind in Maryland.

"My dear Blanca, you really never run out of ideas to make us laugh," said Chedeng.

"Well, we have more fun because your birthday and Tina's are coming soon," said Blanca.

"Oh, yes. Those events will wrap up the year for us," Paco added.

By winter of 2012, Blanca announced the engagement of her daughter. She was over the moon with her daughter's wedding in September. "It was on Valentine's day my future son-in-law proposed. They went to a ski lodge and he went on one knee and said what I've been waiting for," narrated Blanca.

"Did you hear what you just said? It's your daughter that got engaged," Chedeng exclaimed amidst the laughter of the ladies.

"I know, but I was really waiting for the wedding because they've been living together for a while. I am still not comfortable with that set up and finally we have a wedding to be happy about," replied Blanca.

There were more laughter and the ladies began to dance.

Cita got serious and said that she also had an announcement to make. "Chloe is graduating from college in June. I am overjoyed and I am already inviting everyone to her graduation party. If you will recall, she finished high school in 2008 so after four years we are back to celebrate her college graduation. My plan is to host the after graduation party at a seafood buffet in Virginia. I will let you know once the reservation is set," said Cita.

Following the two big announcements of Cita and Blanca, the once a month lunches of the ladies was not followed like it used to be. Cita and Blanca got busy with the coming events in their daughter's lives. Birthday celebrations and trips to the buffett however continued. This was followed by money problems which has plagued many overseas workers. The demand from home sometimes is more than what they can afford to send.

Blanca was first to talk about money when she lost her job and was forced to retire early. She was told that her position had been cancelled. "I was told by management when I came back from my daughter's wedding," bemoaned Blanca.

Lanie was next but begged off to do her hosting. She needed money to finance the paper work related to the petition of her son so he can join her in America. "I requested for him ten years ago. Now he is coming but he needs money for the physical examination. He had to make several trips to the US embassy in Manila. He does not have the money to cover these expenses," Lanie said.

Despite the changing money situation with the ladies, Cita threw a big party to celebrate Chloe's college graduation. "I want to feel again the joy of her graduation for the second time. Remember our get together when Chloe graduated in 2008 – the year our ladies group started, Cita said.

Like Cita, the sisters kept their birthday parties going too. They said their birthday celebrations were meant to thank the group and their other friends who've been with them for years. "Let's not dampen the spirit of the group because some of us are having money problems. We all do at some point of our lives but what we always say, this too will pass," joked Tina.

"Is there anything else we need to hear before we start Karaoke singing?" Chedeng asked.

To everyone's surprise, Jelene announced she was going back to the Philippines for good. A common expression among overseas Filipino worker, it meant she would not be coming back and would stay permanently in the Philippines. Summer, she said was her choice to go home because her *alaga* (ward) Kari would be out of school. I'll leave it to her parents on how and when they will let her know. I hope and pray that it will not be traumatic, "said a sad Jelene.

"Aren't you you just missing your husband? Why not bring him to the States?" asked Tina.

"That sounds practical because we could make more money together. But I really want a life with him in the Philippines. He has done a good job of keeping an eye on things since our wedding. We have a house, a thriving piggery and poultry business and fruit bearing trees. I even had a separate house built for my mother. Thus, all is quiet on the western front.," said Jelene.

The last statement about peace among in-laws generated quite a buzz and lots of laughter with the ladies. "You are one smart lady. You covered everything," said Lanie.

"So our next lunch hosting would be a going away party for Jelene anytime before summer. It's on me ladies. Feel free to bring whatever you can. Jelene's last day with us should be fun but sad because we will miss her," Cita added.

At the going away party, Paco handed her a DVD highlighting her activities with the ladies from 2008-2013. The ladies gave her money gifts as *pabaon* – a Filipino custom to help someone who is leaving to start anew.

Jelene held back her tears watching a video about her. "I could not believe the fun I had with you ladies. It was just like yesterday we were all over Washington DC eating, visiting tourist spots and more. I will miss you but I really have to go back to the Philippines," said Jelene

On their way home to Maryland, Jelene opened up and talked about how her life in the United States. "My bowing and kowtowing to an employer like mine needs to come to an end. "*Iba ang nasa bayan mo ikaw. Hindi ko bayan ang* Cyprus or America (its different when you are in your home country. Cyprus and America are not my home)," said Jelene almost in tears.

"That's what your heart says and you have my support. This is really not about money," added Blanca. She knew Jelene could not be stopped and nothing could change her decision. "I think Jelene has had it with life in America, "surmised Blanca.

By 2013, the ladies focused on other socials. They got interested in the *Ball ng Bayan* (People's Ball) celebrating the Independence Day of the Philippines. They've never been to one. Cita led the selling of the organizer's tickets, something the ladies felt worth buying and dressing up for. The time to prepare for the event had taken over their get together. They went around different thrift stores in the area looking for party dresses.Those stores did not disappoint. The ladies all looked pretty, coiffed, and put together and ready to party.

"All it takes is some patience, and the right matching, and we are ready to go," joked Tina.

"For three consecutive years, you ladies always looked amazing in your cocktail dresses. Even our disappearing Clara who had stopped coming to our lunches showed up and never missed the People's Ball. Your have pictures to show for it," said Blanca over the phone.

"I like that. Your wit and humor Blanca could throw these ladies into laughter for years to come," said Paco while at the going away party for Lanie in the fall of 2014.

"My son has arrived to take over my responsibilities in this house. Ms. Sandra helped me bring Benito to the States. That's the one and only reason I stayed with her for a long time. But like Jelene, I am going home for good too. I have booked a one way ticket for January because it is cheaper.

I am really going she whispered. I am tired of Ms. Sandra, the low salary and the dogs," said Lanie as she walked the ladies out of the house.

The ladies were glad that Lanie spoke out and said something about Ms. Sandra as an employer. Paco said she was speaking from the heart. "We are happy with your decision to leave. It's time to rest.You have trained your son Benito to take over your job and the time has come for you to enjoy life," said the sisters.

"Yes, indeed. Also, I want to thank Paco for the DVD compilation of my time with you ladies. I will watch it tonight and maybe cry," Lanie said.

"I am sure you will cry like Jelene but this time you will be alone. We did not have the time to show it during the party. Ms. Sandra hosted this going away party. We would not be comfortable showing the video at her place," Paco added sadly.

With the two ladies out of the group, the ladies focused again on something they've not done before – going to the beach.

The idea came from Chedeng who had a standing invitation from her employer to use her beach house in Delaware when it's free. "Now that Paco and Lulu can drive us to the place, let's plan on going," she said at Cely's party in 2015.

"It's not too late. Please check if we could go this Labor Day weekend, "said Tina.

"Great! In the meantime, let's finish lunch and then talk about anything under the sun. I am happy to have hosted lunch at this time of the year. Summer is the best time because my employer goes to Italy where they have property. Then they come back in the early fall for Thanksgiving. Given that schedule, it is easy for me to host lunch like what you usually have. You ladies can come and I really don't mind cooking," said Cely.

"Thank you on behalf of the ladies. I understand you are neighbors in Leyte and grew up together," said Blanca.

"*Sipsip lang si* Blanca (she is a suck up) but we really enjoy coming to your place. Antiquity is the theme of your employer's house," said Rissa.

"*Teka* (wait), how do keep this floor shiny?" asked Lulu.

"Johnson Floor wax, it does the job," replied Cely.

She continued and said she has served the family for almost twenty eight years. "The lady of the house can be nasty but the ambassador who is an American is the saving grace. He took care of my immigration papers including my daughter's, so all has been bearable after all these years."

"Who knows? Maybe the ambassador will marry you when his wife dies," teased Lulu.

"I thought Blanca is the person who can make us laugh and now it's you," explained Paco.

The Golden Group left Cely's employer's Kensington home laughing. "Nothing is impossible these days. Haven't you heard stories of employers marrying their housekeepers?" added Lulu.

"That's true," said Chedeng.

5

Holidays and Long Weekends Became a Tradition

"IF YOU WOULD RECALL, CITA STARTED THE 4th of July get-togethers right after Chloe's graduation party. The following month Cita hosted a July 4th cookout in the garage of Mrs. Robinson. So what used to be another day off for us became a fun day. After a couple of weeks, she called Tina to say she will be hosting Thanksgiving. Then on the same night, she said she would be happy to have us to welcome 2009 at her place.

Would it not be fun to keep this going, if Cita wouldn't mind?" asked Chedeng.

"We are afraid our presence might be an intrusion. Also, we are getting worried that you are spending too much money on all these get-togethers," Tina said.

"Like I said before and I will say it again. I take time to celebrate the holidays because I want to keep the tradition my late husband and I had with our daughter. So let's just put it this way, if you have nowhere else to go, come and join us," replied Cita.

Chedeng seconded and said *tuloy ang ligaya* (let the fun continues).

No one refused Cita's sincere invitation to celebrate the holidays with her family. Hencefort, every 4th of July, Thanksgiving, and New Year's Eve had always been at Cita's place in Georgetown. Paco also never missed capturing their activities something the ladies looked forward to.

Not all July 4th events at Cita's were happy and a relaxing one. In 2010, Cita after an early lunch announced the death Rissa's husband by suicide. "It happened last Friday. Ladies let's be prepared to see and comfort her. *Makiramay tayo*(the Filipino custom (of visiting to express sympathy and extend help like cooking etc.)".

By late Sunday afternoon, the ladies went to Rissa's apartment for the repass. "Let's wait until all the guests are gone then talk to Rissa," suggested Cita.

Rissa opened up and talked about what happened.

"I am still numbed and have not cried yet because BJ left instructions to finish everything about what he did last Friday. What just happened was all in his plan. I am sure he did not want to inconvenient us so he had everything planned on a long weekend," smiled Rissa.

She continued and said "I came home late Friday afternoon July 4th weekend and as I entered the apartment, he didn't answer when I said "honey I'm home". That was a ritual to let each other know we're home. But it was so quiet so I checked if he was already home and sleeping maybe. I found my husband BJ slumped in the tub with a gunshot wound to his chest. He had a note that said "do not resuscitate". I ran to the building reception in shock. They called 911. The ambulance came but it was late because he was already dead. The police came after an hour and conducted and investigation. I was told it was a standard procedure. They told me that BJ had really killed himself.

I had no clue he would kill himself. Yes, he was diagnosed with cancer but I assured him we would fight it together. That was our agreement. But it never occurred to me to ask him why he was taking classes on how to shoot. BJ is an economist so learning and reading had been part of his life. I did not worry at all or question him on what he's been up to. He also never asked why I take dancing classes. He knew it is expensive but it makes me happy.

We love each other. He had no other relatives except his mother who lives in India so I will send her his ashes. He loves me so much he wanted to save me from the stress of taking care of him. The clean freak that he was, he did not want his blood on the carpet so he shot himself in the tub," recalled Rissa.

"Everyone laughed. Was he really that clean freak?" asked Paco.

"*Sus Ginoo* (Jesus Christ), Chedeng said sadly.

"What will be your next move Rissa?" asked Cita

Paco asked thoughtfully, "Why don't we ask him?"

Everyone looked at him like he was crazy.

"What if he answers back?" asked Blanca in surprise.

"Then we should all run to the door," said Tina looking nervous.

"Don't be scared ladies. This is just an effort to lighten up a very sad situation. My advice is that it is best for Rissa to remember all the good days because she will never get any answers to all of her questions. Do not beat yourself wondering what you could have done. BJ will not like that," said Paco.

"Some tech person will come this week to help me. BJ put everything in his computer for me. He did not realize I am not computer savvy but that's how organized my late husband was," Rissa smiled sadly.

"Is there someone with you tonight Rissa," asked Cita.

"My cousin from Calgary is still here but will be flying back to Canada early tomorrow," Rissa replied.

"You will be alright. We should be going home now so you can rest. You can call me anytime," said Cita.

"Thank you for coming ladies," said Rissa.

Five years later, at the July 4th event at Cita's Rissa announced her engagement and marriage to a man some of the ladies did not approve. Chedeng and Tina were concerned that he is a divorcee' and had been looking for someone to marry to get a green card. Cita simply said "the ship has sailed and there'aint nothing we can do about it."

Everybody laughed as they recalled the day Rissa became a widow back in 2010.

Lanie spoke up, "I guess you are right and come to think of it, it's her life. Did she have a pre-nuptial before this marriage? You know she is a widow and is probably getting a pension."

"It is too personal to ask but bear in mind that ordinary folks like us can also have a pre-nuptial done before marrying someone. A pre-nuptial is not only for celebrities," added Cita.

"What Cita said is true because we have to protect our million dollar assets too," joked Blanca.

"Let's just wish Rissa all the best. That's all we can say to a friend," said Chedeng.

"Let's toast to Rissa and Juancho," proposed Tina.

"By the way, why was the wedding on a Thursday? It is a workday," Chedeng asked.

"So we cannot attend and say "*itigal ang kasal* (stop the wedding)," joked Tina

Everyone laughed and asked,"Who are we to stop the wedding?"

"I think the fireworks are over for tonight. Rissa's announcement is already our fireworks for this year," said Blanca.

The July 4th celebration at Cita's would not be complete without watching the traditional fireworks from the Mall at Washington, DC. Cita had a different idea in 2013. She treated the ladies to view the fireworks from the third floor of Mrs. Robnson's Georgetown house.

Cita led the way going up at Mrs. Robinson's third floor house to view the fireworks.

"So this is how Georgetown residents watch the fireworks," Blanca said while going up the steps.

The view of the fireworks from the third floor was spectacular. Blanca noticed most of the residents in the neighborhood were on the highest floor of their homes. Everyone was clapping and cheering every time the fireworks went up and exploded with sparkles. They were also a friendly group waving to the ladies.

After the fireworks, Blanca and the sisters went home raving about what they had seen.

I once saw July 4th fireworks near the Capitol. We were coming home from a long weekend with some friends. Our van got stuck while cruising through DC traffic so we had to stop a bit and watch. Other than that incident, we never went back to watch it again. The long lines in the metro after the fireworks could be daunting. Instead we watched the event on TV. But the view of the fireworks from the third floor of a

Georgetown house was something else too. For a moment, I too felt rich and privileged," said Blanca.

"Well, that was also our first time. That was really beautiful," said the sisters.

"Do you know other places near Georgetown with a good view of the fireworks?" asked Blanca.

"Oh! I am sure Cita knows one," replied Tina

She was right because Cita suggested a new place to view the fireworks July 4th of 2014.

After binging on hotdogs, corn, barbecue and potato salad, Cita suggested walking to the Kennedy Center from Georgetown to watch the fireworks.

"Come on, a walk to the Kennedy Center will be good for all of us," Cita urged them.

"Are you sure we will catch up with the fireworks?" asked a worried Tina.

"Oh! If we walk a little faster, chances are we will get there on time for the nine o' clock show," replied Cita.

"Well, I hope you don't mind if I pass. My knees cannot take fast walking. "said Lanie.

They dropped Lanie off at Ms. Sandra's house and proceed to walk to Kennedy Center. The ladies got near the center on time for the fireworks. Tina shouted "Wow! Everybody is here to watch the fireworks with us."

Cita asked the ladies to look for a good spot to sit down that had a view of the fireworks.

"Let's go further away from the center and find an open space to watch the fireworks," Cita not satisfied with their found spot.

When the show finally started, the huge crowd wowed and clapped every time the fireworks shoot into the sky. The shorter ladies like Blanca and the sisters did not enjoy the show at first because the crowd towered over them. Cita noticed the problem and immediately suggested a solution

"To the shorter ladies, please go up to the concrete seats for a better view," said Cita.

"Thank you!" laughed Blanca and the sisters.

"The walk back to Georgetown after the July 4th fireworks proved to be the fun part of their adventure to the Kennedy Center this time.

"That was fun. Maybe we can come back next year in the same spot and watch the fireworks. The walk however may not be easy next time because we are getting older. But it gets easier when you walk with a group like what we are doing right now. Don't you agree ladies?" asked Tina.

"I don't see any reason why we cannot watch the fireworks from that spot next year. It's fun because we are with other people headed to the same place," Blanca added.

"Don't worry. Paco will be taking us home after this walk. Is this not part of the plan Sir?" asked Tina.

"That will depend on how tired I will be," Paco replied.

Everyone laughed at Paco's statement. The ladies were always assured that he was always happy to bring the sisters home. "There's nothing to worry about but let's be nice to him ladies, Blanca added.

The novelty of watching the July 4th fireworks from Kennedy Center enticed the ladies to go back the following year. Cita called the place their hacienda and joked about putting a sign saying the spot was theirs.

The change of place to watch the fireworks in 2014 also changed the way couple Cita and Paco prepared food for their July 4th get-together. Instead of a cookout, Cita had the day catered by a nearby barbecue place. This time the ladies chipped in with the expenses. It's been something the ladies wanted to do but never had the chance because it's impolite to do so. A Filipino host traditionally takes care of everything. Cita in response told the ladies to give what comes from their hearts. That gesture endeared her more to the group.

Cita's generosity to the group did not only cover July 4th celebration. Blanca estimated Cita must have hosted through the years Thanksgiving and New Year get-togethers since 2008. "I will not forget those fun times and the role of Cita in keeping the group together," Blanca reminisced.

One event the ladies loved to talk about every New Year's Eve was Mrs. Robinson's invitation to join her and friends upstairs in welcoming 2015."This is going to be akward," said Tina when she heard Cita talking about going upstairs.

At first, the ladies politely ignored Cita when she said that they've been invited upstairs. They knew Mrs. Robinson was not alone but had friends. Most reluctant to go up were sisters Tina and Chedeng. "We are in our casul jeans and blouse. A little bit fancy compared to our work clothes but still we are out of place because of what we are wearing among other things," said Tina.

"Don't worry about the dress code," said Paco.

"But my dear friends, they are in their formal gowns and tuxedos," explained Tina.

"This is not about how appropriate clothes are but about the spirit of welcoming the New Year," Paco told everybody.

Left with no choice the ladies went up. Mrs. Robinson and her friends greeted and hugged them wished everyone a Happy New Year. The ladies introduced themselves and apologized for not being properly dressed. Mrs. Robinson did not care and said she might join them later for Karaoke.

After all the warm greetings, Cita quietly led the ladies down stairs back to her basement apartment.

"What was that all about?" Blanca asked the ladies.

"*Parang Titanic* (like the movie Titanic)," added Lanie

"What do you mean?" asked Blanca.

"Remember the scene in the movie with the first class passengers wearing gowns and tuxedos for dinner. Or that scene when the captain first announced that the ship was sinking while the third class passengers were scrambling to save themselves by going to the upper deck of the boat? What happened upstairs just reminded me of our well-dressed employers like the first class passengers of Titanic and the casually dressed help in third class section of the boat," smiled Lanie.

"Please let's stop thinking about it. Let's be glad it was just short and is now over," said Lulu.

"You are right. That's how Mrs. Robinson and her rich friends welcome the New Year. They get dressed then go to the party," explained Clara.

For Blanca who had watched tons of movies and TV shows, she likened the scene to the 1970's British television series "Upstairs and Downstairs". The upstairs were the employers and downstairs were the servants. She smiled and said, "It was lovely to see folks dressed formally to welcome the coming of the New Year like the television series, Up-Stairs and Downstairs."

"I hope Mrs. Robinson's invitation to welcome the New Year does not happen again next year. I have not experienced anything like that in all the years I've been working in the States," Chedeng said.

"She was just being nice my dear sister. Mrs. Robinson was always nice and warm to everybody including the help. So before it gets too late, let's go home. It is already two o' clock in the morning. By the way, Blanca will be staying with us tonight," said Tina.

True to what Chedeng said, that awkward New Year's Eve with Mrs. Robinson did not happen the following year. Mrs. Robinson spent New Year with her children in Switzerland.

Also for a change, Cita and Blanca asked the ladies if they would like to join the secret Santa game to welcome 2016. Cita felt it would be nice for the ladies to exchange Christmas gifts New Year's Eve. "Let's do this for a change. We might like it and you'll never know," said Cita.

The ladies did not set steadfast rules with the secret Santa game except a twenty five dollar cap on the gift, no less, but it could be more.

"It's good to know the price cap. It is sometimes difficult to find a gift for less than twenty five dollars," Lulu added.

The opening of gifts was held at the New Year's Eve get-together at Cita's place. The ladies randomly picked a name from a basket of rolled up paper prepared by Chloe at Thanksgiving dinner in 2015.

"Since we do not have rules to follow like the gift should be in this color or soft and shiny etc., feel free to swap the name you pick with another member if you do not like the name you got. He or she will never know unless someone reveals the name of her secret Santa. This is the fun part of the game. Is that okay with everyone?" asked Cita.

"Looks like there is no problem so think about your gifts," said Paco.

However, the secret Santa game did not turn out as expected. Chedeng did not want to give her gift to the member she picked. She wanted Jelene who had gone to the Philippines to get her crystal vases. She said she could give the vases to her *Ninang* Tanya when she goes home to *Dumaguete* (capital of Negros Oriental province).

"But who is your secret Santa Chedeng?" Cita asked.

"Lanie," replied Chedeng.

To cut through the confusion started by Chedeng who seemed not to understand the game, Cita suggested it would be best for the ladies to put their secret Santa gifts on the table.

"Everyone should get the gift they want and if somebody else wants the same item, then, we resolve it by "rock, paper, scissors" game. Fair enough ladies? Cita asked.

In the end, Lanie agreed to give the crystals from Chedeng to Jelene to stop the grumbling. "I would be happy taking Blanca's Timex watch because I need to have one when I walk the dog."

"Do you time dog walking?" asked Tina.

"Not really, but I always want to know the time because I have other things to do in the house," replied Lanie.

Insane as the explanation, the ladies all agreed because Chedeng was still a bit confused with the secret Santa game.

Chedeng was happy that she got what she wanted and that Jelene will be receiving her crystals thru Tanya. Her sister Tina on the other hand, was not pleased after receiving a set of lotion from CVS. Lulu was her secret Santa. Tina could not hide her disappointment. This was followed by the exchange of gifts between Clara and guest Yaya who joined the game even though she had not joined the group. She wanted the fun but got disappointed like Tina. Yaya gave Clara a nice expensive looking handbag. Clara in turn gave her a used scarf.

Cita came to Yaya's rescue and asked the two ladies to pose for a picture with Yaya and Clara holding the scarf around her neck and Clara going around to show her nice bag.

When the game was over and done, Tina asked her sister if she was ready to go home.

"We still have to prepare for tomorrow's lunch at the house," said Tina.

"Do not worry. Let me get the container of the banana bread and off we go, "said Chedeng.

Tina like a disappointed kid started grumbling the minute she got into Paco's car.

"I bet Lulu's lotion was part of her stock on sale from CVS," said Tina.

"Well, at least you have a supply of lotion for the rest of the year," Chedeng teased her sister.

"That's not funny sister. Lulu did not follow the rules. That lotion was not worth twenty five dollars," replied Tina.

"I don't think we will have a secret Santa exchange gift next year," said Chedeng.

"I don't think so," said Blanca

"I agree because some of our folks do not follow rules," Tina smirked.

"It's time to say goodbye before I make you cry," joked Chedeng.

"That's a Victor Wood song from back in the days," said Blanca.

"Let's go to sleep before you and Chedeng start singing that old song," said Tina.

"Good night. Tomorrow should be fun with our other friends. You are welcome to stay for lunch if you want to Blanca," said Chedeng.

Blanca headed for home before the sister's other friends arrive. She felt it was time for the sisters to be with their other friends and for her to rest, make some phone calls to wish family and friends a Happy New Year.

6

The Ladies Enjoy the Sights and Sounds of Metropolitan Washington DC

THE YEAR 2016 WAS A WAKEUP CALL FOR THE ladies to make changes in the way they've been doing things together. They noticed all the eating they've done like lunches, birthdays, long weekends and dance parties made everyone fat and slow.

"I do not need to get on scale to prove that we all have gotten fat. It is documented in the yearly video put together by Paco. We sent those videos to *Leyte* and my daughter got alarmed over our bulging stomachs and arms," said Chedeng.

"Well, my son was not as brutal as your daughter. He did ask why we keep on eating whenever we have a get-together. He asked why was there so much food on the table all the time," said Tina.

"He's just afraid we might end up like *Dabiana* (the famous big and tall Filipino comedian years from years ago)," said Blanca.

"We are not there yet but we could if we do not cut down on the eating. I think I have a double chin now and my face looks bloated," Lulu added.

Everyone checked their cheeks, arms and stomach and just started laughing at themselves for letting their guards down when it came to eating.

"Shouldn't this be like a New Year's resolution for us?" asked Blanca.

"It could be but resolutions are always broken. Why don't we do more activities and eat whatever we can find along the way?" asked Tina.

"What are you trying to say this time?" asked Lulu.

"Let's say for instance, the coming Cherry Blossom Festival this coming April. That would be a fun thing to do, walking and exploring downtown DC like tourists," Tina replied.

"Will you take the lead to get there?" asked Cita.

"Don't worry, I will let you know when to go to see the trees before their blooms fall to the ground," replied Tina.

With the eyes of everyone in Washington DC glued to the TV waiting for the peak of the delicate flower, Tina called the ladies and told them they need to go the first weekend of April. She suggested after the Sunday mass at Dumbarton church.

"We should skip the coffee hour at Dumbarton, take the bus to Foggy Bottom and then walk to the Tidal Basic where most of the trees are. Remember the walk we did during the Obama inauguration in 2009. The distance is probably the same but with less people. I am sure there will be other walkers because walking is the best way to get to the Tidal Basin to see the cherry trees at its peak," explained Tina.

Blanca encouraged everyone to go along with Tina's route. She thought the walk to the Tidal Basin would not be that long until they got to Constitution Avenue. No one said dared to "aren't we there yet", but Blanca almost did.

"I have not been to downtown DC in years but it would have been better if we had gone via 13th and G Streets," Blanca told Tina.

"There is too much delay going your way. We take the bus then take Metro to get to the cherries. Walking via Foggy Bottom is faster. Look, we can see the blooms from Constitution Avenue. Aren't they really pretty?" replied Tina.

The ladies took time to go around admiring the cherry trees. Some sat down because benches are all over the place. Blanca and Lanie enjoyed the performance of live bands playing music for everyone to enjoy. "I feel like I am in a fiesta everyone smiling," said Lanie.

"The whole world is here to see the blooms of these delicate and seasonal flowers from Japan. It is very soothing to the eyes," said Paco.

"Are you not glad we came to the Cherry Blossom Festival? We tend to take this event in DC for granted because we live here. But look at these tourists who came all the way from somewhere else just to see this spectacle. Is this not a beautiful thing to see every year," said Blanca.

"Where do we go from here," asked Lulu.

"You can ask Tina. She is the leader of this trip," replied Paco.

"Here she comes," said Lulu.

"This is how the afternoon will play out. We will walk again towards 13th. There are places to eat in that area. I am hungry, and I think everyone feels the same," replied Tina.

When the ladies got into 13th and G Streets, they could not decide where to eat. There were so many choices.

"There are sandwich places. Can we eat at McDonald's for a change? I want some fish fillet," said Chedeng.

"Okay, McDonald's here we come," replied Cita.

The ladies took time eating at McDonald's. Blanca was able to secure a long table inspite of the big crowd coming from the Cherry Blossom festival. It reminded her of the lunchtime crowd when she used to work in the area.

"You know I used to take the bus to 13th and G. I worked in the area for five years. Had I known Tina's route, I could have saved my visitors some money," said Blanca.

"Well, let's look at it this way. We just went in circles to get here. But it was quite a ways to get here. Walking with a group made it easier ladies. We did not get bored and hardly paid attention to how much we've covered by walking. We must have walked about three miles from the Tidal basin where most of the cherry trees are," said Cita

"The area has changed too. The old Woodward and Lothrop department store or "Woodies" for short is long gone. It was a huge store back then and was real fancy. Its Christmas display was a tradition among Washingtonians. I notice the building has been subdivided to accommodate TJ Max, H & M and other stores I am not familiar with.

Let's go window shopping for a while if the ladies are still up to it then head home by bus. There are busses that go straight to Georgetown from here. We could fill up the front seats or go to the back. It's always fun riding the bus together," said Blanca.

"Let's hit the museums too next time. We had to skip them today because we are all tired and hungry. Checking on one would be a good para *konting culture naman* (a little bit of culture). We have tons of them to visit but we hardly find the time to do so. They are free too. Only in Washington, DC do you get free museums," shouted Tina as the ladies boarded the bus for Georgetown.

Since there were no holidays to celebrate between spring and summer, the ladies decided to visit one a museum the following month in May 2015. Blanca reminded the ladies to decide which one they wanted to see for the day because there are so many to choose from.

"Someone told me it will take two months to see and appreciate all these museums," said Blanca.

"Me, I'd like to go back to the museum of American History. For immigrants like us, it is a reminder of the history of this nation. Of course, I like to see again the inaugural gowns of all the first ladies of the United States. I heard Michelle Obama's gown was really long because she is a very tall woman. It is also interesting to see American inventions that made life easier from era to era. That is one museum I really like," suggested Tina.

The ladies trip to the museum of American History took up most of their Sunday off. They all agreed to take lunch at the museum cafeteria which was a bit expensive. "Let's give ourselves a chance to eat lunch in a museum. I think it would be a good experience," said Cita.

"Well, next time we will go to a different museum that also presents American history in a different way. Maybe we can go in early summer next year, "said Paco.

To everyone's surprise, Paco and Cita took the ladies to the wax museum of Madame Tussauds in DC the following year. Cita told the ladies not to worry about the entrance fee because there is a big discount for a group like the Golden Group. She said it was another way of celebrating her birthday.

"What is this place?" Blanca asked.

"Let's go around first and see why this is also a good way to review American history," replied Cita.

Blanca watched what was going on with the ladies as they go from one replica of famous Americans to another. Immediately, they were preoccupied taking pictures with the different waxed figures of the US presidents, starting with George Washington. Everyone took turns standing behind a copy of US presidents podium as if they were giving a press conference. They all pretended to be a US president in the oval office as seen on TV.

By the way, haven't you realized all these folks are dead except for the Carters, Bushes and the Obamas, if I *remember* right," said Lulu.

"This must be a scary place at night when you only have these look- alikes for company.

They are exact copies of a person's warts and all, and most of them are dead. One thing for sure, I would not come to this place alone regardless what time of day," said Lanie.

"Let's now move to the next area of the museum which is in modern times," said Cita.

"So, we've got the contemporary ones like Beyoncé, Tina Turner, and Jennifer Lopez. Aren't they lovely? Let's pose and sing their famous songs," Lulu said.

Blanca on the one hand skipped the celebrities when she saw the wax figure of DC Mayor Marion Barry standing before the exit sign.

"Well, Mayor Barry deserves to be included in this place. They can joke however they want to about him, but he was a long time mayor of the nation's capital," said Paco.

Everyone took a picture with Mayor Barry as Paco suggested. He said that different cities like London also have wax museums. "This is how we got the idea of taking you ladies here. Who knows you might go to other places. London's

Madame Tussaud had a Queen Elizabeth look alike. We visited the place last year," said Cita.

"Oh! They now travel together like sweethearts ha," Lanie joked.

"Thank you for taking us to Madame Tussaud's. We would not have known about this if you had not brought us here. Is there anything else we missed in this place? If not, then let's have lunch," Tina suggested.

"Would you care to see those enlarged photos of us while we were going around the place? It's also a big part of their come-on," said Cita.

"We will pass on that one. I am sure those enlarged photos are expensive. I think we've had enough for the day ladies," replied Chedeng.

Everyone said yes to Chedeng's suggestion and prepared to go home.

"That was a fun interesting review of US history. There are books to read. But who has the time to go back and read again? Madame Tussaud's just gave us a thorough presentation from these finely crafted images of US presidents," smiled Blanca.

"You are right my dear. It's good to know the important people of this country," said Chedeng.

The ladies' adventure did not stop with festivals and museums. They went to the beach.

"Why are going to the beach?" asked Lulu.

"Well, it's been a standing invitation from Mrs. Leland for years. I don't drive and most of my friends even if they did drive, none of them could come for a long weekend. They could lose their jobs. So all I could say to Mrs. Lelend was thank you everytime she reminds me of her place. But when she told me that her place in Delaware would be free for Labor Day weekend I thought maybe we could go," said Chedeng.

"I think we should go. It is much better than going to Ocean City and staying in a hotel like what Chloe and I do every summer. This is a rare opportunity to be in a private beach house for free. Can we do two nights? *Para sulit naman* (so it would be worth the effort and time)," Cita asked the ladies.

The ladies resoundingly said yes!

"Labor Day is a paid holiday for me. Do you have the same arrangement?" asked Rissa.

"My employer follows the same rule, but I do not know about the others. I can come with you," said Lulu.

"We are coming," said Rissa and Lanie.

"We are coming too," said Blanca and Lulu.

"So we are all set? Bring food for at least two days," said Cita.

"Oh! Chedeng will definitely bring food for more than two days," joked Tina.

The drive to Mrs. Leland's beach house in Delaware took three hours. Paco rented a van to accommodate the ladies. Tina chose the second row seat to stretch her legs. No one knows if she has arthritis, but she was comfortable during the trip. Cita had to be in the front to help Paco navigate. Rissa, Blanca and Lulu took the seat all the way to the back, with little leg room. Chedeng joined her sister in the second row. There was a lot talking in the front and second row seats while Blanca, Lulu, Rissa and Lanie fell asleep along the way.

It was already dark when the group found Mrs. Leland's house beach house. Located in a gated community, Chedeng had the passcode to get into the complex and a key to the house.

"This house is gorgeous, like straight out of a magazine,"Thank you very much for facilitating this opportunity Chedeng," gushed Blanca.

"You are welcome. Let us first select the room we like, then dinner, if some are up to it," said Chedeng.

"That's a good idea. But let's have a house tour first," Lulu suggested.

After the house tour, the ladies said "Blanca is right. The house is like one of those we see in magazines," said Cita.

"Have you chosen your room?" asked Paco.

"Blanca and I want the children's room. Each of us will have the twin beds and cabinets for our personal stuff," said Lulu.

"My sister and I can stay in the adjacent room to the master bedroom," added Chedeng.

Rissa and Lanie took the room next to the sisters while Cita and Paco took the master's bedroom that has an attached bathroom.

"The sisters' room has a bathroom but the rest of us will share the bathroom in the hallway. Don't worry, there are enough bathrooms," said Rissa.

"Please do not forget that there is a powder room off the living room, and if worst comes to worst, we can use the bathroom in the attic," joked Blanca.

"Have you checked the refrigerator Blanca?" asked Tina.

"Well, I saw a well stocked walk in pantry. I guess it's for Mrs. Leland's use or whoever is here on a given day," Blanca replied.

"The fridge looks full but we can squeeze in ours because it's a big one. There shouldn't be a problem because our food is cooked and will only need some reheating. However, we should still put our food in the fridge," Chedeng added.

"That's right," said Rissa.

"Why don't we start dinner?" asked Tina.

"I'm planning on just having some hors d'oeuvres and some wine," said Cita.

"I will put the food in the fridge and those who want to eat should say so now so we can warm it up," suggested Chedeng.

The ladies eventually joined Cita and Paco in the living room. Everyone was drinking and talking. Cita brought two bottles of red and white wine.

"This feels so good and relaxing. No wonder some employers buy places like this to be away from the worries of the city. Like them, it is good to be away from work once in a while. Our lives in the States have all been about work and our families back home," said Lanie.

Chedeng asked the ladies to stay away from anything sad. Everyone began laughing drinking and talking. They had all the time to update each other on their individual lives as well as gossips from the Philippines and their employers.

Lulu said she suspects the wife of her employer will be divorcing her husband. "How do you know when you barely see the couple? Taking care of kids on a daily basis and driving them around takes a lot of our time," added Lanie.

"You are right but sometimes things come out from some unexpected places like the trash can," said Lulu.

"What about the trash can?" Blanca asked.

"While checking each bedroom to dispose the trash, I picked up torn letters addressed to the wife begging her not to divorce him. You see this is the second marriage for my employer. He is a lawyer so I guess he knows what it would entail. He has grown children in his first marriage," explained Lulu.

"Do the children suspect something about their parents? Kids are smart and know what is going on with their parents," said Lanie.

"They try hard to bring their parents together. One of them asked me to help him prepare dinner for his parents. He said he will pay me extra. I told him he does not have to but I could tell the kid was worried. I'm worried about the daughter who is a little bit slow in school. They are not my kids but we've grown closed. I watched these kids grow too," Lulu added.

"Rich folks have their own problems too,' said Lanie.

"Oh! They do and oftentimes it's more complicated because of the money," Paco said.

The ladies stayed up until 2 am. They were like in a state of bliss, no worries, happy and carefree for once.

"Go to bed now ladies. I am just double checking the doors just to make sure we're safe," said Chedeng.

Blanca was first to wake up the following day. "The view of the ocean from Mrs. Leland's house is really something to behold. We are not in the ocean front but distant enough to admire the beauty of the water. This is how rich people live. It's generous of them to share this place with their housekeepers and friends," murmured Blanca.

"Are we ready to go now?" Rissa asked.

"Oh! Good morning everyone," replied Blanca.

"Hold it, first I want to pose in my bathing suit," insisted Lulu.

"That's a good idea. Please take mine too. I want one by the balcony," said Rissa.

"So *kodakan muna* (picture taking), "said Paco.

The picture taking took some time.

"Ladies, we are forgetting the beach. The sun will be intense by ten in the morning. We could get sun burned. We should all be careful even if we have brown skin. Look at us, I am glad we are not embarrassed to be seen in our bathing suits," said Blanca.

"Wow, Rissa you look great in your suit. Is that what dancing can do? It gave you a Coca Cola bottle figure?" Tina enviously looked at her.

"I got this from Lord and Taylor. They really do have nice bathing suits every summer. This is a bit pricey but I do not have kids so I won't feel guilty about the cost," Rissa said cheerfully as she struck a pose.

Chedeng encouraged everyone to head for the water. "But before we do, let's check out the chairs and beach umbrellas of Mrs. Leland. They are all in the shed near the outdoor shower stalls. Mrs. Leland said we could to use them."

"Wow! This place is so complete. It has outside showers to wash ourselves before going back to the house. You think we can come back here next year Chedeng?" asked Lulu.

"Maybe, if we leave the place in order," replied Chedeng.

"Of course, so we can come back," said Lanie.

"Like I said maybe, but let's enjoy for now. Let's talk about next year during dinner," said Chedeng.

The ladies spent the whole afternoon at the beach. "Look, this place is different from Ocean City. The crowd is less because it exclusive to the residents of a gated community.

Oh, rich folks and how they live! We can just lie here and nobody is going to bother us. What more do we want ladies?" Blanca asked.

"I guess nothing for now because it has been overwhelming for me. The sun and the breeze make me fall asleep," said Rissa.

"Ladies look! Tina and Chedeng are in the water. Can they swim? Please be careful ladies, the waves are strong," shouted Lulu.

"Do not worry. We are just soaking our tired feet and legs because sea water helps ease the pain of rheumatism,"

"We are right behind you," said Cita.

Without the usual rice and Filipino dishes, the ladies mostly ate *chichirya* (junk food). Their plan was to eat dinner late that evening and head home mid Monday afternoon to avoid traffic.

At dinner, Blanca watched the parade of food brought out by the ladies. Lulu had *laing* (a dish made from gabi leaves bathed in coconut milk and hot chili). The sisters brought *adobo* and *chop suey*. Lanie prepared a salad of tomatoes and boiled eggplant with a vinegar, sugar, and pepper dressing.

"There is nothing like dinner under the late summer sun in the terrace of this lovely beach house. We are all fresh from the shower after an afternoon at the beach. It's good to have this kind of get together away from the TV and other noise," Rissa spoke lazily.

"This is really rare for me. We always go to the beach with the kids like my daughter, my nephew and niece when they were young. With their need to be cared for at all times for fear of drowning, I just ran around with them. This is different because I am with adults on the beach on a long weekend. By the way, I apologize for not bringing something to share," said Blanca.

"We understand Blanca. Don't worry but Clara is no show again. I think going to the beach or being with us for a long weekend may not be her cup of tea," said Cita.

"Well, I think Clara is focused on her daughter and grand-children. Cita could be right. Going to the beach on a long weekend may not be her thing. Maybe she is *takot sa araw* (afraid of the sun). She is very fair and is not into wearing a bathing suit, let alone letting go of her big bag. Didn't you notice Clara is always lugging her big bag wherever she goes. Did you ever stop to wonder what's in it?" Lulu asked the ladies.

"Hey, that's what happens when you do not join the group for a while. You become the topic of conversation. Call it behind your back, but it happens all the time. Really! What's in Clara's big heavy?" asked Blanca.

The conversation about Clara's big bag resulted into some absurd guesses on what's inside the bag. Everyone laughed at Blanca's innocent question.

"So you mean after all these days, everyone knew what's in that bag," said Blanca.

"Okay, enough for laughing," chided Chedeng.

With Chedeng acting as the official defender of Clara, they slowly cleared the table, put the dishes in the dish-washer, and then moved to the living room for coffee and tea.

They decided to go to bed early that night so they could wake up early and enjoy one last trip to the beach that morning before heading for home.

The plan to leave by mid-afternoon did not happen. The ladies enjoyed the beach like it would be their last time. They ate an early dinner, talked about many things like their other friends, children, and how life had been since their last get-together. There was a lot of laughter and frolicking.

"Alright, Paco intervened, it is time to pack up ladies, otherwise, we gonna crawl like a turtle to get to DC."

The ladies quickly cleaned the table, put everything they used to the trash, and ran to their rooms to pack up their personal belongings. Chedeng did a quick round of the house to make sure everything was left the way they came.

Paco while down by the parking area of the house asked the ladies to hand him their personal things so he could arrange them to fit in the back or top of the stretched van. He said he did not want to put items on the top of the van, because it could fall off and hurt other motorists.

"Wait, wait!" Lanie interrupted. "Can we have some pictures near the flower beds? This could be our first and last trip to the beach so might as well have a nice souvenir."

Paco agreed as long as he got a volunteer to help him sort things. "Call me when everyone is ready for the class picture."

After fifteen minutes of *kodakan*, the ladies boarded the van. "Please take the seats you had last Saturday so we will not waste time," Paco requested.

"Where is Chedeng?" asked Cita.

"She could still be in the house double checking everything. No one should go back or she will get confused," said Tina.

"There she is by the shower stalls checking again to see everything in order," said Lulu.

Chedeng hopped in and said "let's go its getting late."

Everyone clapped their hands as they left the property.

Tina explained, "My sister is protective when it comes to Mrs. Leland's property. It is her responsibility. The house is empty for most of the year. Thieves could get in even if it is a gated community."

On the way home, the ladies talked about on ways to thank Mrs. Leland for the use of her beach house. Everyone agreed to send flowers and card. Cita volunteered to select and order the flowers. The cost would be split among the ladies.

After their Delaware beach trip, Tina suggested they go apple picking in the fall. Blanca was delighted to hear a plan to go apple picking. "I've never been to one," she said. The others were happy too because they haven't done it in a while.

"I remember we've been to an apple farm in Virginia. I do not know any in Maryland,"

Tina said.

"No problem. I will ask Chloe if she would like to join us. She is coming this weekend," said Cita.

Virginia was the ladies' choice to go for apple picking. But the ladies learned they came in a bit late as most of the good apples had been picked. "Late October is not the best time to come," said one of the welcoming staff of the place. The staff greeted the ladies and suggested other activities like hay ride and tour of the pumpkin garden.

"Can we first enjoy looking around the orchard and maybe consider other activities, "said Tina.

"Now everyone please get your *panungkit* (long pole with sharp tip to pick the apple),"

"Well, well, apples everywhere. It's my first time ladies. Growing up Filipino, apples have always been an expensive fruit to have, but some are just on the ground and will rot unless someone picks them up. *Ay buhay America* (this is life in America)," said Blanca

Apple picking was a whole day event. The orchard was a big place to explore. There were also other visitors who were in the same boat as the ladies. Like the ladies, most of the visitors came to make the most of what they could pick from the trees before the weather got cold.

"Ladies, make sure you pick only the good ones. We are all going home with the apples that you picked. It will be weighed per bushel and pay as you go. Let's do the picking while it's still daylight so you get the best and leave the rest on the ground," said Cita.

"So what are you going to do with your apples Blanca," asked Tina.

"I will give some to my neighbor Lilo. She has always been nice to us. I will save the rest for myself. They are fresh off the tree and not like the Penny Saver kind," replied Blanca.

"I hope Chedeng will make some pie. These apples are fresh, juicy and sweet," said Tina.

"After today's apple picking, what other activities are we having in November and December," asked Lulu.

"Well, we have two November birthday celebrants. Chedeng will celebrate hers in December. So far, those are the ones I know about. I have not yet planned on anything for my birthday but I am sure Tina who is another November celebrant will have a get together at their 22nd apartment. These will wrap the year 2015 for us," replied Blanca.

The Farewell Begins

The year 2016 was welcomed by the Golden Group minus one member. Jelene left for the Philippines in the summer of 2013. Lanie after two years also made an announcement that she going back to the Philippines for good.

At the annual New Year's Eve party at Cita's, Lanie spoke and said she had not bought her ticket yet but planned on leaving as soon as her son Benito was ready to take over her position at Ms. Sandra's house.

"Remember, what is the most talked about topic Filipinos like to talk about during parties and other get togethers? The answer is when is the best time to go home? The best so far I heard after all these years was Tanya's. She said when we can no longer take the vacuum up and down the steps,"

Everyone got quiet then they all burst into laughter. Tina said, "It's true. You are no longer physically able to carry on."

Lanie continued and said,"It feels good to know that this hard work for our families must come to an end at a certain point. This is the end for me. My employer kept me as long as I was useful to her, and now my son is taking over. She dangled that sponsorship for my son so I would stay. It worked to her advantage. It is useless to be bitter so I am leaving her," said Lanie.

At a going away party hosted by Ms. Sandra, a guest asked Lanie, "*Paano nayan Lanie, walang* CVS *doon* (what will be your life, there is no CVS in the Philippines)?"

"Then *Mercury Drug* (a chain of drug stores in the Philippines) will do," Lanie replied.

Lanie's reply drew laughter."I have not forgotten the largest drug store chain in the country ladies."

"Will you miss American food?" asked another lady.

"No. I will be returning to an island where there is a lot of fresh fish and vegetables. Have we forgotten life in the Philippines? We were all born and raised in the Philippines so I do not see any adjustment problem. You will have your turn so you know what I am talking about. Please wish me well in this new chapter of my life," said Lanie.

Their conversation got interrupted when Ms. Sandra rang the bell to propose a toast. Everyone gathered around Lanie and cheered with whatever drinks they had on hand and raised their glass to toast her farewell.

"That was gracious of her but you seem indifferent Lanie," said Blanca.

"Well, she never gave me a raise to add to my social security," replied Lanie.

"Don't worry we have something for you to take home," said Cita.

"Would you believe Ms. Sandra said she will drive me to the airport?" said Lanie.

"So the old lady still drives?" said Blanca.

Yes, *kaskasera pa nga minsan* (speed maniac sometimes)," said Lanie.

With Lanie and Jelene gone back to the Philippines for good, the remaining members of Golden Group continued on with their activities whenever schedules allow them to do so. Their trip to the beach was something they all look forward after having gone to Mrs. Leland's place in 2015.

Like in the previous year, Paco again rented a stretched van and packed the ladies with their stuff. Chedeng announced that Mrs. Leland's beach house in Delaware was free Labor Day weekend. Clara could not come so Tina invited her friend Celeste to join the group.

The ladies brought cooked food for the weekend while Cita offered wine and snacks to while away the night before they retiring to their rooms. It was a pleasant evening of conversation centered on the amenities of the house. It was Celeste's first time in the place.

"This is a very nicely done beach house. I have worked for a lot of folks but I was never invited to the beach let alone to use their beach house. By the way, thank you for thinking of me. Sisters Chedeng and Tina have been talking about your group's trip to the beach house of Mrs.Leland. I've met some of you at the 22nd Street apartment of the sister but you have morphed into a group," said Celeste.

"So what are the plans for tomorrow?" asked Paco.

"Let's all sleep in like most of the folks in the village. I remember last year I woke up so early only to find the entire village was still asleep. Let's enjoy the good life folks," said Blanca.

As planned, the group left for the beach around eleven and were back at the house by five 'o clock. They had dinner on the balcony, like the previous year. Chedeng reminded everyone to help out with the clean-up. She wanted the kitchen and countertops cleaned after every meal. "It's a lot easier if we do it each time we are in the kitchen, "smiled Chedeng.

"I think it would be good for us to go to the town center after dinner. Can we check the internet to see if there is a town center and where it is? It is just probably about a 15 minute drive from this place. Is there something to see there?" asked Paco.

"We will never know if we don't go and check out the plaza," replied Cita.

"So let's go ladies. We can come back anyway right away if we do not find anything interesting in the town center," said Paco.

Little did the ladies know that they were in for a surprise in the town center of Bethany. The place was all lit up and had people everywhere, walking and having a good time. An Elvis impersonator was entertaining the crowd. What struck the ladies most was the presence of older adults dancing and having a good time.

"Ladies, this is a fun way to end the summer. Let's stay for a bit and walk around, maybe have some ice cream and see what else is going on," suggested Blanca.

"Let's have some ice cream first. Look, some ice cream shops give bigger scoops than others," said Tina.

"There is a long line but the service is fast. We can walk on the boardwalks from beginning to end. How about that folks? And look ladies, it is a full moon," Chedeng added.

Everyone looked up to the sky. It's full moon lighting up the ocean. Isn't this a lovely evening walking in the boardwalk by the light of the moon?" rhapsodized Blanca.

It was a long walk to the parking lot but everyone had a good time. "How come we never thought of coming to this place before?" Tina wanted to know.

"So now we know about the town center. Then we can come back next year so Blanca can dance more," joked Cita.

"Well, it is always fun to dance with a live band. There is nothing like a live band. Their music is much better than canned music managed by a DJ. The Elvis impersonator got the crowd going? Everyone like Lanie, Paco, Chedeng, Tina and me got transported to an era of rock and roll. A time my oldest sister loved very much," said Blanca.

"Maybe they might have another impersonator next year like Tom Jones," said Lulu.

"Then it will be another night of hip swinging and twisting," said Tina.

After a lovely evening at the town center, the ladies stayed home the following day. Blanca found the no beach morning an opportunity to talk with the ladies. She wanted to know more about Lulu, who obliged but unfortunately, there were constant interruptions from the calls the ladies made to the Philippines. Celeste, the sisters' friends, in particular, was on the phone all morning delaying breakfast and clean-up after lunch.

"This is bad. Looks like everyone is glued on the phone either checking messages or talking to relatives back home," murmured Blanca.

"Ladies, please put away your phones so we can talk while having lunch," shouted Cita.

"Okay, we will put away our phones," said Tina.

"Lunch had just got started when Celeste's phone rang to dismay of the ladies. " I have to take this call from my daughter. We are renovating our house and I want to be updated on the progress," apologized Celeste.

All the ladies could do was to look at each other as Celeste continuously asked to be excused. Blanca smiled and asked "*saan na nga tayo* (do you remember where we left off)?"

"I forgot," replied Chedeng.

"Are we having Alzheimers here?" asked Tina.

"No, maybe the start of dementia," said Lulu jokingly.

Blanca kept the conversation going by asking the ladies about their favorite food, actors, games, TV show and about their plans when they decide to go home. But the conversation faltered due to phone calls and constant checking for phone messages. The ladies were glued to their phones.

"The technology has come and it looks like everyone is hooked to it. We used to reach out to families via long distance calls back in the days. Now, we could talk and see them via skype and other applications. Ladies enjoy the rest of the afternoon," said Blanca.

The ladies left the beach house earlier compared to previous year. Cita suggested dropping by Tangier Outlet Mall on the way home. Everyone liked the idea. Blanca was thrilled with Cita's suggestion. The Labor Day weekend is the best time to check on last minute summer bargains.

"I'm looking at shorts for Chloe. This piece of cloth is forty dollars," Cita groaned.

"This place is not cheap but they do have stuff you won't find in DC," said Tina.

"I got me a handbag," added Rissa.

"What about you Lulu?" asked Cita.

"I got some shorts for my boys. They will like these ones," replied Lulu.

"Let's meet at the parking lot if you need more time to go around. Can I assume you know where Paco parked the van?" asked Cita.

"Of course we do. We will see you at four," replied the ladies.

"Please don't be late. The traffic will be heavy soon. Everyone is going home today because there is work tomorrow,"Cita said.

Everyone was quiet on the way home, but busy with their cell phones. Blanca and Chedeng were the only ones not on a cell phone because they had the old flip kind. Others had the latest smart phones.

Cita asked the ladies for ideas on how to thank Mrs. Leland for the use of the beach house.

Chedeng suggested a pot of orchids because they last longer than cut flowers. She specifically wanted the pot from a garden center in Wisconsin Avenue. Cita reminded the ladies of other places to get the orchid because Hyacinth's is expensive. Chedeng did not budge and insisted on Hyacinth center because it had the best orchids. She said she will meet Blanca on Wednesday to buy the orchids.

Blanca and Chedeng met Wednesday and picked up a pot of orchids for her employer. Chedeng had Wedenesday in mind because it's the day she will be back at the Leland's condo to tidy up. With the pot of orchids in hand, Blanca and Chedeng took the bus to Mrs. Leland's condominium in Chevy Chase, at the border of Maryland and DC.

Chedeng had to the key to the condo. Everyone in the building knew her. She set aside a spot for the orchid.

"I know my way out of the building. Have a good afternoon and I will see you on Saturday, "said Blanca.

During the somewhat lengthy walk from Mrs. Leland's building to the bus stop, Blanca mused over Chedeng's insistence on buying an orchid from the expensive garden center.

"I don't understand why the orchid had to be bought at Hyacinth's Garden Center. Penny Saver had exactly the same pot but cheaper and fresher looking. Maybe she felt Mrs. Leland deserved a pot from a popular garden shop in the district and not from a grocery store. Maybe this whole flower gift thing is part and parcel of her devotion to the lady of the house.

It could have started when Mrs. Leland helped them get an apartment on 22nd Street. Who knows? Chedeng have her reasons for insisting on buying orchid at the garden center. She probably thinking Mrs. Leland deserves the best. On the other hand, I have no doubt Chedeng deserved to stay at the beach house for free Labor Day weekend? I am sure Mrs. Leland knew that Chedeng is one of those rare human beings – honest and caring," Blanca figuring out the closeness between Chedeng and Mrs. Leland.

After the Delaware beach trip, Blanca called the ladies and suggested a visit to Old Town in Alexandria, Virginia. "September is the best time to visit because we are out of the punishing summer heat of Washington DC. We will be joining the throngs of tourists that come to the area at this time of the year. I will take you to see the house of the dentist of George Washington," said Blanca.

Cita called around urging the ladies to go with Blanca's suggestion. "We have not been to the place, so might as well see what they have," she said.

"If Blanca knows her way around the place, it shouldn't be a problem," Tina added.

"I used to work in the area and explored the place during my lunch break. I will be happy to be your tourist guide for the day," Blanca assured Tina.

"So are we meeting at Dumbarton Church or at Cita's?" asked Tina.

"Either one because we will all be taking the bus to Dupont Circle then take the Orange Line to Old Town, getting off at the King Street metro and walking from there. We will be part of the throngs of tourists. The walk from the metro would be fun and easy," explained Blanca.

"Can we leave at ten? If we start early then we can cover more places," said Cita.

"The slow weekend ride on the train was very relaxing. It's a beautiful autumn day. Look there are sailboats and kayakers," said Tina as the train crossed the Potomac River.

"We are also riding with folks going to Reagan Airport," added Blanca.

"Interesting again, there are spots in Metropolitan Washington DC we hardly pay attention to until something like our trip today happens," said Paco.

"Where are you from?" asked one passenger.

"We're from Texas," replied Tina.

"So you came all the way to see Old Town?" another passenger asked.

"We heard that somewhere in Old Town is the house of the dentist of George Washington. We want to check that out," said Chedeng.

Everyone on the train laughed. Blanca loved it. Her story about Washington's dentist clicked. "I hope I could remember where that historic house stands," Blanca murmured.

Tina then asked Cita what state they say they are from. Lulu said Florida because she had been there. Paco said why not just they we're from the Philippines. Everyone laughed at Paco's suggestion.

To avoid getting lost in the Sunday crowd of Old Town, the ladies walked in pairs. "This is like walking in Georgetown, "said the ladies.

"Since I suggested Old Town as our next place to visit and explore, allow me to be your tourist guide. Also known for its cobblestone streets and brick buildings, it has that European feel, like Georgetown. Unlike Georgetown however, Old Town has a sprinkling of bed and breakfast accomodations, restaurants, and boutiques. They are cute and probably family owned. They are really geared to the tourists. Georgetown on the other hand, confined these places in the Wisconsin Avenue corridor.

Did'nt you notice both is predominantly a white neighborhood?" Blanca asked.

"Yes, we agree with you Ms. Blanca but let's now go to the house of the dentist of George Washington. I am really excited about that," said Tina.

"We will get there. So at the end of King Street, we will make a right to Prince Street to check out the house of George Washington's dentist. I want to warn you the house no longer exist but a marker instead saying it's the dentist's house.

"The house had been demolished to make room for a building but in the light of the significance of the house in American history, the Historical Society of Virginia declared the site historical. See ladies the gold historic marker," said Blanca.

She told the ladies about the story she picked up from her co-workers while working in the area. "This could be just a tale who knows.

So the story goes, once upon a time during the Revolutionary War, General George Washington was said to have developed a pain on his molars. So he dropped by the nearest dentist in Virginia to have it fixed. This is the place where he stopped.

Ladies, rumor also has it that the dentist also made Washington's first denture," said Blanca.

Paco suggested they should do a fact check one day. "A visit to Washington's house in Mt. Vernon could shed some light on the myth of his alleged dental problem back then. We should plan on visiting Washington house next time. It should be one of our day trips."

"Ladies and gentleman, smile and show our teeth before we leave the spot where George Washington's dentist used to live," joked Tina.

"I hope you found the story interesting even if you saw only a landmark,' said Blanca.

"Well, after a historic site let's look for a place to eat," begged Chedeng.

"There are lots of places to choose from. Can we do it by voting?" asked Lulu.

Everyone agreed on a Thai restaurant by the river. Tina reminded the ladies to let the server know the level of heat they want for their entrée. "Remember ladies everyone has a different level of tolerance for hot food," Tina added.

For dessert, the ladies stopped for an ice cream. The line was long and so were the the rest of the other ice cream kiosks.

"Did you notice Star Bright Ice Cream scoops are big and generous?" said Lulu.

"You're right. You have to hurry with your ice cream or they will melt and gets soupy," added Tina.

When everyone was seated, someone asked who would be the first to finish their ice cream. Tina got ahead of everyone because her ice cream melted faster compared to the other ladies. Other customers noticed the game did the same with their group.

"Wasn't that fun? Since when did eating ice cream become a game? But it did. It was really about who could finished their ice cream first," joked Tina.

Blanca interrupted and said, "a visit of Old Town would not be complete without visiting the Torpedo Factory and the year-round Christmas store. The Torpedo Factory has been hosting art exhibits and classes for years so there is always something to see on most Sundays. There is also art to buy but a bit pricey. Most art works range from one hundred dollars to a thousand."

"You're right. We cannot afford these paintings. Where is our next stop? I remember Blanca talking about the all year Christmas store," said Tina.

"I was so delighted when I found this year-round Christmas store during one of my walks in the area. What makes a Filipino smile? It's Christmas," said Blanca as they cruised the narrow aisles of the store.

"Yes, they do have rare Christmas stuff, but they're expensive. Sorry but we can't afford anything here," said Chedeng.

"You don't need to buy. Just enjoy the place like the lights and décor'," said Blanca.

On the way out of the Christmas store, Paco told the ladies about a ferry that could take them to DC instead of the metro. "Let's go and see where that ferry is docked. It should be nearby. Let's follow these tourists and maybe we get to see the ferry or we can always ask," said Paco.

"Wouldn't it be fun ladies if we take the ferry to go home?" asked Blanca.

Everyone said yes but they had to fall in line because the tourists also took the ferry to get to the other side. The pier had benches for passengers to sit on until everyone gets on board. But the ladies preferred to sit under the sun by the elevated sidewalks. With tickets in hand, they quickly boarded to look for a good spot to sit down and view the scenery.

"The ferry ride from Old Town to DC was a breeze. Everyone got sleepy but was kept awake with Blanca's story about the ferry she used to ride with her mother and brothers. "I cannot believe those ferries from *Batangas*. They would take as many passengers, without fear of sinking but that was still safe back in the days. I remember I could touch the water as the boat sails. But this ferry is high tech, we hardly hear the motor, yet it is fast and comfortable. It feels great cruising in the Potomac. Let's do this again ladies," said Blanca.

"Thank you for giving us to a tour of Old Town. We loved the ferry ride. That was refreshing," said the sisters.

"You are welcome. I'm glad you enjoyed coming to Old Town. It was part art, exercise and shopping. The ferry ride was something I was not aware until Paco remembered the ferry service from Old Town to DC," said Blanca.

"Well, the ferry ride saved us from walking back to the King Street Metro and another bus to Georgetown. A bit more than metro and bus fares but it was something new and different from our past activities," added Lulu.

"Is there anything else you want to do different next time?" asked Cita.

"We do not know yet but let's keep checking and visiting other places away from Georgetown," said Chedeng.

It did not take long for the ladies to come up with another Sunday activity. The ladies went to Atlantic City even if no one was into playing at the casino. Their trip was the topic of conversation at Chedeng's December birthday party.

"How did you get to Atlantic City? Did you drive to the place?" a guest asked Chedeng,

"Someone told Cita about a bus to Atlantic City every Sunday. We don't know who manages the trips. Years ago, my sister and I used to join trips organized by this Filipino lady Marcela. She had bus trips to the casinos in Atlantic City, Niagara Falls in New York and outlet shopping in Pittsburg. We love all these activities but could not go because we don't have cars and can't drive. Renting a car and hiring a driver were not an option. So Marcela was really what we might call God sent. She took us to places we dreamt of seeing one day.

The business was not big but Marcela found her niche – the Filipino workers. She made them affordable and fun. We need a break from work. Remember a Filipino saying,"All work and no play, makes *Juan* a dull boy". But ladies, she would even serve *pansit* and soda either lunch or dinner. Can you beat that?" smiled Chedeng.

"Amen," said everyone.

"Yes, we all know Marcela. Is she still around and doing those trips? I have not heard any news about her for some-time. Are we just out of the gossip loop here?" asked Tanya.

"Marcela has gone back to the Philippines to take care of family. Rumor has it that the business has taken over her life and needed the break. But really those trips with Marcela's bus were fun," replied Chedeng.

"So Marcela is gone. But when are you going back to Atlantic City? Please let us know," asked a guest.

"Let me go back to the new bus to Atlantic City, before we got hooked to Marcela's life story. This is what I know. There is a designated bus stop in Bethesda every Sunday morning bound for Atlantic City. If it gets filled, then the bus will leave for Atlantic City," said Cita.

"Here is the number you can call. So to all those casino lovers, get ready with your money for the bus fare. I do not know about the money for the casino,"said Paco.

7

Sickness and Death Befalls the Golden Group

AMIDST THE FUN AND FROLICS THE GOLDEN group had for years, the inevitable health issues started to creep into their worn out bodies. As Blanca loved to say, they were no spring chickens when they got together in 2008. Lanie, Clara and Paco were already in their mid-sixties when they met at Chloe's high school graduation party. Chedeng was also in her late sixties while Tina and Blanca were in their late fifties. Jelene and Cita celebrated their 50th year birthday with the group. "So like cars, some parts are starting to breakdown because of wear and tear. The mechanic could replace some parts to keep it going but there's a limit to what he can do. Again, like an aging car, our bodies have limits to what it can do," said Blanca.

Lanie was the first to succumb to what the ladies feared all along. She had a knee replacement two years in a row in 2014 and 2015. She said physical pain cannot be ignored all the time especially when it is a recurring one.

"No amount of medication could alleviate the pain on my knees. It would go away for a little bit and then comes back worse. So its time to end my agony," said Lanie.

Tina was the first to know where Lanie had gone after the procedure "I know where that rehab place is. It's in Aspen Hill, Maryland. I have a part time job in the area. I will be happy to take everyone this Saturday to visit Lanie,"Tina told the ladies.

At the rehab, Lanie was candid about her knee replacement. She was in high spirit joking about a gadget attached to her foot. "See, it moves up and down with my foot. The purpose of which was to make sure my knee does not get locked. *Araguy* (Visaya word for ouch pain) screamed me after the doctor asked me to stand and walk the following day. He said not to be stubborn. If I heal well then the other knee follows next year. Why one at a time? Someone of my age cannot take a one time double knee replacement proecedure. One knee either left or right for now then the other next year,"explained Lanie.

On their way out of the rehab, Cita said she admires Lanie's calmness about the decision to have a knee replacement. "You kind of wonder how those knees are replaced but this is about quality of life. She will be happy again when she recovers. I have seen her walk the dogs mindlessly bcause of the pain. *"Engkang, Engkang yan"* (she walks wobbly).

From knee replacement to woman's problem when she gets to a certain age, Lulu announced she will have her own procedure. She was quiet about it and said it was best to keep the matter in wraps because her issue is a delicate matter to talk about.

The health situation with Lulu came to the fore after six months when Lanie was starting to walk again but with a cane. The ladies went to visit her at her employer's home one weekend after a hysterectomy procedure at Georgetown Hospital. It was their first time to see where she lives in

Georgetown. They were impressed with the housing provided by her employer. Lulu received the ladies in a separate
small house like a one bedroom apartment at the back of the
property. "I'm glad that this privacy allowed me to recover
faster because it is quiet. The kids do not come here out of
respect I guess," said Lulu.

The ladies had a good time during their afternoon visit of
Lulu. She got flowers to put beside her bed. She said she does
not have much food. "Don't worry we got food from Penny
Saver," Tina said. They ate and watched Filipino shows. Lulu
had a Filipino channel subscription. "It's an added expense
but it is entertaining not only at night but in times of recovery from sickness like now," said Lulu.

Stories about sickness did not seem to stop at Lanie's and
Lulu's procedures. Paco told the ladies about Cita's breast
cancer scare during their annual New Year's Eve party at
Cita's place.

"After a routine mammogram, a tiny lump was found in
Cita's left breast. She underwent a minor operation to remove the lump for biopsy. It turned out to be benign and so
this is best time to let the ladies know about it.

"Where did you have the procedure?" asked Tina.

"She had it at the rival hospital of Georgetown, Sibley
Hospital," replied Paco.

"As a precaution, the doctor advised Chloe to have a regular mammogram too,"added Cita.

"I am not a doctor but I heard that breast cancer can run
in the family," said Tina.

"I hope that's not the case for us but a yearly mammogram is recommended for women," said Cita again.

As the cancer scare went away, Cita called the ladies one late November afternoon to say that Tina got hit by a car on her way to the bus stop by Calvert Street.

Chedeng said she got a call from the police about the incident and was told to come with them to the hospital. "My sister was going up the hill when a car hit her on the back while the driver was maneuvering to get out of a tight street parking space. The driver happened to be a doctor working at Georgetown Hospital. It was not a surprise a doctor hit my sister. Many doctors live in our area because it is near the hospital. What probably caused it too was poor visibility. It was raining and maybe the driver did not see Tina because of her height and black umbrella.

Tina was taken by an ambulance to George Washington Trauma Center. I remember President Reagan was taken to GWU hospital when he got shot years ago. It was my first time to ride an ambulance. What an experience! I was told I am the nearest of kin so I have no choice but to ride in the ambulance with Tina on it. Honestly, I was scared and felt sick too. The feeling went away fast. All I wanted to know was the extent of Tina's injury.

Tina is now resting with a brace on her back. I do not know when she will be discharged from the hospital but I will keep you ladies posted," said Chedeng.

Cita asked if they are filing a case or do they need a lawyer? Chedeng said the doctor's insurance will take care of the case. Cita suggested it's still best to get a lawyer. But Cita did not hear a word from Chedeng about her suggestion.

The ladies on the other hand, got quiet about Tina's case. Because of work and lack of time to even to talk to their employers some of which are lawyers or would know a lawyer who could help Tina, the ladies unanimously agreed to leave the sisters alone to deal with the case. Cita still offered to help because she had the most flexible work schedule but to no avail. "Maybe we can just put together some money and play it by ear as to what the sisters really need at this time," said Cita to the ladies.

Tina got out of GWU hospital but was not able to work for a month because of her injury. "Avoid unnecessary bending in the days and months to come," Tina's doctor said. She agreed only for a while. "I need to get back to work soon even if it's against doctor's advice. It would be tough to keep up with the rent coming from Chedeng's salary. I will keep my back brace and buy a gadget that picks up stuff from the floor and work," Tina told the ladies.

The health problems some of the ladies faced did not stop at Tina's accident. "Ha! This is was we could say "when it rains, it pours "when she learned about Chedeng's mild stroke a week before her 75th birthday in 2016," Blanca reacting to Cely's news.

"It is unfortunate that we stopped talking to each other. It must have been caused by the cancellation of the beach trip to Delaware last Labor Day weekend. I know someone in the group did not like the sudden inclusion of my family to the trip. But no one among us talked about why it got cancelled on the eve of our departure for Delaware. All I got from Rissa was a very short call to say it's cancelled,"said Cely.

Blanca could not get any explanation from anyone too. "Let's resolve not to beat this issue to death and instead focus on Chedeng's condition this time. Thank you for calling Cely. Otherwise I would not have known that Chedeng had a stroke. It looks like I am out of the loop since the cancellation of our trip to Bethany last Labor Day weekend. Did the ladies call you about Chedeng's condition?" asked Blanca.

"No. I found out about it because the sisters and I are still in speaking terms with each other and will always be no matter what is going on with the group. Like I said before, we grew up together in Leyte and got reunited here in the States. What we have is like an unbroken bond. In the meantime, I want to help Chedeng get better even if I sacrifice my off days. She needs help to go up and down the steps of 22nd to get to the doctor. In the meantime, you and the ladies should talk to each other again. The silent treatment we are getting from the group is getting worst," replied Cely.

She went on and further said that the sisters never had a health insurance because they had chosen not to get one. "That was a big mistake. Tina thinks health insurance and hiring immigration lawyers are a waste of their hard earned money. And it's ironic she always pulls Chedeng to think the same way even if the older sister thought otherwise.

You see between the two, Tina is the bully and Chedeng is the peacemaker. The older sister sometimes may disapprove on just about anything regarding their lives, Tina's ideas and plans always prevail.

Take for instance the use of free clinics in the district when they are sick. They could not use them for fear of getting caught by Immigration. The sisters knew being undocumented is really a pain but refused to solve the problem. Why?" Cely asked.

"What do you think? It is a very sensitive issue and an expensive one. I asked Chedeng once about it. She said she relied on Filipino lawyer to help her in 1986 when the amnesty law was passed for undocumented people in America. She never heard from him after he got paid.

Tina on the other hand, said their children are already over age to get petitioned. Hiring an immigration lawyer she said to legalize their presence in the States is a waste of money. I never had the the heart to say she was all about money but as it turns out, that was her concern for years. But for now let's just concentrate on how we could help Chedeng first," replied Blanca.

Cely then continued and said," so for non-serious illnesses like minor aches and pains, they would order medicines from friends going home to the Philippines. Do you still remember *Cortal* (famous brand of pain reliever in the Philippines in the 60s) and an antibiotic I cannot recall the name? Maybe it all ran out or was not working anymore for the pain she was having. Chedeng took one of those over the counter pain relievers from CVS. That caused the mild stroke and luckily she got to the Emergency Room right in time according to the doctor.

I know that they used to go a Filipino doctor on Nebraska Avenue but I learned he is gone. I have no idea how much damage the mild stroke did to Chedeng. But I will let you know. Right now, I use and save my off days to take Chedeng to the doctor. She has trouble walking and in pain. It takes her time to go down the steps let alone go upstairs, "said Cely over the phone.

"What about Tina? Can she not take her sister to the clinic in Columbia Road?" asked Blanca.

"Oh! Not in a million years. Tina's policy is she will never miss work unless she is very sick or there is a snowstorm and hurricane. She said Chedeng can get a cab and eek herself out of the building to go to the doctor," Cely replied.

"I am sorry to hear that Chedeng can no longer work. That lady prepared one week of food for me when I fell and ended up with crutches for a week. I will never forget that kindness. Did Tina say something about their future plans?" asked Blanca.

"None so far but the big concern that I see right now is the apartment rent. Tina cannot do the rent alone in the coming months. Everything at 22nd is split half," Cely explained.

Everything happened so fast for Chedeng. Much as she was hoping to get back to work, her recovery was slow. Most of her employers like Mrs. Leland told her it's time to go back to the Philippines and enjoy her house and life. Rumor has it that Mrs. Leland requested her friends to stop hiring Chedeng not to spite her but to force her to stop working.

Decisions also had to be made about her condition and what's next for her in the States. Cely spoke of Chedeng going home for good by February 2017. Tina wanted to stay for at least a year more because she was still financing a four unit apartment in *Leyte*. The rent would be her only retirement income. Chedeng took the cash value of a life insurance she bought years ago. "Between the two, Tina somehow prepared for the inevitable," said Cely.

Unexpected but not a surprise on the sudden departure of Chedeng to the Philippines for good, the ladies and Chedeng's other friends put together a going away party for her. Blanca who was left in the dark about what's going on with her group did not know about the party. Cely who had been a fixture at 22nd Street told Blanca she attended and helped out in any way she could to make the party fun and memorable.

"The going away party for Chedeng was a far cry from other going away parties when one of us goes home to the Philippines for good. Everyone was happy with lots of singing and dancing. Chedeng's was sad because she did not want to go home yet but had to because she was sick," said Cely over the phone.

Cold was Cely's description of the the ladies at the party. Rissa and Lulu were at the party but hardly mingled and smile. Mel and Paco dropped by late that afternoon but did not stay long. The couple told the guests that they had an earlier commitment. "What a lame excuse,"Blanca commented.

"Everyone gave cash gifts to Chedeng since she really did not have much to bring to the Philippines. Everyone knew she is going home without social security because she and Tina had chosen to stay undocumented.

Chedeng also helped not only her daughter and grandchildren for years but also relatives. She was very generous to them. This is the reason she does not have savings for her old age. Tina on the other hand, did not care help other relatives. Instead she saved to build a rental apartment. It is not easy to tell a friend "I told you so", Cely said.

Blanca did not allow her disappointment with the group to ruin her friendship with Chedeng. "I thought I found a Filipino group that would not succumb to division and alignment of its members to serve egos and agendas. In the end, we were no different after all. What is important now is to see Chedeng before she goes back to the Philippines," Blanca reminded herself.

Blanca travelled all the way to DC to visit Chedeng one morning to give her some cash. She told Chedeng she sold her house so she is a rich lady. Chedeng laughed and cried.

On her way out, Blanca promised Chedeng she would come back for one last and final visit. Blanca kept her promise. She caught up with Chedeng for the last time by the bus stop at Calvert Street a day before her departure for the Philippines.

Again, Blanca gave Chedeng some money and got off at Wisconsin Avenue while Chedeng continued on to Dupont Circle for her last doctor's visit. There were no hugs but Blanca stopped by a corner gas station and cried as Chedeng waved to her from the back of the bus.

"Thank you Chedeng for all the cooking and the care that came with it. I wish you all the best. It is time for you to rest and enjoy life while you can," murmured Blanca.

While no one died among the ladies over the years they were together, some of their family members in the Philippines passed away. Cita's mother passed away in 2014. Her mother was in her late eighties and had been sick for a while. "It was best to keep her comfortable because there is nothing else doctors could do for her. I am glad I caught up with her before she passed," Cita said when she came back from the Philippines.

"That's how we love our parents in the Philippines. While most of our relatives get greedy and envious of remittances we send them, we do it to support any living parent. Its part of our culture," added Paco.

Blanca asked if the ladies could give a money donation to Cita. "From where I come from in the Philippines, we always give *abuloy* (money donation) when someone dies," said Blanca.

"But from where Cita comes from, money donations are accepted before the burial only," replied Tina. "It's good to know that different areas in the Philippines have their own customs when it comes to donation for the dead. Let's observe whatever they are to avoid offending anyone," replied Blanca.

Paco's reckoning with death compared to his dear friend Cita came differently. He stayed away from the ladies as far as possible while they were sightseeing at Gaylord National Harbor during a Sunday lunch. The ladies wondered what's happening with him.

"Is he not in the mood?" asked Chedeng.

"No. His favorite sister passed away. She requested him not to come for her funeral because she had been sick for sometime and had helped her a lot financially. That hurt him but he has to abide with the request. Let's allow him to cry in this open field away from us but I assure you he will be back before you know it," replied Cita.

The death of Mel's mother and Paco's sister were caused by sickness. Both have led a full life. But the death of Lanie's son Benito in 2017 of lung cancer and Clara's daughter Sherrie of breast cancer a year after surprised Blanca and Cely. They came to know about the story after some months have passed.

"Who told you of the passing of Benito and Shirley?" Cely asked Blanca.

"Lanie's cousin. I called him to confirm about Benito's death otherwise we will never have known. How come no one among the ladies in Georgetown cared to call to let us know? We knew those kids because of their mothers. They've attended our get together like July 4th and birthday celebrations. Filipinos almost always set aside differences when it comes to the unfathomable sorrow related to death of a family member. We all grew up thinking that way. We are all just a phone call away. I find that strange my dear," Blanca lamented.

"I guess that's what happened because we've not been talking to each other since the summer of 2016. I am new in your group but I know those kids. We should have been told about the death of Benito and Sherrie. But things happen and I am not surprise at all," Cely smiled.

"Why? Is there something else you missed to say?" Blanca asked.

"Well, I realized over time that I've been deleted from the chat group of Cita, Lulu and Rissa formed to test and play around with their new phones. I was in that group before and after the cancelled trip to the becach. I had a new phone like the smart kind so they included in the chat. The connection gave me access to what was going on in your group but boom I was ousted and deleted by some conspiracy and secrecy we will never unravel, "Cely laughing so hard.

"Did you know about Sherrie's death, the daughter of Clara from breast cancer? " Blanca asked.

"That's sad. She could be a bit older than my Minnie. I do not know much about Clara," Cely replied.

"Well, Clara left the group a long time ago. Her differences with Lulu never got repaired. The ladies did not want to take sides because we were friends. The issue between the two ladies is a long story. It could be our topic the next time we see each other. But I feel for Clara because they say nobody recovers from the death of a child. Remember the saying you do not bury your child but they should bury you.

Sherrie's children are still young. The oldest is a girl around eleven or twelve. I am sure Clara will play a big role in her grandchildren's lives. Let us keep in touch from now on because it looks like it's only the two us from now on," laughed Blanca and Cely.

8

Leaving for Good

CHEDENG'S SUDDEN DEPARTURE FOR THE Philippines in 2017 triggered some serious conversations among the ladies and other friends. It centered on the question of when is the best time to go back to the Philippines after working in the US for years like sisters Chedeng and Tina. Cely who was at the going away party for Chedeng told Blanca that it happens all the time when one of them gets sick and could no longer work. "It comes and goes. Chedeng's going away party was one of those. Our discussions always turn out to be a blame game with lots of ifs and buts.

"I was just listening to the way their old friends from way back talk about how Chedeng should have gone back much earlier. I heard someone asked how is Jelene. She went back to the Philippines while she was still young. Someone replied and said she has a husband to go home to otherwise the husband would leave her for another woman. That made everyone laughed like crazy because it's true. Let's not name names but I know a lot of women who lost their husbands to another woman because we are working overseas," said Cely.

What about Lanie's decision to go home, asked another guests. Tina replied and said her knees had been replaced withTitanium, and they hurt when the weather gets cold.

The ladies just laughed how heavy work leads to broken hips and knees. Everyone agreed that there is a time when one knows it is time to go home. They quoted Tanya who loves to say the time to go back to the Philippines is when one can no longer bring the vacuum up and down the steps.

"But hear this. One guest asked Chedeng if she really wants to go home. Chedeng replied and said she still wants to stay because she has not saved enough money for retirement. Deafening silence engulfed the room like something scary was about to happen but it was too late to stop it. The fear is because some of us are also in the shoes of Chedeng. We hardly save for ourselves only to realize it's too late. We love our family too much.

Social Security is something to rely on when we retire. Some employers do not pay but claim they do. The only time we know we have it is when we start receiving letters from Social Security office giving us an update about it. Chedeng for a while received some when she turned sixty five but was cut off when Social Security found out she was undocumented.

With Chedeng's departure for the Philippines coming into a reality, Tina announced at Chedeng's going away party of her possible departure in the fall of 2017. Again, Cely told Blanca of Tina's predicament. "She is now alone in paying rent. All her prospective roommates could not agree to a six hundred dollar share in the apartment. It's too much for a housekeeper working only part time in Georgetown. That's what it boils down to. Keeping an apartment like what the sisters did for years is an expensive proposition to any Filipina working as a housemaid. Tina sooner or later will have to give up their 22nd Street apartment," said Cely.

Reality sank in withTina barely three months after her sister's return to the Philippines. She gave up their 22nd Street apartment and moved in with one of her part time employers in Chevy Chase, DC. Cely said Tina was having a hard time adjusting to the life of a live-in-maid. Tina was not used to serving late dinners and sleeping late. She was used to a big living space and privacy they had at their 22nd Street apartment.

Cely added thatTina tried to make it work for a while for two reasons. First, her long time employer happened to be the lawyer that helped settled her accident case with the Georgetown doctor. Having done a good job with her accident case, the lawyer earned her trust that she offered to work full time for his family. Second, working for the lawyer can help her extend her stay in the US because he knows immigration laws.

She was however told that they no longer need a full time housekeeper because the kids are grown and done with college.

Tina was not surprised with turn of events with her part time employment with her lawyer. She never really wanted a full time job like a live in maid eversince she moved to the States. "It was just one of those options that might help me stay longer in the US," she said.

A little shaken, Tina kept her her usual happy spirit. She was grateful for the basement apartment and some money from the lawyer in exchange for her part time services. But what really broke Tina's heart in terms of her options to extend her stay was her diminishing part time jobs. "Those jobs kept me up float as I navigate new life without Chedeng, "Tina lamented.

She told Cely her problems came soon. No one wants to hire her after the accident." I became slow and somewhat moody. As job offers got less especially after Chedng left, I found myself killing time in the mall then go home to the lawyer's house to serve dinner and clean after. I think it was probably time to go and enjoy life with Chedeng in the Philippines. I do not see any light at the end of the tunnel for me at this point," Tina said jokingly.

Most of Tina's old time friends, including Cely, did not let her go without a bang. They put together a going away party at her employer's home. She had their blessings to use the house for a going away party. Tina's closed friends brought already cooked food and drinks. Most were grateful and happy that her employer allowed them to use the house for Tina's going away party. The 22nd Street apartment where they've been for years to party was gone.

Blanca was invited and once again was amazed at the venue of Tina's going away party. "So this is Westmoreland different from Georgetown but had that antique feel except the former really smell like more money and power," Blanca said with a smile.

Lulu, Rissa and Lanie were already in the living room when Blanca stepped into the house. "This is really akward and of all people why does it have to be them the minute I walked in," Blanca smiled tried hard not to show her disgust.

Initially, Blanca walked around the living room to admire the décor of the house. She then focused on Lanie. She held her hand and expressed her deep condolences on the death of her son Benito.

"You know I came back to the US to be with my son Benito as he battled cancer to the very end, "smiled Lanie.

"That must have been really helpful in your healing," said Blanca.

Lanie talked about keeping her cool during the last days of her son. She said Ms. Sandra paid for her ticket to come back to the States to be with her son. But what made Blanca cried was Lanie's story about Benito's request for her mother to sing songs she used to sing to him when he was a kid. "How can our children remember songs we used to sing to them?" Blanca asked.

"I guess they do remember all those lullabies because it calms them down and put them to sleep," replied Lanie.

Blanca again held Lanie's hand and apologized for missing out on what happened to her son. Lanie got hold of her bag and gave Blanca a copy of the memorial service for Benito.

"Thank you. I don't know what else to say but what happened to your son is really sad and hard on you. We will never know how you feel because no one recovers from loosing a child. So before we both cry, let's join the the rest of the ladies to bid goodbye to Tina. I think the rest of the ladies have moved to the dining and kitchen areas," said Blanca.

Lulu and Rissa followed walking behind Blanca and Lanie. They exchanged greetings and said they have not seen each other since the cancellation of the ladies' trip to the beach. Rissa and Lulu did not say a word to Blanca's mentioned of the beach trip.

Blanca did not let go of the opportunity to talk to them about the cancelled beach trip. In her mind, there should'nt be any hesitation this time because what happened with the group was hurtful and rude. She did not get anywhere when she diplomatically asked the ladies.

To evade Blanca's contionous query on why the beach trip got cancelled, Lulu and Rissa kept moving around the big dining and kitchen areas. Blanca then asked Lanie. She said she had no idea why the trip got cancelled. "I really do not know anything about that trip," Lanie whispered.

"They were evasive and encouraged me to forget the cancelled trip to the beach incident. Lulu and Rissa were ready to say what happened was all in the past," Blanca told Cely as they tried to talk to each other during the party.

Annoyed as she was by the evasive tactics of Rissa and Lulu, Blanca cherished the company of Lanie and Cely. She admired Lanie's courage who somehow managed to keep smiling despite the recent death of her son. "This is not the time for reckoning things with our friends we've not seen for sometime. Let's enjoy Tina's party because we might never really see her again. She is going back to *Leyte* permanently," Lanie again smiled.

"Thanks Lanie for reminding to stop nagging them. I get it. Hovering around them won't work because they will move again. They are now across us. It's like our *patintero* (hop-scotch)," said Blanca. They could not help but laughed about what was going on with the ladies.

"Look Tanya is about to propose a toast. Get your glass. This is not something to be missed. I will never forget when you ladies proposed one for me back then. Those good wishes gave me confidence and I am sure Tina will feel the same," said Lanie.

Tanya called everyone to lift their glasses and wish Tina good health and blessings for a job well done. Emotions ran high as everyone held back their tears. With the afternoon of fun and goodbye finally coming to an end, Tina was unusually quiet and looked overwhelmed by what was going on.

Someone came to her rescue.The young lady she took care of for years stood behind her egging her to keep smiling. She said she was happy to see Tina honored and appreciated by long time friends.

Blanca called Cely the following day to ask for her final thoughts on the sisters' decision to go home and their future.

"Tina would be fine in L*eyte*. She has that apartment building finished before she goes home. Do you know how she fast tracked financing its construction? She used her *paluwagan* savings. Smart lady, but I doubt if her son saved money for his mother's return.

They lived like rich folks when Tina was at the height of her working life in the States. Oh, they're spoiled rotten brats who did not care to get any employment. They put up businesses but were never hands on so they all folded up.

I could go on and on about the sisters's spoiling their children and grandchildren. Chedeng went home penniless and never did anything to correct her situation. I predicted this was bound to happen because I go home to Leyte often. I saw how their families live and the parties they would throw to show off all coming from remittances overseas. Remember, they never missed to send money every time I go to the Philippines. This is on top of the monthly remittance she sends religiously. You will wonder what's left for them to live on in the States.

What a sacrifice!? Our families back home have no idea that we work regardless how high the snow is every winter. Live out maids like the sisters know what I am talking about except we never let our families know because we do not want them to worry or feel bad.

Spoiling their families has been going on for years but nothing could be worst when they did not spend money to legalize themselves in the States. Like I said before, they had their chance during the amnesty of 1986. Tina was against asking the services of an immigration lawyer because of the fees. Rumor has it that immigration lawyers charges four hundred dollars an hour. Chedeng went along with her because Tina could boss her around. We all know between the two, Chedeng was always for peace,"

"By the way, who drove Tina to the airport?" Blanca asked.

"Tanya did. She is the most flexible and reliable friend they have in Georgetown. Also, to let you know, Cita took the sisters to a spa in Georgetown as a going away gift," said Cely

"Oh! I am not surprise. She knows it's good to go to a spa once in a while," replied Blanca.

"No, *sana pera na lang* (gift money would have been better). Money is more practical because they really need the money especially Chedng. The sisters have no social security when they go back to the Philippines. They also choose not to contribute to the Philippine social security either. Their families should have known better," lamented Cely.

"They're gone and they did what they feel was right for them at that time. I will miss them, and I wish them well," said Blanca.

"I think their families knew that Tina and Chedeng no longer have visas to stay legally in the States. I never talked about their immigration status everytime I go home to the Philippines. They never asked either. Besides, their families especialy Chedeng's daughter never cared to see me whenever I am in Leyte. She would send her maid to pick up the money from her mother. Your eyes probably lit up. Yes, Chedeng's daughter has a maid paid by her mother of course.

"I do not know what to say but it is what it is. All we could do right now is wished them well," replied Blanca.

9

Graduation and Wedding Bells

"HEY CELY, HAVE YOU HEARD? PACO AND Cita finally said "I do," said Blanca over the phone.

Cely laughed like crazy and asked, "when did this happen?"

"I don't know but I saw them in messenger as Mister and Mrs. Paco Ramos. They were holding a baby boy. I suppose it's their grandchild by Chloe and her husband" replied Blanca.

"That's great. Remember the Filipino saying *pagkahaba-haba man daw ng prusisyon,sa simbahan din ang tuloy* (no matter how long the procession could get, it always ends up in the church).

"Ha, ha, ha, *Sus Ginoo* (Jesus Christ). I love that Filipino saying. It has happened to a lot of couples I know. *Sana* (I wish) it happens to us too. Wish *lang* (only)," said Cely.

"I am really happy for them because the last time Cita and I were together without Paco was in 2014. We met at Pentagon City. Cita said Paco lives in the area. Did I ask if she had a weekend date with Paco? No, that's too personal. What I did was to focus on the place because Pentagon City shops are mostly boutiques those one of a kind thing.

Yes, indeed because I got me an orange scarf for my birthday. The generous Cita got me one. We continued our walk until we saw some bridal shops. I wondered why we went to several and checked on gowns and other wedding paraphernalias. Cita's eyes lit when I asked if she was getting married again. Guess what? She said Chloe just got engaged and wanted to know how my daughter and I prepared for the big day.

All I could say was to leave the planning to the bride and groom. The conversation then got into the Filipino custom of the groom taking care of the wedding expenses. I told her times have changed. The groom and bride shares the cost of the wedding these days. But what about the American way of the bride taking care of the expenses, Cita asked and I replied it's no longer the case. People these days are now practical when it comes to weddings. It would not be good to start married life mired in debts.

The fun part of my day with Cita was we hopped from store to store that sells wedding things for the mother and father of the groom and the bride. We laughed trying everything from pins to hats. Cita had a good time trying them. I suspect most of the merchandise are not available in upscale bridal shops in Georgetown.

But you know what, Chloe's wedding for all the excitement Cita and I had that afternoon turned out to be a small one. *Sila, sila lang* (just the family). I got a picture in the mail. It was obviously a family affair. I do not want to speculate why it went that way but I think I know why. Cita once mentioned the difficult logistics of a big wedding. It is a quite a distance to travel from the groom's house to Georgetown. He grew up in the farmlands of Maryland.

But the marriage of Cita and Paco came to me as a surprise. I thought they would be an unmarried couple because Paco was divorced from his first wife. She is a Filipino too.

Philippine law does not recognize divorce issued in America although I heard that had changed too in recent years. I' m not a lawyer so I rather keep my mouth shut on the matter," said Blanca.

"How did you know all these about Paco?" asked Cely.

"Paco told us in passing. He said that his Filipino wife left him years ago. She married an American she met in Subic or Clark. I do not know which one among the bases. He also mentioned that his ex was a radio personality in Tarlac. I can't remember the reason what led him to talk something personal and private but we let him do it and we listened. First, he said he is proud that her daughter joined the US army then he talked some more. Paco we know is very quiet so we all got surprised," said Blanca.

"My daughter petitioned me so I can come to the United States. Her mother first petitioned for her then me. That's how immigration works. A mother can request for her children then children can request for a parent like me," explained Paco.

"You are amazing Blanca. How did you convince him to talk about his past? No one among us could engage him in a lengthy conversation like his immigration status," said Cely.

"Don't forget I used to be a reporter. But I did not dig in. I think it's more out of respect for Cita that the ladies did not care to ask anything else about Paco. But the ladies are not dumb. Everyone knew he was not single the first time we met him. He was already in his sixties when he came into Cita's life so maybe at a certain point he thought it was best to open up to the group. We also know that our community is full of married men and alleged divorced ones. Which one is he? Also, he already knew a lot about us too. Should'nt we need to know something about him too," replied Blanca.

Still on the subject of weddings, Blanca reminded Cely of the number of ladies who got married since the group started in 2008. "First, was Jelene who got married 2012. She went home for the wedding and married the love of her life to the dismay of her family because he was not an American. They had a big one like the entire *baryo* (town) was invited. We laughed watching Jelene's wedding video one Saturday night at 22nd.

Then, Rissa ceased to be a widow and married Juancho in 2015. We should be happy for them because they found love again," continued Blanca.

"I hope they had a rehearsal before the wedding. Remember what Tina said about the importance of wedding rehearsals? Because if you don't, delays and other embarrassing moments are bound to happen during the ceremony?" asked Cely.

"What did Tina say? Blanca asked.

"She will have a rehearsal when her time comes so that the crying and faux pas at Jelene's wedding will not happen at her wedding," replied Cely.

"Like what wedding faux pas?" Blanca asked.

"Like the flower girls did not want to walk and the ring bearer cried. Did you see the parents pushing the kids to walk and begging them to stop crying? Guess what happened? As a result, Jelene's walk to the altar got delayed, "said Cely.

"Oh! I miss Tina and her jokes like that one. But we should really be happy because our friends' lives came in full circle and found happiness again. Can you believe these turn of events. You know the song "Love is lovelier the second time around. Maybe it's true," said Blanca.

"You are right. Our friends' love stories do not happen every day in our community.

"It's like a fairy tale. The prince charming finally came, like in Cinderella. Sometimes it takes a long time for things to happen. Like would you believe Chedeng and Tina's exes are now widowers? Who knows love would be lovelier the second time around for the sisters too?"Blanca said.

Cely laughed so hard and said she might find someone too.

"Let me remind you again of our saying" *huwag mag-sasalita ng tapos* (never say never). Miracles do happen. The truth is, their children are all for the reunification of their families now that their fathers' first wives are gone. Tina however, was against it when told her ex got free.

Do you remember her famous line? Blanca asked.

"What is it this time? You really remember a lot what everyone said back in the days." said Cely

To quote Tina, "where were these men when we needed them for support? Tina will never agree to a reunion with her ex," said Blanca.

"You turned your back on me before so why be friends now?" Tina loves to say. "It's all water under the bridge for the sisters when it comes to their exes," said Cely.

"Let's turn to something light. Mine graduated in 2008 and got married in 2012. Time flies when it comes to our children. Cita's Chloe graduated in 2012 too and got married after four years. Both of them are now settled on their own.Cita and I shared our milestones of our daughters like graduation and wedding," said Blanca.

"Mine is not wed yet but she gave me a grandson. I am happy having one but I reminded her that child did not happen like an accident. It is now important that you know the responsibility and I will try to help whenever I can with my "apo" (grandchild)." said Cely.

"You seem not to be happy about Minnie's situation," said Blanca.

"Well, kids sometimes make bad choices. But I will always be supportive of whatever this couple plans for their future. That's what parent does. Right?" asked Cely.

"I agree because we really do not have control over everything even if we want to," replied Blanca.

"Sorry but I've got to go. I heard a voice from upstairs. Call me Thursday," said Cely.

"I can't promise but I will keep Thursday in mind," said Blanca.

"Hi, do you want to hear the latest on the sisters? Cely asked

"I am glad you called. It's been more than a month since our last conversation," replied Blanca.

"Are you ready for an hour or two update tonight?" asked Cely.

"Of course I would love to hear from you. I know you have the latest happenings in Leyte from your family," replied Blanca.

"It is sad to see Chedeng looking thin and old now. She now stays in the first floor of her house so she can manage to get what she needs during the day. She is left alone in the house.

Everyone is working. Her grandchildren have their own families and live in another town," said Cely.

"If I remember right, Chedeng has a grandchild who is a nurse. So there is nothing to worry about. She knows the condition of her grandma by now. Also, it is good for Chedeng to lose some weight. We do not need more weight as we age. What about Tina? How is she after months of adjustment?" asked Blanca.

"Oh Tina is fine. She got it all figured out when it comes to her retirement. She is busy tending to her rental because you cannot have empty apartments in that kind of business. The son has acquired a van that takes tourists around the city. That could be Tina's plan too and would be more hands on because all the businesses of her son failed while she was away. There is nothing like being home to orchestrate your own affairs," Cely said.

"Their families need time to adjust and so do the sisters. It's vice versa. One thing they will all miss are the goodies coming from Costco. That went on for years. The flow of money from the States will also be missed and the sisters will also miss what they used to have. In the end, Tina's son and Chedeng's daughter finished school. That was all they cared about. They wanted to give them a comfortable life and now it is their turn to carry the torch," said Blanca.

"But what are you plans now that your daughter is married. You are now an empty nester," said Cely.

"I'm now living in senior housing in Aspen Hill. I freed myself from the care of a house so I can travel when I see reasonable flights and places to see. I promised myself I will keep on traveling while I still can. I have a small kitchen, but we can cook. It's not yet late to learn how to cook like you do. You've always been a good host to the ladies. I like how you feed us with a few good dishes and top off the meal with good coffee and of course, those hilarious talks that could last to five in the morning," Blanca reminisced.

"So where is your new place?" Blanca asked.

Minnie's place is in Layhill Road so I take a bus from Connecticut and Georgia Avenue," replied Cely.

"Then you won't have any problem coming to visit me. I am in the area and any bus from Georgia and Connecticut like Layhill Bus 10 passes by my new place. You won't miss stops because the bus announces each stop. The name of our building is Hillcrest House located on Hillcrest Road. You will know you are in the right place because there is a bus stop in front of our building.

Let me know when you can come. I have quite a busy life too. I am not one of those seniors who gets thrown into oblivion somewhere in Florida," joked Blanca.

"Oh I will call you first but I would love to see your new place," said Cely.

"You are welcome anytime," said Blanca.

"This will be all for now and I will see soon," said Cely.

"Wait, don't go yet. What is the latest on Jelene? I know she lives in another province," asked Blanca.

"Well, guess what? She was able to get back all the lands her mother pawned years ago.

Apparently, that's what she's been working on every time she goes home. She had a house built for her mother to avoid any friction between her husband and mother in law. That lady really had it all figure out when it comes to the use of her savings accumulated while working in the States," replied Cely.

"How did she deal with City Hall, the Register of Deeds and the folks who got the lands?

"Simple my dear! She got herself a lawyer who did all the paper work and paid everybody involved. *Paandarin mo ang pera* (let you money talk) *Day* (short for my dear in Visaya).

"By the way, Tanya's husband died of heart attack while in the vacation house of her employer in Baltimore. Story goes he went to the bathroom and dropped dead. He was cremated fast. That's how practical and cold Tanya could be. Her husband calls her square meters because of her penchant for buying lands in their town. He is gone now. I don't know much about him but friends say he was a good man. Faithful to Tanya who took care of their only son, their marriage is rare in the community.

Men like him are rare in the community. We all know that once a Filipina leaves to work abroad, her husband will get another woman," added Cely.

"Oh! I've met her son who to my surprise is a nurse. He struck me as a good match to my daughter but I did not push the idea. He might think I'm crazy. Now his mother and I call ourselves in laws that never happened.

I am glad Tanya was open about our kids checking on each other but it was late. Miren already has a boyfriend. They met in school. Still, Tanya and I would have fun talking about matching our kids every time we each other at the sister's apartment," said Blanca.

"Aren't you surprised that we could talk for hours? To think that I was never a member of the group and here we are the last men standing. I guess friends come and go. There is no point crying over spilt milk. No one among the ladies could explain what happened to us. So let it go Blanca girl. Please go now for your walk," Cely laughed.

10

The Wall of Silence-
The Golden Group's Demise

AFTER THE SISTERS WENT BACK TO THE Philippines for good in 2017, Cely and Blanca agreed to keep in touch with each other. The two ladies found a common bond in wanting to know the truth behind the cancellation of the Golden Group's trip to the beach in 2016.

"Just think about the food that had gone bad. It's not bad to share food with your neighbors or eat off it for a week, but still that was a waste of food. Chedeng made a big pot of *adobo, pansit* while I baked *embutido* (Filipino meat loaf)," Cely recalling the effort everyone made to make the beach trip fun.

"I am not a good cook but I really wondered where all that food went," added Blanca.

The two ladies burst into laughter and said goodbye to each other.

Since Blanca and Cely could not get any explanation from the ladies about the cancelled trip to the beach, Blanca and Cely moved on with their lives. They called each other regularly, especially during Cely's day off. But no matter how long their conversations, the memories of the beach cancellation and the questions remained.

"Could it be that Paco got tired of us once he and Cita officially became a couple? You see, some men if you let them, will control you once they get you. I heard Cita say a couple of times "I will stand by my man". This was during the time I was part of their chat group before I got deleted.

Why did she have to say those lines from that famous song? She must have a reason to say that. Who was the man? Paco was the only male in our group who was also her boyfriend then and now her husband.

Then I heard them talk about overcrowding at Mrs. Leland's beach house because my

Family was added to the guest list. Cita even talked about getting a hotel instead because the beach group got bigger. Then the group chat realized I was listening. Though novice as I was in the smart phone group chat etc., I think Paco and Cita decided to do the last minute cancellation of the trip and the ladies went along with it.

Cely thought she knew why. Paco did most of the driving of the ladies all the time. Cita had always been generous to the group to a point that she was owed a lot. That was the kind of clout the couple had over the group. They got whatever they wanted from the group without asking for a consensus.

None of the remaining members of the group will say anything more. This is how some of us are in the community. We become groupish, cliquish and secretive over time. Once chaos and confusion has been created, no one is brave enough to own up to the trouble they've caused.

I've been with all kinds of folks in our community. What happened to the Golden Group is a common occurrence. Don't get me worked up. Someone in your group did not like my presence. I could have caused the end of it but no one among the ladies will have the guts to say it in my face," Cely said.

"Your readings and speculation could have some basis. What I did not like was the well-orchestrated response of Lulu, Rissa, Tina and Chedeng at the time I was probing about what really happened. They all said not to talk about the cancellation of the trip to the beach anymore because it was all in the past and suggested to forget about it. That really infuriated me, because they had become these cold people," replied Blanca.

Given what Blanca and Cely picked up from the group chat's conversations, they agreed not talk about it anymore until Blanca got a call from Cita in the fall of 2018.

"Hi, I was driving and I saw you walking on Reservoir Road early morning today. What brought you to the the area? You seemed to be in a rush,"Cita asked.

"I have a doctor's appointment at Georgetown Hospital. It's good to hear from you. What's up with you these days?" asked Blanca.

"Why don't you come to our place for lunch after your doctor's visit? Just call me when you're done with your appointment and I will come and pick you up," Cita suggested.

"Sure, why not? That should be nice," replied Blanca.

After her doctor's appointment, Blanca called Cita to confirm she was ready to meet with her. Cita said there was a change of plan. She said Paco did not want a meeting in the apartment for lunch because their place was a mess.

"Why don't I pick you up now and we could go to that coffee shop in front of the Seven Eleven on Wisconsin Avenue. How about that?" asked Cita.

To Blanca's surprise, Cita came alone, driving a brand new Subaru. 'What an evader," Blanca mumbled her disappointment at seeing Cita without Paco. She was really looking forward to seeing the couple to congratulate them. Blanca was also ready to ask what happened to the group, but instead she found herself engaged in the phoniest conversation she had experienced in years.

"He did not come because he knew I would ask them what happened to the group. I would ask why the trip to the beach was cancelled. He knew I would speak up. We belong to the same generation so he would not dare mess with me," Blanca laughed to herself while waiting for the bus to go home to Maryland.

Blanca immediately called Cely about her lunch with Cita.

"That lunch with Cita was so phony. We were talking about the weather like everyone does in Washington," Blanca told Cely.

Blanca and Cely burst into laughter because both ladies hated the ubiquitous Washington weather talk. "But given the situation, sometimes we have to just tolerate it or be gone because you feel like throwing up," Cely said while reeling from their laughter.

Several months passed, Blanca got another call from Cita inviting her to their Christmas presentation at the Blessed Sacrament Church. "Our choir will be singing during the mass. It would be nice if you could come. Rissa and Juancho are coming because Rissa is also member of the choir," Cita said over the phone.

At first she thought of saying yes because of the opportunity to see and talk with the couple. She did not mind the tight parking situation in the area a problem because she could always take the bus. The truth was she could not stomach another encounter with Cita and her husband Paco. Blanca politely declined the invitation and said she had some guests from out of town for the holidays.

"So there is still some communication between you and Cita. The couple and the remaining ladies of the group are on Facebook now. I know what is going on with them despite the group's demise. To test the waters as we love to say, why don't I put together a lunch this spring and invite everyone like I've done before? Let's see if they would care to come this time," said Cely.

"I will not call them but mail the invitation. I will pick up some invitation cards from the thrift store and send them early February. I kept their addresses because I send everybody

Christmas cards during the holidays. Let's see if they will reply. You call me anytime if we could pull off this reunion at your employer's house," suggested Blanca.

A week later Cely called Blanca to confirm that her employer's place was still available. "They are coming back for the summer and then leave in the fall," said Cely.

"Great! I have mailed the invitation to Lulu, Rissa, and Cita and Paco but I have not received any reply so far," Blanca informed Cely.

When the third Sunday of March came, only Rissa and Juancho showed up. "Can my daughter and cousin join us? Juancho asked.

"No problem. We have enough food to feed everybody," replied Cely.

The lunch get together went well. Cely prepared food like her first hosting back in 2015. She set up the food buffet style in the kitchen then directed her guests to sit and eat in the dining room.

"Cely, it was just like yesterday that the Golden Group was here laughing so much nobody wanted to go home. Let's now focus instead on our newlywed couple Rissa and Juancho," Blanca said.

Juancho said he went home for two months because he had I have not gone home in years. "I had a good time," he said. It felt good to see family and friends. My daughter is here with us now and that meant a lot to me. Thank you for hosting lunch today. The food is great and of course I'm enjoying the company of you lovely ladies," said Juancho.

"*Bolero pa rin si* Juancho (Juancho is still a smooth talker)," joked Cely as she and Blanca reviewed what happened.

"Isn't it incredible he was able to bring his daughter to the US without any hassle? He got his green card," said Blanca.

"Oh! Well, that's his luck. I remember he's been looking around for a woman to marry so he could get a green card and he found one in the person of Rissa," added Cely.

So, our lunch invitation did not work. Rissa was the only one who cared to come.

Cita and Paco did not come. As the protocol and etiquette person in the group, I was surprised she did not even send a reply to say they were not coming. That was it for me. The message was loud and clear! We don't want you anymore," fumed Blanca.

"Surprises have a way of coming into lives Cely. Guess who called me a few days ago in the middle of the pandemic?" Blanca asked.

"Who was it this time? Were you in Georgetown Hospital again and Cita saw you walking?" Cely asked.

"No. Doctor's visits there days are done virtually. It was Lulu from out of the blue," replied Blanca.

"Why? How did she find you?" asked Cely.

"She said she was going over her contact list and found my name and DC number. So she called the number to check if anyone would answer. She thought it wasn't me at first but mentioned our group and I got comfortable and talked. So here is my update on what had happened to Lulu.

First, she had left her Georgetown employer two years ago. It was not a surprise she said because the kids are already grown. They have left for college except the youngest. They are now all driving. It happens all the time in the kind of job that we do. Of course, you are the exception because you are still with the same employer.

She now lives in Maryland, does babysitting and is no longer a live-in-maid. Lulu shares an apartment with some friends. She said she is now enjoying the freedom and flexibility that Tina and Chedeng loved to talk about. Lastly, she suggested a get together when this pandemic is over. *Say mo* (what do you say to the idea)," joked Blanca.

"Well, well, this is a good sign. Once this pandemic is really over, I would love to host lunch even if Lulu and you are my only guests," said Cely.

The two ladies laughed thinking "Maybe we will have another group in the making."

Appendix

The exploitation of the Filipino domestic worker is worth writing about in other books. In fact, much has been written already and more will be documented in the future. However, unless US immigration laws are changed to allow these workers full U.S. citizenship should they desire it, their plight will remain as little more than indentured servants to the rich and famous in this country.

It is an ugly stain on U. S. diplomacy and has been going since wealthy American began recruiting Filipino domestic helpers in the 1960's. Most of these workers remain in this country until they are too old to continue their jobs and eventually have return to the Philippines, barely better off than when they came. Without green card status, or permanent residency, not to mention access to full U.S. citizenship and all the privileges (such as the right to vote, the rights to social security) they have few if any means to move beyond domestic worker status.

Make no mistake, there are some employers even those in this elite Georgetown community in the US capital, who work with their maids/housekeepers to help them obtain at least green card. However, it is long, tedious process, is the exception and is rarely successful.

In the meantime, the day- to day lives of these women (primarily) consists invariably of cleaning homes of their employers, cooking meals, catering to guests, caring for their elderly relatives, serving as nannies to their children, running errands (yes, some are provided with driving instruction and obtain licenses and are even given cars), walking dogs, and performing other tasks. The pay is low, with some who live-in and are on call-24 hours a day with wages that are so low they never able to live independently. Those who do manage to earn enough to live independently are forced to have roommates to make ends meet.

This is a cursory look at what goes on behind the scenes for these workers. Their individual stories are many and varied, and often unbearable to hear. This book however, exposed the resilience of these women, bolstered by their strong cultural identity, their love of family and friends, their strong religious beliefs, and their determination to enjoy each other and as much of American life they are allowed. Their adventures as chronicled in this book over a span of eight years and provide inspiration for us all to have the "audacity to hope" in overcoming adversity.

The author wishes to thank all these women who allowed her to share their fun filled journey over the years. It was an inspiration getting to know and enjoy their individual personalities.

Glossary of Filipino Words and Expressions

- Aakyat siya ng ligaw – home visit to start a courtship
- Abuloy – cash donation to the family of a deceased
- Adobo – sauted dish of pork or chicken marinated in vinegar, garlic, bay leaf, soy sauce
- Ang tigas ng accent – heavy accent
- Ang Pasko Ay Sumapit – A Filipino Christmas carol meaning Christmas is here
- Ay buhay Amerika – this American life
- Alaga – ward or someone to take care of like children
- Ang haba – something is taking long
- Ang galing – brilliant
- Aguy – equivalent of "ouch" in Visayan dialect
- Amo – employer
- Apo – grandchild
- Artistas – actors
- Asim – sour
- Ate – big sister and polite way to address an older lady
- Bahay kubo – bamboo house
- Bacolod – capital of Negros Occidental province
- Bagong salta – a newcomer to the town
- Baon – bagged food for lunch, snacks or dinner
- Balikbayan box – back to the homeland or Philippines refers to care packages sent by Filipinos to relatives in the Philippines
- Balita - news
- Baryo – innermost part of town
- Ball ng Bayan – People's Ball or party for everyone
- Baligtad – opposite
- Balita – news
- Beso beso – kissing and hugging
- Baka sakali – possibility, maybe
- Bagets – Filipino slang for senior citizens
- Beauty na smart pa – smart and pretty

- Bisaya tayo Day – we are all from Visayan region ladies
- Bibingka – steamed rice cake
- Bulalo – soup from beef bone marrow
- Bolero – smooth talker
- Burloloy- hanging decorations common in fiestas and occasions like Independence Day
- Bongga – lavish
- Bunot – dried coconut husk use to shine floors
- Buto-buto – beef or chicken bones good for soup flavor
- Capitana – female leader or head
- Chichirya – snacks mostly junk food
- Cortal – well known pain reliever in the 60s
- Culture naman – turn to a little bit of culture
- Day, Filipino ka talaga – you are really a Filipino
- Daya-cheating
- Daig ng maagap ang masikap – hardworking people oftentimes are beaten by the more forward looking one
- Dabiana – famous plus size Filipino comedian
- Daghan salamat – thanks a lot
- Dating – aura
- Dinuguan – a dish mad from pig's blood with vinegar, spices and meat
- Diningding – a dish from the Ilocos province mostly vegetables
- Eksena – a scene
- Entrega – put in the care of like babysitting
- Embutido – Filipino meatloaf
- Engkang engkang – wobbly walking
- Feel na feel – combined English and Tagalog expressing a heartfelt feeling
- Gabi – tarrow root
- Galing talaga ni Manang Chedeng – Chedeng is really smart
- Gising – wake up
- Halo – halo – dessert mix of sweetened plantain, yams, black beans, jack fruit and shaved ice with milk and sugar or condensed milk
- Hindi ko bayan ang Cyprus at America – Cyprus is not my home and country
- Hindi masama- not bad
- High tech na rin – updted in the technology too
- Huwag magsalita ng tapos – never say never

- Ilonga ka Day – Miss, are you from the Iloilo province?
- Irog – endearment for a sweetheart
- Iba na ang nasa bayan mo ikaw – it's different when you are in your country
- Inggit- envy
- Kabayan – compatriots
- Kabisera – seat at the head table usually reserved for the father or mother or host of a party
- Kalabaw lang ang tumatanda – reference to the Philippine work animal water buffalo carabao that plows the ricefield
- Katas- juice
- Katulong- maid or housekeeper
- Kasu kasuan – muscles and joints
- Kodakan – picture taking derived from the famous brand film company Kodak
- Kuya – older brother but polite address to an unrelated older male
- Kuwento – story
- Kung saan nadapa, doon babangon – come back from where one fell down
- Lako – a door to door vending
- Latag ang banig – spread out the sleeping mat on the floor
- Lang – only
- Ligawan – courtship
- Lola – grandmother
- Lumpia – spring rolls
- Mikidi – Filipino slang and short cut for McDonald's
- Mindanao – of the three regions comprising the Philippines
- Misa de Gallo – a Spanish term also known as Simbang Gabi- dawn mass in anticipation of Christmas and the birth of Chris. It starts in early morning mass usually at 4 AM from December 16 – 24.
- Monggo – soup made from a pack of green beans usually available in Asian stores
- Mag-aama – collective noun for a father and children
- Madre – nun
- Makiramay – express sympathy
- Maagap – someone who is always ahead
- Makabayan – patriotic
- Makabagbag damdamin – touches your heart

- Makupad - slow
- Maraming Visaya din – lots of people from Visayan region
- Manang – polite name for an elderly female like aunt but no relation
- Mga Manay – addressing or calling ladies from the Visaya
- Matudnila – a Visayan song meaning It is said so
- Maria Clara – female role model refinement and propriety
- Masikap – hardworking
- Maayong gabii sa imo – Good evening in Visaya
- Mayabang – bossy
- Nagoyo tayo – we've been scammed or tricked
- Noranians – diehard fans of famous singer actress of the 80s in the Philippines
- Ninang – godmother
- Nakakaloka – going insane in disbelief
- Nakataga sa bato – not written in stone
- Nakakatuwa – happiness over something
- Oy – hey
- Oy,Oy, Oy – hey, hey, hey
- Oo na Day – yes my dear in Visaya
- Pera yan – that's money
- Patay malisya – pretending not to know
- Pakbet – a dish from the Ilocos region in Luzon
- Paluwagan – pooling money from members distributed in rotation per month until
- Paano nayan walang CVS doon – What is life without a CVS in sight
- Paandarin ang pera – let your money talk
- Paimportante – the need to feel important
- Patak patak – share the bill, installment plan
- Pansit – a noodle dish made from a mixture of chicken broth, green vegetables, carrots, and slices of meat like chicken, pork or shrimps
- Panungkit – long pole with a sharp tip to pick apples, mangoes, and other fruits
- Pangasinan – a province in Luzon region
- Pasko at Bagong Taon – Christmas and New Year
- Pasuring suring – walk woobly manifested by a drunk or disoriented person
- Palayaw – nickname

- Palitaw – round rice cake dipped in boiling water serve with shredded coconut, sesame seeds sprinkled with sugar
- Patay tayo – two people in trouble
- Prom di – born and raised in the province
- Pobreng Alindahaw – A Visayan song about a little bird
- Pabitin – the Filipino version of Piñata but candies and other goodies are tied to a woven bamboo square design hang in tree pulled up and down by an adult while kids reach for the candies and chocolates
- Parang di mahulugan ng karayom – so tight place one can drop a needle and it won't be felt
- Panata – a Catholic practice of promising to visit a shrine or pray over a certain period of time to ask for something difficult to get or achieve
- Pampagueño – a native of the province of Pampanga in Luzon Island
- Parang mga bata din sila – they are like children too
- Paksiw – fish dish boiled in vinegar and salt
- Pikot – shotgun wedding
- Pusod – a hairstyle similar to a bun
- Salabat – ginger juice
- Sari sari store – nickel and dime
- Sabay sabaw – equivalent of the expression "when it rains it pours"
- Sabit lang – tag along
- Sabi nga ni – someone said so
- Sa muling pagkikita – till we meet again
- Sako sako – lots of sacks
- Salamat – thank you
- Sana pera na lang – money could have been better as a gift
- Santacruzan – May procession where young ladies called sagalas dressed in gowns representing different saints like Saint Marta patron saint of cooks
- Sagalas – chosen young ladies in different towns to join the Santacruzan parade
- Sitsit – a Filipino way of hissing
- Sinabi mo – an expression to confirm that something said was right
- Sentido kumon – common sense
- Sinigang na buto buto – sour soup from beef or chicken bones

- Siguro – maybe
- Sila sila lang – just among themselves
- Sipsip lang – suck up
- Sus Ginoo – Jesus Christ in Visayan dialect
- Sama ng loob – gripes
- Sinigang – sour stew
- Suwerte- luck
- Talaga – really
- Takot sa araw – afraid of the sun
- Teka – wait
- Tama ka – you are right
- Talak – senseless continuous talking
- Taglish – combined use of Tagalog and English
- Teleserye – Filipino term for soap opera
- Tambiolo – lottery wheel
- Tisismoso – one who gossips
- Triangulo – triangle shaped firecracker
- TNT – an acronym "tago ng tago" meaning an illegal Filipino overseas always in hiding
- Torotot – horn use to welcome the New Year
- Todos Los Santos – All Saints' Day
- Tsismis – gossip
- Tuloy ang ligaya – keep going with the fun
- Tawag ng Tanghalan – a popular amateur radio singing contest in the Philippines during the 50s and 60s.
- Utang – debt
- Umuusok ang tambutso – smoky tailpipe
- Ulam – main dish goes with rice
- Usahay – a Visayan song "Sometimes I Dream of You"
- Vilmanians – fans of famous Filipino actress Vilma Santos in the 60s and 70s
- Walang bale yan Day – it does not matter my dear
- Walang ganyanan – reply to someone who is rubbing on something in the form of a joke
- Walis tinting – stick broom made from anahaw leaf cuttings
- Waray pa rin – someone who never lost being someone from Leyte province
- Waldas – squander money and other assets almost bankrupt
- Yaya – babysitter

- Yuyugan – nonstop dancing characterized by swinging hips and lots of fun

The Department of Migrant Workers DMW
(Kagawaran ng Mangagawang Mandarayuhan)

Said to be long time coming but still in its infancy, President elect Feredinand Marcos Jr. (May 2022), has been tasked by his predecessor Rodrigo Duterte to bring to the forefront the newly created Department of Mingrant Workers (MMW) that will formulate plan, coordinate, promote, administer and implement policies and undertake systems for regulating, managing and monitoring Overseas Filipino Workers (OFWs).

Background - The DMW came officially into being on December 30, 2021 under the Department of Migrant Workers Act (Republic Act No. 11641) signed by then President Duterte. Organizationally, the functions and mandate of the Philippine Overseas Employment Administration (POEA) will serve as the backbone of the department and absorbing the seven offices of the Department of Labot (DOLE) and the Department of Foreign Affairs) namely the Office of the Under-secretary for Migrant Workers (OWWA)of the DFA, Philippine Overseas Labor Office (POLO), International Labor Affairs Bureau (BLAB), National Reintegration Center for OFWs (NRCO) and the National Maritime Polytechnic (NMP) of the DOLE. The Overseas Workers Welfare Administraton (from DOLE) will serve as its attached agency and DMW Secretary will serve as the concurrent Chairperson of OWWA. As an attached agency, OWWA collects membership fees to cover health insurance of registered members.

The department is also mandated to closely coordinate with the Bangsamoro Ministry of Labor and Employment

(MOLE) on the training and protection and regulation of deployment of Overseas Bangsamoro workers, *Department of Migrant Workers, Wikipedia, November 14, 2022.*

Susan Ople

The daughter of the late Labor Secretary Blas Ople, Susan "Toots"Ople was one of the first appointees of the newly elected President Ferdinand Marcos Jr. in June 20, 2022. Tasked to  head a unified Department of Migrant Workers, Susan is not new to her job. She has long been in the forefront of protecting OFWs and is the founder of the Blas T. Ople Policy and Training Center that provides assistance through legal help and reintegration of services upon a person is return to the Philippines. The center has been consistently focused on the forced labor and trafficking aborad. It also sits on the Inter-Agency Council against trafficking that combats modern day slavery.

Following the footsteps of her late father, Susan reiterated the contribution of the OFWs wherever they are deployed. To quote her initial statement with journalist Malou Mangahas in Mangahas Interview, *"hindi dapat tratuhing busabos ang OFW ng mnga recruitment agencies dahil nagbabayad sila ng fees at mayroon siyang talento o skills na dala sa gawaing inaaplayan niya. Hindi yan one way, OFWs should be treated with respect and not like a slave. She worked hard for her money to pay whatever is required or asked by agencies. It takes two to tango, the employer and the worker. Sometimes, agencies would padlock the dorms where a pro-spective OFW from the province is temporarily staying."*

The Informal Recruitment of Overseas Filipino Workers (Ofws)

While there's been an earnest effort on the part of the Philippine government to regulate the hiring of Filipino workers for abroad through collaboration between local and foreign recruitment agencies, a record number of Filipinos found their way overseas through informal channels. These informal connections save a prospective OFW from a collection of fees leaving an applicant in debt before going overseas.

According to the Overseas Recruitment Rules and Regulations Rules and Regulations, Philippine recruitment agencies may charge their overseas counterparts for service fees, visa fees, airfare, POEA processing fees and OWWA membership fees. A Philippine recruitment agency may charge its hired workers a placement fee equivalent to one month's salary, plus documentation costs for passports, NBI, police, and barangay clearances, authentication of documents, birth certificates, medicare, trade test if necessary, inoculations if required by host country and medical examination fees.

The circumvention of formal recruitment channels for overseas employment also appears to be common. Some Filipino domestic workers travel to Singapore or other regional cities on tourist visas, and then enter into work after arrival. Bangkok has also been identified as transit cities, since Philippine "tourists" for Thailand. Once there, some OFWs acquire visas for other countries within the region as well as Europe and the Middle

East. Another type of informal recruitment involves overseas domestic workers who source among friends, neighbors and relatives back home. In some cases, these domestic workers receive a commission form the recruitment agency overseas and charge the new hire a recruitment fee as well. There are also illegal recruiters by non-license agencies or licensed ones but with unauthorized agents. In some cases, local agents in the provinces find recruits for Philippine employment agencies who then pass the recruit to an overseas placement agency. In other cases, local agents work directly with overseas counterpart, sometimes help illegal immigration with false or no documentation. In a study of recruitment of Filipino workers in Malaysia, Dana Wong found that a well-organized network of sub-agents existed between Malaysian employment agencies and sub agents in the Philippines. They are in the barrios and small towns run by well-known people of the province. Bribery is rampant. Once an OFW gets to an employer, changes could happen in the contract like less salary with poor working condition. These could happen in both formal and informal recruitment. Some recruiters used the fly now pay later scheme throwing the worker into debt, *Sayres, Nicole J., International Labor Organization An Analysis of The Situation of Filipino Domestic Workers pp. 18-19.*

The Ladies' Favorite Recipes

MONGO (GREEN BEAN SOUP)
Corazon dela Santa Version

1 pack of mongo green beans from Asian Store
3 garlic cloves
1 medium size onion
3-4 strips of ginger (optional)
1 pack or bundled spinach
4 cups of chicken broth (canned or homemade)
1 cup of water
Optional ingredients: dried shrimps, pork strips, chicken strips and veggies like ampalaya (bitter melon, tomatoes

Wash monggo beans to weed out dirt and other impurities such as black beans. Boil the beans until mushy and tender. Saute garlic, onion, ginger and preferred add ons like dried shrimps, pork strips. Pour mongo to pot and mash to your liking or how much you want to retain bit and pieces of the pork strips and beans. Add chicken broth and water. Bring to boil then add spinach or veggies of choice until wilted. Add salt and pepper. Serve hot.

Preparation and cooking time: 1 hour
Serves 4

L U M P I A
(Spring Rolls or Egg Rolls)
Corazon dela Santa

1 medium size cabbage
4 celery stalks
4 medium size carrots
1 medium size kamote (sweet yam)
1 cup chopped onion
1/4 tsbp.chopped garlic
1 pack store bought spring roll wrappers from Asian Store (comes in either 25 to 30 wrappers)

Cut all vegetables julliene. Carrots maybe also grated but press to take juice out.

Saute garlic and onion then start putting vegetables into the pan celery first sweet yam, carrots and cabbage last. Mix well keeping veggies crispy. Season with salt and pepper.

Using a colander, allow vegetable fillings to cool and excess juice to drip. Put fillings in fridge overnight if possible. This will allow mixture to blend and stick.

Thaw frozen spring rolls wrapper, keep them in fridge until ready to use. Gently separate wrappers and cover with slightly wet paper towels while wrapping each roll. Most store bought wrappers have a step by step instruction on how to wrap the rolls.

Prepare slurry a mixture of flour and water to seal the spring rolls.

Frying spring rolls: put one cup of cooking oil to high heat start with the first batch then turn heat to medium to fry the remaining ones. Give each roll space in the pan when frying. Cool rolls in baking rack to let excess oil drip. Pat fried rolls with paper towels.

Dipping sauce: Filipinos love vinegar with salt, pepper or chili, chopped garlic and a hint of sugar. Asian stores also carry sweet and sour sauce. La Choy and Kikoman are two popular brands.

Variation: vegan all vegetable fillings, shrimps or pork maybe added for flavor. Bean sprouts (*toge*) and green beans can also be used.

Preparation and cooking time: for 50 rolls take 2 hours chopping ingredients and sautéing,

Serves 10

SINIGANG NA BABOY
(Pork in Sour Broth)

From: Filipino Cooking and Entertaining Here and Abroad by Eleanor R. Laquian

1-1/2 pounds riblets or pork ribs country style cut to pieces
1 medium icicle radish or 10 radishes cut into 1" pieces
5 cups of water, 1 tsbp of patis (fish sauce)
1/4 green beans
4 medium tomatoes, sliced
1/2 pound kangkong or spinach trimmed
1 medium size onion, sliced
5 medium ripe tamarind fruit

In a large pot, bring water and pork to boil. Add tomatoes, onion, salt and tamarind. Simmer covered for an hour or until tender.

Remove tamarind (or substitutes) and mash with some of the broth. Strain juice back into pot.

Bring to boil. Add green beans and radish. Cool for ten minutes. Taste and adjust seasoning. Stir in kangkong or spinach, cover. Remove from heat. Let it stand for 5 minutes and serve. Along with adobo, sinigang is a favorite disih of Filipinos nationwide. Aside from pork, there is also beef, fish and shrimp siningang. It is often prepared as a dish in one.

Variation: Beef (stewing, brisket, shank or plate) may be used in a place of pork. Adjust cooking time for each. Fish or shrimps may also be used. Add just before the spinach and cook shrimps 5 minutes, fish 6-10 minutes.

Notes on Substitution: A 14 oz. sinigang mix or tamarind soup base may be used instead of the real fruits. This mix is sold in most Asian food stores and even in the Asian food section of regular grocery stores. Other substitutes to sour the flavor of sinigang are: 2 tsbp.. Add lemon juice or 2-3 stalks of rhubarb may be used in lace of green tamarind fruit. Add lemon after the spinach; add rhubarb, cut into 2'lenghts, with tomatoes. Mustard green or watercress may be used in place of kangkong or spinach.

Preparation and cooking time: 1 hour and 30 minutes
Serves 4

PANSIT GUISADO
(Sautéed Rice Sticks)

From: Filipino Cooking and Entertaining Here and Abroad by Eleanor R. Laquian

2 pound chicken fryer
1 pound bihon (rice vermicelli or rice sticks (soaked in warm water for 15 minutes and drained
1/2 pound pork
2 galic cloves
1 medium onion, sliced thin
1 tbsp. salt
3 tbsp.canola
1/4 tsp. pepper
1 tbsp. Patis
2 hard cooked eggs, shelled & quartered
1/4 shrimps, shelled, deveined and halved
2 green onion and chopped
1 1/2 cup cabbage, shredded
2 tbsp. lemon juice
1 medium carrot cut into strips
1 cup patis for sawsawan

Cover chicken and pot with water in a pot and bring to boil. Simmer 15 minutes. Drain but save broth.

Remove meat from chicken and slice into this strips. Cut pork about the same sizeas chicken meat.

In large skillet, sauce garlic and onion in hot oil. Add meats and patis. Saute for 3 minutes. Add 2 cups of broth, simmer for about 10 minutes.

Stir in shrimps and vegetables. Bring to boil. Reduce heat and add bihon, salt and pepper. Cook stirring until bihon tender.

Add more broth if mixture becomes too dry before noodles are done.

Garnishwith eggs, green onion and lemon wedges. Mix 1 tsbp. lemon juice with 1/4 cut patis in a small bowl for extra seasoning.

Variaton: Birthday Pancit served at birthday parties but most of the ingredients or cut in rounds to symbolize prosperity. For example, whole hard boiled eggs are used in place of quartered hard cooked eggs. Carrots and celery stalks are cut in rounds instead of strips. Small fish balls, boiled squid rings. Chinese sausage and shrimps cut into this rounds are added to the noodles.

Bibliography

Heyman, David. The Georgetown Ladies' Social Club: Power, Passion, and Politics in the Nation's Capital, pp. 8-9, Atria Books, 2003.

Laquian, Eleanor R., Filipino Cooking and Entertaining Here and Abroad, pp.61,117,156, National Bookstore, 2009.

Lang, Thomas, Steadwell Books World Tour Philippines, p.11, 2004.

Mangahas, Malou, Mangahas Interview, Youtube Channel, June 2022

Mildenstein, Tammy and Cordstier, Samuel, Modern World Nations, The Philippines, p.110, Chelsea House Publishers, 2005.

Sayres, Nicole J., International Labor Organization An Analysis of the Situation of Filipino Domestic Workers, pp.18-19.

Overseas Filipino Workers, Wikipedia, February 2, 2021.

Wikipedia, April 14, 2014.

About the Author

Corazon N dela Santa hails from the province of Boac, Marinduque and Quezon City, Philippines. She is a trained teacher and was a Foreign Service Staff Officer for the Foreign Service of the Philippines. Her foreign postings included Hong Kong and Vancouver, British Columbia, Canada. Corazon attended University of Santo Tomas, the University of the Philippines and American University in Washington, DC. She works as a substitute teacher for the Montgomery County Public Schools in Maryland, USA.